ACCLAIM FOR JAMES PATTERSON'S HOTTEST SERIES!

COUNT TO TEN

"ONE OF *PRIVATE*'S MOST INTRIGUING AND ENTERTAIN-ING INSTALLMENTS TO DATE."　　　—BookReporter.com

MISSING

"*MISSING* IS, IN A WORD, TERRIFIC. This is a one-sit, fast-paced read that fully satisfies but nonetheless will leave you wanting more."　　　—20somethingreads.com

THE GAMES

"FAST PACED...THERE IS NO DOUBT YOU CAN FINISH THIS BOOK IN ONE SITTING."　　　—Blograma.com

PRIVATE PARIS

"THERE'S NO FLUFF OR DEAD WEIGHT, AND REVELA-TIONS COME FAST AND HARD...This story is drenched in realism and really strikes a chord, proving to be a worth-while read."　　　—matthewrbel.blogspot.com

PRIVATE VEGAS

"NEVER A DULL MOMENT IN THIS ACTIONPACKED PAGE-TURNER."　　　—Writerswrite.co.za

PRIVATE INDIA: CITY ON FIRE

"IT IS UNPUTDOWNABLE AND DEFINITELY A PAGE-TURNER...ONE IS FORCED TO KEEP READING TIL THE END, THOUGH THE END IS OVER 450 PAGES AWAY."

—Winnowed.blogspot.com

PRIVATE DOWN UNDER

"FAST-PACED AND SUSPENSEFUL."

—Upinstitchesblog.wordpress.com

PRIVATE L.A.

"A GREAT READ DEVOURED IN ONE SITTING... [I'M] LOOKING FORWARD TO SEE WHAT HAPPENS NEXT FOR JACK MORGAN AND HIS TEAM(S)."

—RandomActsofReviewing.blogspot.com

PRIVATE BERLIN

"FAST-PACED ACTION AND UNFORGETTABLE CHARACTERS WITH PLOT TWISTS AND DECEPTIONS WORTHY OF ANY JAMES PATTERSON NOVEL."

—Examiner.com

PRIVATE LONDON

"THE STORY CONTINUES ALONG QUITE QUICKLY WITH THE TWO-PAGE CHAPTERS FLYING PAST FASTER THAN YOU CAN IMAGINE. I READ THIS BOOK IN ONLY AN EVENING. If you are a Patterson fan then you will probably enjoy this one as well."

—TheFringeMagazine.blogspot.com

PRIVATE GAMES

"PATTERSON, HE OF SIX DOZEN NOVELS AND COUNTING, HAS AN UNCANNY KNACK FOR THE TIMELY THRILLER, AND THIS ONE IS NO EXCEPTION...A PLEASANT ROMP."   —*Kirkus Reviews*

PRIVATE: #1 SUSPECT

"[THEY] MAKE ONE HECK OF A GREAT WRITING TEAM AND PROVE IT ONCE AGAIN WITH [THIS] CLASSY THRILLER, THE LATEST IN A PRIVATE INVESTIGATION SERIES THAT'S SURE TO BLOW THE LID OFF A POPULAR GENRE...If you want to be entertained to the max, you can't go wrong when you pick up a thriller by Patterson and Paetro."   —NightsandWeekends.com

PRIVATE

"*PRIVATE* WILL GRAB YOU FROM PAGE ONE AND FORCE YOU TO SIT THERE UNTIL YOU TURN THE VERY LAST PAGE...A GREAT START TO A NEW SERIES FROM THE MASTER OF FAST-PACED THRILL RIDES."
                                        —LorisReadingCorner.com

ALSO BY JAMES PATTERSON

PRIVATE NOVELS

A list of more titles by James Patterson is printed
at the back of this book.

PRINCESS

James Patterson
AND
Rees Jones

GRAND CENTRAL
PUBLISHING

NEW YORK   BOSTON

Hachette Book Group supports the right to free expression and the value of copyright. The purpose of copyright is to encourage writers and artists to produce the creative works that enrich our culture.

The scanning, uploading, and distribution of this book without permission is a theft of the author's intellectual property. If you would like permission to use material from the book (other than for review purposes), please contact permissions@hbgusa.com. Thank you for your support of the author's rights.

Grand Central Publishing
Hachette Book Group
1290 Avenue of the Americas, New York, NY 10104
grandcentralpublishing.com
twitter.com/grandcentralpub

Originally published in May 2018 by Century, a division of Penguin Random House UK
First U.S. edition published by Grand Central Publishing in May 2018

Grand Central Publishing is a division of Hachette Book Group, Inc. The Grand Central Publishing name and logo is a trademark of Hachette Book Group, Inc.

The publisher is not responsible for websites (or their content) that are not owned by the publisher.

The Hachette Speakers Bureau provides a wide range of authors for speaking events. To find out more, go to www.hachettespeakersbureau.com or call (866) 376-6591.

Library of Congress Control Number: 2018934477

ISBNs: 978-1-5387-1443-0 (trade paperback), 978-1-5387-1444-7 (hardcover library edition), 978-1-5387-1452-2 (large print), 978-1-5387-1445-4 (ebook)

Printed in the United States of America

LSC-C

10 9 8 7 6 5 4 3 2

To the fighting men and women of the United States Marine Corps

Princess

Prologue

CRACKED LEATHER TOUCHED rich soil. Knee in the dirt, the man thought of what was to come, and smiled. A broken nose took in the smell of the damp earth, memories carried in its dank scent. Memories of digging spades, pleading eyes and shallow graves.

The owner of the gloves wiped them against his camouflage trousers, his memories cleansed as easily as the leather. To him, the image of those graves was as inert in his mind as the way a postman views the mail. It was his job to fill holes in the ground, and with pride—the man knew that he was good at it. Better than good. He had been born as just another shitbag on the estate, but now he was a hunter.

He was a killer.

He'd tracked in forests, stalked in deserts, kidnapped in jungles and killed in cities. He had done these things for service, for his country and for his brothers. Sometimes, he'd done it for money.

Today he did it for pride.

He did it for *justice*.

The hunter-killer turned his eyes up to the sky. Rain was beginning to fall, bouncing from the thick green leaves of summer. The hunter-killer welcomed it. It was his ally. It would cover him as he slid and crept his way closer to his target. Closer to justice.

He could see his prize now, and the proximity caused his heart to beat against his scarred chest, endorphins flooding his body as he pictured his kill and the satisfaction it would bring.

It had been a long stalk, but the prize would justify the suffering and the cost. This kill would come at a price—a great price—but he would not shirk it. The butcher's bill would be paid in full, and then there would be *justice*.

Fifty yards away now, and the hunter-killer begged his heart to still, despite the thrill of what was only moments away. Wet branches pulled at him as he moved forward, checking his pace. He forced himself to slow, too close now to fail.

He looked down at the pistol in his hand, checking it for dirt. There was none, as he knew there wouldn't be. Inside the weapon in his hand, a bullet rested snugly in the chamber, ready to shatter on impact, and to tear out a great chunk of flesh in the body of his prize.

The hunter-killer smiled as he pictured that carnage.

Then he brought the pistol up into the aim, and centered its sights on the back of his target. A target that had caused pain and misery and suffering.

With a smile on his face, the hunter-killer pulled the trigger.

Chapter 1

One day earlier

JACK MORGAN WAS alive.

For a former U.S. Marine turned leader of the world's foremost investigation agency, Private, that could mean a lot of things. It could mean that he had survived knife wounds, kidnap and helicopter crashes. It could mean that he had survived foiling a plot to unleash a virus on Rio, or that he had lived through halting a rampaging killer in London.

Right now, it meant that he was twenty thousand feet in the air, and flying.

Morgan sat in the co-pilot's position of a Gulfstream G650 the private jet cruising at altitude as it crossed the English Channel from Europe, the white cliffs of Dover a smudged line on the horizon. To the east, the sun was slowly climbing its way to prominence, the sky matching the color of Morgan's tired, red eyes.

He was exhausted, and it was only for this reason that he was a content passenger on the flight and not at the controls.

The pilot felt Morgan's hunger: "You can take her in, if you'd like, sir," the British man offered.

"All you, Phillip," Morgan replied. "Choppers were always more my thing." He thought with fondness of the Blackhawks he had flown during combat missions as a Marine. Then, as it always did, the fondness soon slipped away, replaced by the gut-gripping sadness of loss—Morgan had walked away from the worst day of his life, but others hadn't.

What is it the British say on their Remembrance Day? "At the going down of the sun, and in the morning, we will remember them." Morgan liked that. Of course, he remembered those he had lost every minute between the rising and the setting as well. Every comrade of war, every agent of Private fallen in their mission. Morgan remembered them all.

He rubbed at his eyes. He was *really* tired.

But he was alive.

And so Morgan looked again at the printed email in his hand. The friendly message that he had read multiple times, trying to draw out a deeper meaning, for surely the simple words were the tip of a blade. As the sprawl of London appeared before him, he was trying to figure out if Private were intended to be the ones to shield against that weapon, or if it would instead be driven into the organization's back.

He was trying to figure this out because the email had not come from a friend. It had come from Colonel Marcus De Villiers, a Coldstream Guards officer in the British Army. Though no enemy of Morgan's, he was certainly no ally, and when in doubt, Morgan looked for traps. *That* was why he was alive.

But De Villiers was more than just an aristocratic

gentleman in an impressive uniform. He was the head of security for a very important family. Perhaps the greatest and most important family on earth.

And *that* was why Morgan was flying at full speed to London.

Because Jack Morgan had been invited to meet the powerful people under De Villiers' care.

He had been invited to meet the royal family.

Chapter 2

MORGAN STEPPED FROM the jet into a balmy morning of English summer.

"Beautiful day, isn't it?" the man waiting on the tarmac beamed.

Morgan took in the uniformed figure—Colonel Marcus De Villiers was every inch the tall, impressive man that Morgan remembered from two years ago, when Private had rescued a young royal from the bloody clutches of her kidnappers. De Villiers had been a sneering critic of Morgan and his agents then, and Morgan was certain that, beneath the smile, the sentiment was still strong.

"It is a beautiful day, Colonel, but you weren't so keen to exchange pleasantries last time we met," Morgan replied. "After I refused to cover up the Duke of Aldershot's involvement in the kidnapping of his own daughter."

"All's well that ends well." De Villiers shrugged, trying hard to keep his smile in place.

"The Duke died before he got to trial and faced justice." Morgan shook his head. "I wouldn't call that ending well."

"One could say that death is the most absolute form of justice, Mr. Morgan, but that's beside the point. The whole business went away quietly, which was very well received where it matters."

"If you've brought me here to boast that a royal scandal stayed out of the papers, Colonel, then you're wasting my time. I took this meeting out of respect for the people you represent, but I'm ready to step back onto this jet and head home if you don't tell me in the next ten seconds why I'm here."

"Very well, Mr. Morgan. I didn't bring you here to boast about avoiding a royal scandal. I brought you here to prevent the next one."

Chapter 3

MORGAN JOINED DE Villiers in the blacked-out Range Rover that waited beside the landed jet. The Colonel would divulge no more information, but he had said enough to get Morgan's attention.

The men were driven from London's outskirts into the lush green countryside of Surrey, where multimillion-pound properties nestled in woodlands. It was beautiful, and Morgan watched it roll by the tinted windows as he considered who he might be heading to meet, and why.

The British royal family was large, with Queen Elizabeth II at its head and dozens of members tied in by blood or marriage, but Morgan had some clue as to who they were driving to see in the English countryside. Colonel De Villiers had once told Morgan that the family's inner circle was his concern, so the American was either on his way to meet the Queen herself, or one of her closest family.

Morgan allowed himself a smile at the thought. Here he was, an American—and once an American serviceman at that—driving to meet the monarchy that his nation had fought against for their independence. The fact that the bloodiest relationships could be repaired made him pause and look to De Villiers. There were enough people in the world that wished Morgan dead. Why not take a lesson from the United States and the United Kingdom?

"Thank you for inviting me here," Morgan said to the Colonel. "It really is a beautiful day, and a beautiful country."

"It is." The Colonel nodded. "But don't let it fool you. At this time of year, you can get the four seasons in a day."

The Range Rover left the main road and entered a long driveway flanked by woodland. It would have been hard for anyone to spot the two armed men camouflaged among the trees, but Jack Morgan was not just anyone.

"Relax." De Villiers smiled, seeing Morgan tense. "They're ours."

As the Range Rover came to a stop and crunched the gravel, Morgan took in the exquisite Georgian farmhouse of ivy-covered red brick that stood before him.

"It looks like something out of a fairy tale." He smiled, allowing himself to relax.

But then, as the house's green door opened, Morgan's pulse began to quicken. It was not the sight of more armed men that caused it, but the figure that walked by them and into the dappled sunshine.

Morgan stood straight as he was approached by one of the most famous women in the world.

Her name was Princess Caroline.

Chapter 4

THE PRINCESS PUT out her hand, offering it to Jack Morgan as he stepped away from the Range Rover.

"It's a pleasure to meet you, Mr. Morgan," she said.

"Please, call me Jack, Your Highness," Morgan answered, feeling himself bow on instinct.

"Let's take a walk, Jack. De Villiers tells me that you're the person I need to speak to."

Morgan looked to De Villiers, surprised that such praise would come from the Colonel. De Villiers' face gave nothing away, nor did he move to follow as Princess Caroline led Morgan away from the courtyard.

"It's too nice a day to be inside," she explained as they entered a walled garden. Bright red strawberries clung to the planters. "Try one," she insisted.

Morgan raised his eyebrows as he bit down on the fruit and the juice hit his tongue. With food in his mouth, he had the excuse he needed to keep it shut—introductions to a mission always worked better when he let the client do the talking.

Nothing brought out the little details as well as just keeping quiet and allowing the other person to fill the dead space.

"This place belongs to a friend of mine," Caroline offered up against the silence. "Aside from my security detail, there aren't many people who know that I come here. I like it. It's quiet and it's close enough to London that I can sneak off here for some peace without it being noticed. I hope you know how to keep a secret, Jack."

Morgan nodded, but said nothing.

Princess Caroline smiled. "You don't say much."

"It's not every day I meet a princess, Your Highness."

Her smile grew, but from insight, not flattery. "I think it's more that you like to let your clients do the talking, to see what they may let slip."

Morgan couldn't help but grin. She was smart.

"I like to read about crime, and detectives," the Princess admitted, her smile then falling. "I didn't ever think that I'd be needing one."

Morgan held his tongue and waited. She gathered herself, and he noticed the briefest trace of sadness pass across her face, and something else: fear.

"I need you to find someone for me, Jack. A dear friend of mine. She's missing, and I need her found. Her name is Sophie Edwards."

"Are the police looking for her?" Morgan asked, knowing the answer before her reply.

"No," Caroline said.

Morgan knew that he would not be standing here if they were. More than that, he was certain that Princess Caroline's fear was an indication that this was more than a simple missing-person case. Where there are complications, people tend to want to avoid the shining beam of the law.

"De Villiers said there's a scandal to avoid," he said bluntly. "It's easier to avoid if I know what it is."

"He shouldn't have told you that," she whispered after a moment.

"I'd have been back on the jet if he hadn't."

Princess Caroline nodded, but instead of talking, she walked toward the far door of the walled garden. Morgan followed, and they stepped out into the woodland that butted against the house. Shafts of warm sunlight cut their way through the canopy.

"Do you believe in second chances, Jack?" she asked, her eyes on the path that wound ahead through the trees.

"I do," he answered, his eyes to the trail's flanks—some fifty meters away, armed men moved parallel to the royal who was third in line to the British throne. They were her deadly shadow. The guardians who protected her at all times.

"There are things in Sophie's past—things in her life— that should not be public knowledge," she explained. "I live life under a microscope, Jack, because I was born into it. I wouldn't change that. But for Sophie? She hasn't lived with it. She hasn't trained for it."

"And what are these things in Sophie's past?" Morgan asked.

She walked on in silence for a few moments before giving her answer. "Sophie is a young woman who's lived her life, and in doing so—like all people—she's made some bad decisions."

Suddenly she stopped. She turned to face Morgan, her expression earnest. "She doesn't deserve to have those bad decisions made public as a consequence of being *my* friend. Do you understand, Jack?"

Morgan did. He also understood that those under the

closest scrutiny became guilty of the sins of their company, and guilt by association was never more magnified than in the scandal-hungry media of the twenty-first century. Morgan knew that Princess Caroline was a reflection of the time she had been born into—a people's royal who connected to the country on all levels, leading a life that seemed as close to their own as was possible, given her position—but the same machine that had built her reputation could savage her overnight.

Caroline read his thoughts. "It's in the country's interest that the monarchy avoids scandal, Jack. We're the benchmark. The example. I should be someone whom people look up to."

"And you're not?" Morgan asked directly.

It was a long time before she replied.

"I'm human, Mr. Morgan. De Villiers will give you everything you need. I hope to see you again soon."

She turned away from him then and continued to walk further into the woodland. Out in the trees, her armed shadows moved with her.

"I didn't say I'd take the job," Morgan said to her back.

"You didn't need to," Princess Caroline replied without breaking step. "Your eyes did. You should learn to be a better liar, Jack."

Morgan said nothing, because she was right.

He would take the job.

He would find Sophie Edwards.

Chapter 5

ALONE IN THE woodland, Morgan pulled his phone from his pocket. He was surprised to see he had such good reception, but then reasoned that residents of one of the wealthiest regions of England would be unlikely to put up with poor service.

His call was picked up on the first ring.

"Hello, Jack," Peter Knight answered in his London office. The head of Private London, Knight had been side by side with Morgan through some of their toughest scrapes. He was also the American's friend. "The office told me you diverted here. Business or pleasure?"

"Business, Peter. Let's get together and talk about it. I'm going to send you my location."

"What's the case?" Knight asked, knowing that their calls were encrypted to government levels and stood no chance of being monitored.

"Missing person with connections."

"I might need to send you a team in my place, Jack. I had a case come in a few days ago. A man named Sir Tony Lightwood was found hanged in his home a few days ago, and his daughter wants us to take a look into it."

"What have the police found?" Morgan asked, disappointed that it appeared he would be working without his British right hand.

"Said it looks like a straight-up suicide. Daughter wants a second opinion."

"Why?"

"Says suicide doesn't fit her dad."

"Everyone says that. The truth's hard to accept."

"True," Knight mused, "but the *Sunday Times* did list him at number fifty-two on their Rich List."

"You'd better run with that case," Morgan agreed. "Money doesn't buy happiness, but..."

"It does give people a good reason to want you dead," Knight finished.

Morgan was about to follow up, but then movement along the trail caught his eye.

De Villiers.

"I'll meet you at your site," Morgan told Knight, then hung up and walked over to join the tall figure of the Guards officer.

"Did you get everything you needed from the Princess?" De Villiers asked.

"She said Sophie had some things in her past, and that she made bad decisions. Can you be a little more specific?"

A look of distaste passed over the Colonel's face. "Sophie was a good friend of your pal Abbie Winchester, if that helps," he revealed, referring to the hard-partying royal whom Morgan and Knight had rescued from murderous kidnappers.

"I need more than that," Morgan told him, but the officer shrugged, enjoying the moment.

"You're the world's greatest investigator, Mr. Morgan." De Villiers smiled. "So let's get you back to London. *Then* you can begin investigating."

Chapter 6

MORGAN DECLINED COLONEL De Villiers' offer of being driven to London. Instead, he asked to be taken to the nearest helicopter landing site. There he was collected by a flight chartered by Private and flown back into London. Morgan's mind was full of questions, but after asking his team to come up with a background file on Sophie Edwards, he forced himself to sleep on the short flight—experience told him that such luxuries would be in short supply during the investigation, and he needed to be sharp.

Collected by car from the heliport, Morgan peered at the London streets as he was driven to Eaton Square, one of the many homes of business tycoon Sir Tony Lightwood. Eaton Square was one of the most expensive places to live in the UK, with an average house price of £17 million, and Morgan could see why. The buildings' white stucco facades gleamed in the sunlight, and Bentleys and Rolls-Royces lined the street. Everything about the area screamed opulence. Only one thing seemed out of place.

It stood in the street, all smiles beneath a mop of red hair, a West Ham United football shirt tucked into skinny jeans.

Morgan stepped from his car and greeted the man. "Good to see you, Hooligan. Really good."

The men shook hands. Jeremy "Hooligan" Crawford was a double Cambridge graduate turned MI5 tech guru turned Private London legend. He was also a diehard Hammers fan, and a man who had helped save lives several times over for Private—Morgan's amongst them.

"Good to see you too, boss," the East Ender replied, still shaking Morgan's hand. "The rest of them are inside."

Morgan turned and followed Hooligan toward the entrance of the home. The building wasn't large, and was adjoined at both sides to its neighbors, but its colossal price could buy someone an entire village in the north of the country.

"Sir Tony wasn't shy about flashing his cash," Morgan noted.

"You can say that again, boss," Hooligan agreed. "Inside looks like the Saatchi Gallery."

"Contemporary art a passion of yours, Hooligan?" Morgan asked, trying to hide his surprise.

"Bloody hell, no." The Londoner laughed as they stepped inside. "I heard her say it."

"Her" was Jane Cook, former British Army major, and newest agent of Private London. Astute and striking, Cook had worked alongside Morgan as they'd raced to save Abbie Winchester's life before the Trooping the Color parade, two years previously. Their mission had ended with Abbie's release, but their time together in London had not. Morgan had delayed his flight back to the U.S. twice before a critical case had finally pulled him from Cook's bed.

"Jane." He smiled.

"Jack."

Hooligan opened his mouth to speak and excuse himself, but quickly realized he had already been forgotten. Chuckling to himself, he moved away along the richly appointed hallway.

A moment of silence held between Cook and Morgan.

"Peter here?" Morgan finally managed.

"Upstairs. I'll follow you up," Cook said softly.

Morgan was forced to brush by her in the narrow entrance. It was the slightest touch, but he felt as though he'd been shoved into a flame.

"After you, boss," Cook teased, adding fuel.

Morgan walked on, glad to have the beautiful woman out of his vision. He had been recovering from a deep knife wound at the time of their brief affair, but not even the pain from his injuries had held them back in their passion.

With such sexual tension in the air, he was almost relieved to enter Sir Tony's study. Surrounded by mahogany furnishings, Peter Knight was on his hands and knees, fastidiously working every inch of the room for a clue that would suggest the rich man's death was suspicious.

"You don't have to kowtow," Morgan joked. "A simple bow would be enough."

"Good to see you, Jack!" Knight grinned as he got to his feet and took Morgan's outstretched hands. "It's been too long!"

"It's always too long," Morgan agreed, having missed the company of his trusted British friend and colleague. "How are things looking here?"

"Sir Tony was found hanging from this beam," Knight began, pointing to the ceiling. "No note has been found, which is one of the reasons his daughter is certain it wasn't suicide."

"What are the others?"

"That he was happy, successful and wanted to continue to be that way," Knight answered. "From the people we've interviewed, it does seem out of character."

"You never know what's going on inside someone's head," Cook added.

"You don't," Knight agreed, but he could make a good guess at what was going on inside Morgan's and Cook's—the pair seemed almost at pains not to look at one another, and so it was with a little surprise that Knight heard Morgan's next words.

"I've got nothing to start with on this missing-person case, Peter, so I'm taking Cook with me. Going to need to cover a lot of ground."

"I can handle Sir Tony's case alone," Knight agreed. "Where are you going to start looking?"

Morgan hadn't been given much to go on from Princess Caroline, so he drew on the initial information Private's office had been able to gather.

"Sophie moved here from the country," Morgan explained. "And when someone comes to a big city and gets in trouble, there's a good chance they run for home."

"And you think she's in trouble?" Knight asked.

"From what I can see so far, she doesn't seem like the kind to just drop off the grid. She was a friend of Abbie Winchester's."

Knight nodded. "Abbie Winchester was in the papers as often as the prime minister. If Sophie was in her circle, then it's likely she tried to live her life *on* the grid as much as possible."

"So we start at her home?" Cook asked.

Morgan nodded. "We're going to Wales."

Chapter 7

THE HELICOPTER CUT its way through the sky above a patchwork of fields and villages, the spires of local churches reaching up to Morgan and Cook like long-lost friends.

"I love this country," Cook said proudly, her eyes on the ribbon of a river that glimmered silver in the morning's strong sunlight.

Morgan glanced at Cook and smiled. "It has its charms."

Cook let the compliment hang in the air before pulling a tablet from a packed rucksack that held a few changes of clothes, wash-kit, and all manner of items that ranged from torches to bolt-cutters. Cook had learned in the army that she should always be ready to deploy on short notice, and this pre-packed kit had been waiting patiently in her Private London office for an occasion such as this.

"Did you bring sandwiches?" Morgan teased.

Cook rummaged in the rucksack and pulled out a packet of freeze-dried rations.

"Close enough?"

Morgan laughed and waved the food away. "Never again." He smiled, thinking back on his military days. "Did the background come through on Sophie?"

Cook gave a curt nod. She was all business now—the woman who had risen to become a major in the British Army, earning an OBE for her leadership in Afghanistan. "Sophie Bethan Edwards, born on the third of December '89 in Brecon, Wales."

She went on to describe how Sophie had been raised in a middle-class family, and how she had excelled in school, winning a scholarship to the London School of Economics. No sign yet of the mistakes that Princess Caroline had alluded to.

"What did the Princess's protection team send us on her?" Morgan asked—he had pushed De Villiers further for information.

"Not a lot that's helpful." Cook shook her head. "The Princess met Sophie at a closed-doors party in London. They became friends quickly, but due to Sophie's reputation as a party girl, their friendship was kept behind closed doors as much as possible."

Morgan thought on that for a moment. Looking out of the window, he saw that the helicopter was approaching the wide mouth of the Severn Estuary. They would soon be in Wales.

"What do you know about these 'closed-door' parties?" the American asked Cook, the former officer having spent many years in London.

"You only go if you're invited, and the only people giving out the invitations are celebrities, sports stars, movers and shakers, or in our case, a member of the royal family."

"And who gave you your invitation?" Morgan asked with a wry grin.

"*That's* not in the briefing," Cook warned. "But what I will say is anything goes at these places. I'm not saying it's one of Caligula's orgies, but they're private for a reason. I saw more than a few well-known celebrities and sports personalities with white noses."

"So Sophie met the Princess there. I wonder who else she met," Morgan said, speculating on who in such circles could wish harm against her. "Anything in the file about a boyfriend, or exes?"

Cook shook her head. "Aside from saying that the girl likes a party, there's nothing really in here. Maybe this is as straightforward as Knight's suicide, and the girl skipped town?"

"No," Morgan said with certainty. "People don't go missing without a reason."

Chapter 8

"YOU WANT COFFEE?" Peter Knight asked Hooligan, looking up from the pathologist's report into Sir Tony Lightwood's death spread before them.

"Soon as the boss shows up you get stars and stripes in your eyes!" the East Ender laughed. "I'll take a tea, like a true Brit."

Knight got to his feet and crossed a lab that was filled with the most cutting-edge technology that money could buy, before stopping in front of a battered kettle that was probably older than he was—some designs just couldn't be improved upon.

He was about to pick up the finished brews when there was a knock on the lab's door.

"You must be Perkins," Knight said to the squat man in the doorway. He gestured for him to come inside.

"I am," the man confirmed, shaking hands and making his introductions to both Private agents.

Knight had been expecting the new arrival. Perkins

worked for De Villiers in a similar role to Hooligan. He would act as a liaison between the Colonel's team and Private.

"You military or police?" Knight enquired.

"Neither. I was in the navy, back in the day, but I'm a civvie contractor now." He turned to Hooligan. "West Ham fan, are you?"

"What gave it away?" Hooligan smiled, looking down at his West Ham shirt, steam rising from the West Ham mug in his hand.

"Not sure we can work together then, mate." Perkins smiled slyly. "I'm a Lion."

"I'll have no Millwall supporter in my lab!" Hooligan barked.

The two men laughed and launched into passionate speeches about why their chosen club was the greatest, and why the other should be consigned to football's toilet bowl.

Knight gave a sigh, knowing he would be flying solo until they ran out of steam. Hooligan was a hard-working prodigy—two university degrees before the age of nineteen was proof of that—but he was also Hooligan, and nothing was more important to him than his beloved Hammers.

And so, while Perkins reminded Hooligan of Millwall's 7–1 defeat of West Ham back in 1903, Knight looked once more at the pathologist's conclusion as to Sir Tony's cause of death: strangulation caused by a rope tied around his neck. No signs of struggle or foul play. Verdict: suicide.

Having read the path and police reports front to back, conducted exhaustive interviews with family, friends and business associates, and having worked over the scene of death himself, Knight found himself at the same conclusion.

It was suicide.

He pushed himself away from the desk and onto his feet.

Beside him, the two football fanatics stepped down from their clubs' soapboxes.

"You all right, Peter?" Hooligan asked.

Knight gave a brave smile. He didn't look forward to what was to come. He could give the results of his investigation over the phone or via an email, but that wasn't his style. "Sir Tony's daughter doesn't live far from here," he explained. "I'm going to go and see her, and let her know that her father took his own life."

Chapter 9

KNIGHT SAT ACROSS a pristine marbled table from a young woman. Her name was Eliza Lightwood, and following Knight's conclusion that her father had taken his own life, she had said nothing. Instead, she stared with intelligent eyes at a point beyond Knight. There was not a tear or an emotion in sight, but he could sense the calculation that was taking place inside the impressive woman's mind.

And she *was* impressive. Knight remained still, but his own eyes took in the setting for their silence. The huge penthouse was modern in design, sleek and minimal in its furnishings. On their first meeting three days ago, Eliza had explained that she hadn't taken a penny of her father's money since graduating from university. The paper trail of that education sat proudly on the walls, an abundance of achievements from London's prestigious colleges and financial institutions. Twenty-seven-year-old Eliza Lightwood was an investment banker, and even in that cut-throat industry she was proud to be known by her colleagues as a "killer."

Knight could see why. If she was this composed in the days following her father's death, how cool must she be when handling hedge funds?

"I'm about to offend you," Eliza said suddenly, almost startling him, "because I don't think you've come to the right conclusion, Mr. Knight. I know you're a pro—that's why I came to you—but . . . my father wouldn't kill himself. He just wouldn't."

For a moment Knight said nothing. He wondered if this would be the point where the dam holding back Eliza's emotions would burst, but there was nothing. Just the face of a woman who had the utmost certainty in her words.

"You're going to tell me that everyone feels that way," Eliza pre-empted. "I understand that. If I say that this is different, you'll tell me that they all say that, too."

There was no hostility in the words, only a cool understanding of human nature and the desire to believe that one's loved ones were not so unhappy as to wish to take their own lives. "I can't imagine how hard it must be for the families, wondering if they could have done something. Stopped it. Have you ever lost someone close to you, Peter?"

"My wife," Knight said solemnly, picturing the face of his true love and mother of his two children.

"My mother died of cancer." Eliza sighed. "My father was always a huge supporter of cancer research and charities for people suffering the disease."

"As are you," Knight noted, paying the woman her dues for her incredibly generous donations.

"You looked into me?" She almost smiled.

"I look into everyone. That's why you brought us in. And I'm sorry to say, Eliza, that your father killed himself."

Slowly, as if breaking the news to a child that Santa is a

myth, Eliza explained why Knight was wrong. "You know, this is the first Sunday in months that he hasn't spent here. He was as much my friend as my dad. We'd always have guests over—sometimes a lot—and we would laugh so much. If Dad drank too much wine, he'd stay over, and we'd watch *Blackadder* together. He even has—*had*—his own room here. That was how close we were, Peter. I'd know if he was planning suicide."

"He had a room here?" Knight asked, interested, and a little chastened for not having known earlier. *Never assume*, he cautioned himself.

"You want to look at it?" Eliza guessed. "I haven't touched it since he was last here."

Knight followed her through the apartment.

"I'll be in the kitchen," she told him, opening the door.

Knight stepped inside. Unlike the rest of the modern apartment, the bedroom reflected Sir Tony's style, gaudy and opulent—this truly was *his* room.

He set to work as he had done in the Eaton Square home, covering every inch, looking for clues or evidence that would set off an alarm in his investigative mind.

He was back on his hands and knees when he found it.

Taped beneath the bed was a USB thumb drive.

Chapter 10

IT WAS EVENING by the time Jack Morgan and Jane Cook had landed at Cardiff airport, collected their four-by-four rental and driven to the small town of Sophie's childhood. Brecon nestled amongst the spectacular scenery of the Brecon Beacons mountain range, and Morgan marveled at the beauty.

He was also impressed that Cook navigated the winding roads without any need for a GPS.

"The army does a lot of its training down here," she explained. "See that peak over there? That's Pen y Fan. One of the toughest tests we do—*did*—is the Fan Dance."

Morgan smiled inwardly at Cook's use of "we." No one who had served was ever truly a civilian once they left. Morgan felt the same way about the Marine Corps.

"Pen y Fan?" he asked, butchering the Welsh pronunciation.

The former soldier laughed. "And that's one of the easy ones to say."

She was not wrong. Morgan saw tongue-twisting place

names like Caerphilly, Merthyr Tydfil and Llangadog as they drove past roadside signs.

"There's a Cardiff in San Diego," he told his driving partner.

"I've never been to California," Cook hinted.

"Are you still surfing?"

"When I can. Not many spots for it in London."

Morgan smiled, and forced his mind away from the image of Cook on a Californian beach.

"We'll split up tomorrow," he told her. "I'll go to the family, you canvass the town and try friends. Sophie's social media has been quiet for days, and most of her circle seems London-based, but Brecon looks like a small place. If you ask the right questions to the right people, you might be able to dig something up."

Cook nodded. She didn't need to ask what those questions would be, or who those people were. She had proven herself to be an excellent investigator during her first year at Private. She was still a rookie, but one with a bright future in her new field.

"This is it." She smiled, pulling the car to a stop outside a quaint hotel that brandished three gold stars above its doorway. "Probably not the luxury Jack Morgan is used to, but there's no Shangri-La hotel in Brecon."

Morgan smiled. "Check us in. I'll get the gear out the trunk."

"It's called a boot."

"These are boots." Morgan pointed to his feet. "I'll see you inside."

After a few minutes to check in with Private HQ and carry their bags inside, Morgan joined Cook and followed her up the stairs. His heart beat faster as he walked, and it had nothing to do with the heavy baggage. The attraction to Cook today had been magnetic, and it had taken all his focus to keep his mind on the task and his hands off her body.

They stopped outside Jack's room.

Cook turned to face him and he could sense she felt exactly the same.

He leaned to kiss her, but she turned away.

"I'm sorry. I misread the situation," he said.

Cook shook her head. "You didn't, Jack. But I'm with someone now."

"Oh, I didn't know."

"It wouldn't be right."

"It wouldn't."

"I should have told you sooner."

"There's no harm done. You're a good person, Jane, that's why we hired you."

Cook nodded. Clearly there was a part of her that, in this moment at least, did not want to be a good person.

"Good night, Jane."

Morgan opened the door and stepped inside his room, closing the door without looking back.

Chapter 11

AFTER A LONG day of travel, Jack Morgan needed a shower. After his moment with Cook, he made it a cold one.

Looking in the mirror, he told himself that it was for the best that nothing could happen with Jane. Last time they had been together, they were civilian and soldier, not boss and employee. With a sudden stab of emotional pain, Morgan remembered other affairs that had ended in more than a little heartbreak—they had ended in death.

There was a knock at the door.

Morgan's heart pumped instantaneously—she'd come back.

"Who is it?" he called as he picked up his jeans from the bathroom floor and pulled them on.

The delay saved Morgan's life.

Bullets pumped through the hotel room's wooden door, sending splinters flying, the rounds chewing into the desk, biting pieces from the television and carefully laid-out refreshments. The sound of the shots was muffled, almost like a heavy tutting—whoever was out there was using a silencer. Morgan subconsciously counted the blasted rounds. They stopped at seventeen.

He took his chance and bolted from the bathroom. There was just a split second to take in the riddled doorway before he twisted behind the wall that separated bed from bathroom. He was out of the line of fire, but he expected the door to be kicked open at any moment. Whoever had fired would come through to finish the job.

Morgan looked to the window. The hotel was privately owned, and unlike with the big chains, the windows were not held almost shut to prevent suicides. He could make it out, he knew, but if the assassin had a partner, that's where they would be waiting.

He looked above him at the ceiling panels. The time from the gunshots to his decision took mere seconds. Morgan pushed away a tile and hauled himself up into the cavity. Dust cascaded onto the bed, where it fell alongside pieces of splintered furniture that had flown across the room. Pressed in between floors like a coal miner in a seam, he scuttled backward, pushing by cabling that snagged at his feet. In moments, he had pulled the tile back into place.

And then Morgan held still.

If he made any noise he knew he would be an easy target through the thin ceiling panels. And so he waited as quietly as he could.

But there was no crash of the door being kicked off its hinges. No more gunshots. There was only the sound of terrified screams from other rooms in the hotel, and then a fire alarm. Morgan held his breath and held his position.

He waited.

He waited, and then he heard her.

"Jack?"

Chapter 12

MORGAN DROPPED DOWN onto the bed. He saw a rush of relief wash over Jane Cook as she realized he was uninjured.

"We need to go," he told her. "Now."

"The police are here," she replied.

"That doesn't mean we're safe."

"They're armed. At least, she is."

Morgan followed Cook's eyes to the doorway. There was a woman standing there wearing dark jeans and a hoody, and in her hand by her side was a Glock 17.

He tensed.

The magazine of that weapon held seventeen rounds. The same number of bullets that had cut apart his hotel room.

"Who are you?" Morgan asked, wondering if she had reloaded, and if he could cover the distance to the woman before she could raise the weapon.

"I'm PC Sharon Lewis. I'm on Princess Caroline's protection team. De Villiers sent me."

"Call De Villiers," Morgan instructed Cook.

Lewis laughed. "I've got a gun and you're standing around half naked." Her Welsh accent was thick to the point where Morgan almost struggled to understand her. "If I wanted you dead, well…"

Morgan said nothing. The words made sense on the surface, but he was ruling nothing out. Until he knew more, he would treat this woman as suspect.

Cook hung up her phone call. "De Villiers didn't send her. The Princess did."

"She sent me to see if there's anything I can help you with," Lewis explained, toying with the broken crockery of the tea set. "My guess is, that would be a place to sleep that isn't a shooting range?"

Morgan allowed himself a wry smile. "It would be nice to go to sleep without wondering if I'll wake up dead."

"Get your stuff," Lewis told them. "We'll leave now."

"Where are we going?" Cook asked her.

"You wouldn't be able to say it even if I told you." The Welshwoman grinned, pausing in the corridor to allow Morgan to finish dressing, and for Cook to grab her rucksack. "All ready?"

They were, and as the riddled door swung shut behind Morgan, one thought was clear in his mind.

Someone did not want Sophie Edwards to be found.

Chapter 13

COOK BROUGHT THEIR rented Range Rover to a stop. Ahead of them, the red brake lights of Lewis's car were bright as she stopped at a gate and spoke to a pair of men who stood guard beside it.

After a moment of conversation, Lewis stepped from her car and walked over to Morgan's window. She was followed by one of the men, who held a dog by a leash.

"Step out, please," Lewis instructed. "He's going to search you both, and the car."

The Private agents complied, both watching with respect as the search was carried out with expert skill.

"Go ahead," the man told them, and the pair climbed back into the vehicle. They set off again, following Lewis along a winding drive that was only one car-width wide.

"Wouldn't want to run into a car coming the other way," Cook noted. It was an attempt at small talk to break a long silence. The atmosphere in the car had been tense, but that had less to do with sexual chemistry than with the attempt on Jack Morgan's life. As they had driven from Brecon, Morgan's mind had been churning over why someone would be willing to kill to prevent Sophie Edwards from being found. Knowing as little as he did, he could form no solid motives, only wide-ranging theories, and such a lack of concrete intelligence had pushed him into a simmering silence.

"I doubt they get many visitors here," he made himself say, not wanting Cook to feel isolated after such an evening.

"Here" was the royal residence of Llwynywermod. Morgan had been expecting a castle when Lewis had told him of their destination, but what he found instead was a rectangular barn and farmhouse conversion painted white, its profile low against the dark shape of brooding hillsides that surrounded it.

The place was barely lit, the hour now late, but Morgan had no doubt that thermal imaging cameras would be filming their arrival with the clarity of daylight—Lewis had assured him that security at the residence was high tech, and lethal. Morgan saw no reason not to believe her, but he was not about to trust her—Lewis's choice of sidearm and timing had raised the hairs on the back of his neck, and Jack Morgan was still alive today because he had learned to heed those instincts. For her part, Lewis seemed equally as cautious as Morgan.

"You go where I say, when I say," Lewis told the pair as they exited the Range Rover. "Your rooms have bathrooms, and I've had some snacks and drinks put in there, so there's no reason for you to go wandering. If you try it, the security detail will shove a taser up your arse. We've got a competition going to see who can zap the most dickheads in a year, so don't tempt us."

Morgan said nothing, but he caught Cook giving the slightest roll of her eyes at Lewis's bluster.

"Right. Time to turn in," Lewis told them. "We've got a big day tomorrow."

"We?" Morgan asked.

"Yes. We."

Private's investigation team had grown by one.

Chapter 14

JACK MORGAN COULDN'T sleep. The image of the splintered door and the suppressed thwacking sound of the bullets were still fresh in his mind. So too was the picture of Jane Cook as they had lingered outside the hotel room.

Morgan was alone in his bedroom, a quaint space decorated in the typical fashion of a farmhouse—the furniture plain and practical, wooden beams crossing the ceiling and climbing the walls. The structure reminded him of prison, and that was how he felt—trapped. Trapped with no clear leads and his head seemingly in a noose that he could not see.

Thirty minutes of press-ups and crunches did something to clear his mood, his skin slicked with sweat, muscles pumped with blood. He looked to the Rolex on his wrist, seeing the hands creep delicately onto the hour. It was 6 a.m., and time to call Peter Knight.

"Jack," Knight answered. "The rest of the night was quiet?" Morgan had briefed him about the attack the moment they had left the hotel.

"Security is tight," Morgan assured his friend, "but we're useless while we're here. We need to get back to Brecon, and find out what's worth killing me over."

"I'm sure there are a few things," Knight replied, trying to lift Morgan's mood. "Do you think they'll call off the hunt?"

Morgan had asked himself the same question. Princess Caroline hiring an investigation agency to find her friend was one thing. Having one of the agents killed in that search was another. The whole point of hiring Private was to avoid public knowledge and scandal, and Morgan's brains on his bed sheet could hardly get buried in the back pages.

"If they don't, I'll need more manpower," he told Knight.

"I can be there in a few hours."

"Thanks, but no," Morgan said, abreast of Knight's own investigation. "Stick with Sir Tony. Has Hooligan cracked the USB's encryption yet?"

"Not yet."

"Then you have to stay with it. If someone's gone to that much trouble to hide what's on that USB, then there must be a good reason."

"Or a bad one," Knight added.

Morgan heard footsteps and turned to the bedroom's door. This time it was knuckles against the wood, not bullets. "Come in."

It was Sharon Lewis.

She took in the sight of the sweat-shined American. If she was attracted to the man, she showed no sign. "Take a shower, Morgan. You've been invited to breakfast with a princess."

Chapter 15

PETER KNIGHT PUT his phone away and poured himself another coffee. Despite having a major investigation under way, he was still responsible for the running of Private London, and so he was casting his eye over the agency's ongoing tasks when a call came through from Hooligan's lab. He let it go unanswered. Instead, he ran down to the facility.

"You cracked it?" he asked as he entered the lab, certain the call would be to signal the successful decoding of the USB drive.

"Cracked it?" Hooligan replied. "I'm a delicate instrument, Peter, not a hammer. I slipped inside that code like a Navy SEAL."

Knight listened patiently as Hooligan spent the next two minutes telling him that the encryption would have collapsed in on itself and wiped the data clean had he come at it like "a bone-headed Neanderthal."

"Nothing but class and finesse here," Hooligan concluded.

"You have stains on your shirt," Knight smirked, proud of his technician.

"That was Perkins' fault!" Hooligan shouted. "He told me Millwall would win the FA Cup this year and I spat me brew out!"

Knight began to laugh, but the sound died in his throat as Hooligan tapped at his keyboard and the contents of the USB stick flashed up onto a big screen.

"Not good, is it?" Hooligan said.

Knight shook his head. "No, it's not."

"It gets worse."

Hooligan hit play on a video. Knight's jaw dropped.

Revealed on the screen, in graphic detail, was the reason for Sir Tony's death.

Chapter 16

JACK MORGAN SHOWERED quickly, feeling underdressed as he pulled on a pair of jeans and a black T-shirt. The American wasn't certain what you were supposed to wear to breakfast with a princess, but he was fairly certain that it wasn't the rumpled clothing from his travel bag.

Morgan found Sharon Lewis waiting on the other side of the door. "You didn't tell me she was here."

"It's your job to tell *me* things, Morgan, so that I can pass them on to her. This is a one-way system until she says otherwise."

Morgan didn't bother to press the issue. He could see that Lewis was dedicated and loyal to Princess Caroline to a fault—unless the royal said jump, Lewis would stand in front of an oncoming truck.

"Have you been with her long?" he asked as they walked through the barn conversion. Aside from the cameras and bulletproof glass, it could have been any other home in the countryside.

"Five years," Lewis answered proudly.

"That's a long time to be in the same detail."

"I asked to stay."

"Why?"

"I've worked with a lot of politicians, and a few royals. Princess Caroline's different."

"Different how?"

Lewis came to a stop. "The kitchen's in there. Go ahead."

"Do I bow?"

Lewis laughed, but said nothing. Morgan walked inside. If he was expecting silverware, waiters and a stuffed boar on the table, he was to be disappointed. Princess Caroline stood at a breakfast bar. She wore yoga pants and a hoody, and was pouring herself a bowl of cereal.

"Morning, Jack." The royal smiled. "Help yourself to cereal, or there are bacon and eggs in the fridge. I could make you some, if you'd like?"

Morgan's appetite had been stoked by his workout, but even had he been full, he would not turn down the chance to eat bacon and eggs cooked by the potential future monarch of the United Kingdom.

"Bacon and eggs sounds great, Your Highness. Thank you." Morgan wondered if anyone had ever uttered those words before, thinking of what a story this would make for his grandchildren—should he live to have any.

Perhaps Princess Caroline read his thoughts. "You had an eventful night," she said simply, laying the bacon into a pan where it sizzled and spat.

"Not the greatest room service," Morgan said, trying to make light of it.

"I'm sorry that happened to you, Jack. I really have no idea why."

"You don't?"

"I don't."

Morgan held his tongue. The kitchen was quiet but for the sound of the bacon frying.

"Do you still want the job?" Caroline asked eventually.

Morgan was taken aback. Despite the danger, he had not for one second thought about backing away from the mission. "Of course."

Caroline appeared relieved. "Then I'm sending Lewis to work with you. She's a Welsh speaker, Jack, and that could be useful. She can also legally carry a firearm."

After last night's attack, a firearm on Morgan's side could be more than useful.

"How do you like your eggs?" she asked.

"Scrambled," Morgan answered, before pulling the conversation back on course. "Your Highness, somebody fired seventeen bullets into my room last night."

"The police are investigating," she assured him quickly.

"I'm sure they are, but people don't get shot at because they're out looking for a young woman who liked to party a little too much—even if she is the friend of a princess."

He let the statement hang in the air, and with it the implied question—what wasn't he being told?

The Princess broke her eyes from the American and turned back to the cooker top. For a few quiet minutes she stirred eggs in a pot, then slid the bacon and eggs onto a plate, which she placed on the breakfast bar in front of her guest.

"Eat up, Jack. It's going to be a long day."

Chapter 17

THE DRIVE TO Brecon was quiet. They took the Range Rover, Cook behind the wheel with Lewis riding shotgun, where she would be in the best position to react to any attack. In the back seat, Morgan regularly looked over his shoulders, but saw no sign of a tail—the winding roads of the Brecon Beacons, combined with the light traffic, made it difficult terrain to follow and remain inconspicuous. It would be different once they reached the town. That would be where they were at their most vulnerable, but it was where they had to go.

Despite the attack of the previous night, the team would still split into two: Morgan and Lewis to meet Sophie's parents on the town's outskirts, and Cook to track down possible friends in the town center. Morgan considered changing the plan and keeping everyone together, but Cook convinced him not to.

"They took a swipe at you in a quiet hotel in the middle of the night," she explained. "I'm going to be in a town center with witnesses and police around. I served in Afghanistan," the former soldier reminded him, "I can handle Brecon."

Morgan relented. The truth was, in a missing-persons case, every second was vital. Keeping the team together meant doubling the time to work the same leads, and that time was a luxury Sophie Edwards may not have.

The Range Rover came to a halt and Morgan took Cook's place behind the wheel. "You don't leave the town center," he repeated to her.

"Think about your own safety, Jack. It wasn't me who ended up in the ceiling."

Morgan *was* thinking of his own safety, fully aware that if Lewis had been the one to shoot up the hotel room, then he could be dead before he ever reached Sophie's parents' house. Prepared for such an eventuality, he was ready to hit the brake hard if he saw the officer move to draw her weapon. He hoped that would buy him the split second needed to pull out the steak knife he had liberated from Princess Caroline's kitchen, and which now resided inside his right boot. It was risky, but it was all he had. That, and putting his trust in Princess Caroline and her appointed officer.

"Have you met Sophie?" he asked Lewis as they drove on.

"I have."

"Tell me about her."

"She was the Princess's friend, not mine."

"You're a police officer. You're observant. What did you observe?"

Lewis held her reply for a long moment, instead turning her eyes to the green hillsides that surrounded the town and the growing clouds above them. "It's going to rain. So much for the good weather."

Morgan suppressed his frustration and kept his tone neutral. "Sophie, Lewis. What did you observe about her?"

The police officer shook her head. "That she got what she had coming," she told him.

"Why do you say that?" he pressed, but Lewis would offer no detail to back up her statement. Instead, the GPS announced their arrival at the home of Sophie's parents.

Frustrated and more wary of Lewis than ever, Morgan told her to wait in the car while he headed for the front door of a light-brick home set in a quintessential British middle-class estate.

Morgan rang the bell. He saw shapes moving behind the glass, and then the door opened to reveal a short woman with jet-black hair, and large eyes behind wire-rimmed glasses.

"Mrs. Edwards?" Morgan guessed.

"Yes?" she replied, eyebrows raising in wonder at his American accent.

"Is Sophie home?"

"Sophie?" Mrs. Edwards sounded confused by the question. "She hasn't lived here for years. Can I ask who—"

"My name's Jack Morgan, Mrs. Edwards. I'm a private investigator."

The woman in the doorway said nothing, but her face said it all. Morgan saw the first traces of fear and placed a calming hand on her shoulder.

"May I come in?"

Chapter 18

PETER KNIGHT WAS searching for a parking spot on a busy London street when the call came through his car's system. He saw Morgan's name and answered.

"Go ahead, Jack."

"I talked with Sophie's parents."

Morgan's tone suggested that the meeting had not proved fruitful, but Knight asked how it went anyway.

"According to them," Morgan answered, "Sophie went missing when she left for university. They said that she never got tired of telling them how much she hated it in Brecon."

"Any suspicion of the parents?" Knight asked.

"No," Morgan answered, trusting his gut. "They looked worn down by her, but that was about it. Both schoolteachers. Not the kind of people to have the connections to set a shooter loose."

"So they're a dead end?"

"They're a dead end. Have you broken the news to Sir Tony's daughter yet?" Morgan asked. Knight had forwarded him the contents of the USB stick. "That took some watching," the American added. "It was hard to hold down my bacon and eggs."

Knight sighed as he finally found a place to park. "No. I'm just arriving now."

"I don't envy you this one, Peter."

Knight let out a long sigh as he slotted the car into position and pulled on the handbrake. "It won't be easy. Stay safe, Jack."

"Good luck."

Knight ended the call and stepped out into the street. One look at the clouds told him that the good weather was close to breaking. Complaining under his breath about the British summer, he walked the short distance to the home of Eliza Lightwood. He had called ahead, and she was working from home to accommodate his visit. The security guards in the apartment building buzzed him inside and escorted Knight to the lift.

"Hello, Peter," Eliza greeted him at the door. Her handshake was firm and she looked optimistic. "You have something?"

"I do," Knight confirmed. "Better I tell you in private."

Her eyes narrowed slightly. Then she led Peter inside her penthouse apartment.

"Is it bad?" she asked, the slightest tremor of doubt in her voice.

Knight nodded. There was no way to soften what had to be done, and so he came right out with it. "Eliza, your father was being blackmailed by a prostitute. The USB drive we found in your father's room contained a graphic video that the blackmailer was threatening to share publicly."

If he had been expecting a dramatic reaction at the revelation, he didn't get it.

"Oh" was all that Eliza said.

"I've seen it before with blackmail," Knight said. "People don't think they have a way out, so they choose death over—"

"Shame?" Eliza finished for him, taking a seat as the dam of her strength finally showed signs of cracking. "That stupid old fool. I couldn't have given a shit if he was sleeping with every prostitute in London. He was my *dad*."

Tears appeared in the corners of her eyes. Knight could see that the realization of her father's suicide was finally hitting home. "Stupid old fool." She sighed again.

"I'm sorry, Eliza."

"It does seem clear now, doesn't it?" She wiped the tears from her eyes. "I suppose you can put me in with all those other deluded people who just couldn't accept the truth staring them in the face. I still can't believe it. That he'd take his life over . . . a whore."

"Blackmail is a terrible crime. It pushes people into a corner."

"Who was it?" Eliza asked, her voice hardening.

"We don't know. The face of the woman in the video was obscured and there are no obvious clues."

She shook her head angrily. "You did your job, Peter. You proved to me my father committed suicide. You can close this case. Close this one, and open another . . . Find the bastards who blackmailed my father."

Chapter 19

JANE COOK HAD mixed memories of Brecon. As a soldier she had often trained in the mountains, and those memories were of being cold, wet, hungry and tired—no, exhausted. But then there were the good memories. Memories of camaraderie. Memories of shared challenges, and shared victories. That was what Cook had loved about being a part of the army, and that was what she loved about being a part of Private.

Cook had approached the Welsh market town as she would an Afghan one. That was not to say she sought out traps and ambushes—though she was vigilant—but that she talked in a friendly manner to shop owners, police officers and anyone who was happy to give her their time. She did not question these people directly on Sophie, but used her as bait, telling them she was visiting Brecon based on the recommendation of a university friend who had been born there. Inevitably, in such a small town, people would ask for the name of that friend.

"Sophie Edwards," Cook would tell them.

"We know Sophie!" the two girls serving in the coffee shop told her, excited.

"Such a small world, isn't it?" the taller of the pair said.

"We were in the same school year," the shorter one explained. "Haven't seen her since leaving day," she added without prompting.

"That must have been about the time she went off to London, and met you?"

"I suppose it was," Cook replied. "She didn't waste any time leaving here, did she?"

The shorter girl snorted. Her body language told Cook that although she knew Sophie, she might not have cared too much for her. "Well, she wouldn't, would she? All we heard through school was how shit this town is, and how she was going to move to London and not come back."

"Really?" Cook said. "She always said how beautiful this place is."

"Not in school she didn't," the taller woman replied, adding the finishing touches to Cook's coffee. "One pound fifty please."

Cook paid with a five and put the change in the tip jar.

"Do you guys keep in touch with her?" she asked.

The two young women shared a look. The taller one answered. "I don't think anyone's seen her since she left."

The other one shook her head. "She didn't want anything to do with her life here. She wouldn't even accept my Facebook friend request."

Cook's first instinct was to smile at that statement, but then a thought hit her like a cold slap to the face. Where else would you search for a young woman in her twenties?

Chapter 20

JACK MORGAN PULLED the Range Rover to a stop outside the coffee shop. To avoid being a static target on the street, Cook had waited inside, her eyes on the door, an emergency exit route planned through the back, behind the counter. At a gesture from Morgan, she moved to join them.

"Tell me something good," the American asked of her, pulling out into the light traffic.

"Sophie's a ghost here," she told him, confirming Morgan's own experience at the parents' house.

Morgan nodded. "If she ran away from London, she didn't come here. We'll head back to..."

"Llwynywermod," Lewis finished, pronouncing the name of the royal residence for the American.

"We'll have the helicopter meet us there, and take us back to London."

"London?" Cook asked.

"She's not here. Next step is to see if she's hiding, or being hidden, under everyone's noses."

"I'm going through her social media to see if there are any clues on there," Cook informed him.

"HQ have already done that. There was nothing. No movements. No recent updates."

"I know," she replied, "but there could be something else. A pattern, maybe. *Something.*"

"OK," Morgan allowed. "Follow your nose—"

He was about to add more when he saw Lewis looking anxiously behind them. "What is it?"

"Black BMW. I've seen it three times today."

"Can you make out the plates?"

"No. Too far back."

"I'll pull over. See if you can get the plates as they go past."

Lewis nodded. Morgan noticed that her hand was on her pistol.

He pulled the car onto the side of the road.

"Shit," Lewis growled. "They went up a side street."

"That's a hell of a coincidence."

The police officer nodded. "He was following us."

Morgan pulled back onto the road. "At least we shook him."

He called in to Private London's headquarters. "What's the ETA on our security team?"

"I'm sorry, Mr. Morgan," the operative in the personnel department replied, "but all our agents are in the field."

"What about freelance contractors?" Morgan asked, confused. There were dozens of personal security companies that could be hired in these situations.

"I'm afraid none of them are bidding on the contract," the

operative explained. "It's really quite unusual, Mr. Morgan. I've never come across this before. I have no idea why no one is taking the job."

But Morgan had.

The reason's name was Michael Gibbon.

Chapter 21

MORGAN HUNG UP the call. He looked into the mirror, and Jane Cook's eyes meet his.

"It's Flex, isn't it?"

Morgan nodded. Michael "Flex" Gibbon was a former SAS soldier who owned and operated one of the biggest private security companies in the country.

He had also taken an embarrassing beating two years earlier at the hands of Morgan and Cook as they'd searched for Abbie Winchester. Flex had broken no laws when he'd facilitated the hiring of the men that carried out the kidnapping, but he had broken Morgan's code. For that, he had suffered a ruptured knee, and now Morgan could see that Flex was enacting his revenge.

"He's blacklisted us with the other companies."

"Can he do that?" Cook asked.

"Enough of the bigger companies are run by former SAS that he only needs to bring a few onside. The others will fall in line because they don't want to piss off the big boys."

"We can do this without their help," Cook assured him.

"We can," Morgan agreed, no trace of doubt in his voice as he pushed the subject from his mind and addressed Lewis. "You have anything more to tell me about Sophie?"

Lewis did not.

"So tell me about the Princess. Tell me who would want to hurt her."

"The Princess?"

"Right now, we have no reason to suggest why someone would want to hurt Sophie. My guess is that there are plenty of people who want to hurt the Princess."

Lewis nodded. There was a pistol in her shoulder holster for a reason. "Terrorists are the biggest and most obvious threat. They'd love to take out a politician or a royal."

"But they've stopped going after hard targets," Cook put in.

"That's true," Lewis agreed. "Recent terrorist attacks have been more focused on soft targets—driving into crowds of defenseless civilians and so on. They know their chance of success is small if they come after high-profile targets. We're bloody good at what we do."

"The best," Cook acknowledged, deeply proud of her country's security services.

"Then who else?" Morgan asked.

"There are anti-royalists, but they don't tend to be violent," Lewis explained. "Of course, there are always lone wolves. Weird little bastards who just get obsessed with the Princess, try to sneak into places to see her, or steal her laundry."

"You've seen that?" Cook asked.

"I've seen bloody everything. There are some very strange people on this planet."

"It's the dangerous ones I'm concerned about," Morgan told her.

"As you well know, there are plenty of those too. So where do we start?"

Morgan had no concrete idea. He only knew that, in a missing-persons case, time was everything.

And theirs was running out.

Chapter 22

PETER KNIGHT RUBBED at his eyes. It had been a long night, and the stress of having to deliver bad news to a family member always sapped his energy levels. Now he was in Hooligan's lab, and hours of staring at bright computer screens was threatening to turn his eyes the color of tomatoes.

"I don't know how you can look at these all day," he said to the man beside him.

On the screens in front of them were long lists of numbers, files, and all kinds of digital code that Knight could only guess at. He was an intelligent man, but Hooligan's explanations went over his head.

The men—mostly Hooligan, Knight admitted to himself— were looking into the digital records of Sir Tony Lightwood. As next of kin, Eliza had granted them permission, and now they were searching the man's digital footprints for anything that could be useful—contacts, payments, patterns. In the modern world, it is impossible to live a life without leaving a trail of digital data behind, and Hooligan followed the path like a bloodhound. It was down to him to find the patterns in the data, and it was what he was most brilliant at.

"Here's another one." Hooligan pointed at the screen.

Knight leaned forward. He was looking at a receipt. It was the sixth one they'd found for the same boutique hotel—the Mistral in Kensington.

"Four hundred quid a night?" Hooligan snorted at the price. "Do they pay someone to sleep for you?"

"It's another Wednesday," Knight noted. "They've all been Wednesdays." Then something in what Hooligan had said triggered a thought in his mind. "Do you think you can access their CCTV footage from those nights?"

"You mean *steal it*?" Hooligan exclaimed in mock horror. "Yeah, no problem. You're the boss. I was just following orders, your honor, that was all..."

It took Hooligan less than twenty minutes to find what he was looking for. "Didn't even have to do anything illegal." He shrugged. "The Mistral needs to fire whoever runs their security. OK, here it is."

CCTV footage came up onto one of Hooligan's screens. Using the check-in time shown on the receipts, they were able to quickly find Sir Tony's arrival. For Knight it was a bizarre, eerie feeling to see the now-dead man run up the steps, all smiles as he shook the hand of the hotel's porter. That he could go from this bag of joy to dead by his own hand within weeks...

"I'll take close-ups and screenshots of everyone who enters," Hooligan told him, freezing the frame on a pair of wealthy-looking men. "Who are you expecting?" the East Ender asked, stopping the film to screenshot the next person.

Knight opened his mouth to reply, but no words came out.

Because on the screen was the face of Sophie Edwards.

Chapter 23

THE RANGE ROVER moved at speed along the winding Welsh roads.

"You know we have speed limits here?"

Jack Morgan ignored Sharon Lewis's comment.

Peter Knight's caller ID appeared on the car's system.

"Peter. What's the ETA on the chopper?" Morgan asked.

"Thirty minutes, Jack, but I'm not calling about that. Am I on speaker?"

"You are."

"Then you may want to take me off."

Morgan looked for a quiet stretch of road to pull over. Leaving the engine running, he told Cook to get behind the wheel. "If you see that black BMW, hit the horn." He left the back door wide open so he could jump inside if they needed to make a quick escape.

He walked away from the car and held his phone to his ear. "What is it, Peter?"

When Knight told him about who had followed Sir Tony

into the plush London hotel, Morgan thought that he'd misheard.

"Sophie Edwards," Knight confirmed. "We went over the footage for every night Sir Tony stayed there. Sophie arrives after him within thirty minutes, every time. We even checked the nights that Sir Tony wasn't a guest. There's no sign of her unless he's there."

Morgan thought over the inevitable conclusion. "It has to be her. She's our blackmailer."

"I agree," Knight told him. "There are seven instances. It isn't a coincidence."

"And she's been missing longer than Sir Tony's been dead. He killed her then couldn't live with the guilt."

"Ties up nicely, doesn't it?" Knight agreed.

Morgan looked out over the rolling hills and mountains. The highest of them was now in cloud. The rain was coming. A British summer could never be perfect.

And neither could a crime.

"I don't know, Peter. Sophie graduated with a first from the London School of Economics. If she was a prostitute, why? She could have been making an easy six figures with that education."

"She could," Knight agreed. "And then there's the shooting."

"Exactly." Morgan's thoughts were gathering speed. "If Sir Tony is responsible for her disappearance, then how is he sending shooters after the investigators from the other side of the grave?"

"It doesn't tie up that nicely after all," Knight conceded.

"It will," Morgan promised. "We just don't have all the pieces yet."

The two men lapsed into silence. Knight knew that his boss was thinking, and gave him his time.

Morgan eventually spoke. "The shooters are the best lead we have, Peter. We get them, we find out who wants to put us out of action. We get that, we know who took Sophie."

"But we can't get you a protection team, Jack—" Knight began.

"I don't need one," Morgan cut him off, friendly but firm. "I've got an armed police officer and a decorated soldier."

"If you're sure, Jack . . ."

"I'm sure, Peter. Call back the chopper. You keep digging in London, and I'll find our shooters."

The men said their goodbyes, and Morgan walked back to the Range Rover's open door. "We're staying in Wales," he told the two women, before focusing on Lewis. "I need to talk to the Princess."

Chapter 24

JACK MORGAN ENTERED the stables of Llwynywermod, the acidic tang of dung and straw thick in his nostrils. Three beautiful horses stood proudly in their stalls. Tallest amongst them was a magnificent chestnut mare—Princess Caroline was lifting a polished saddle onto its back.

"Tennessee Walker." Morgan smiled, recognizing the breed. "She looks fantastic."

"You know horses?" Princess Caroline moved the saddle into position. "Come out with me, if you like. You can take Felix here. He's a great ride."

Morgan held his tongue, and she took that as him thinking over the offer.

He wasn't. "I'd rather we just get to the truth, Your Highness. Sophie Edwards is a prostitute, and a blackmailing one at that."

If Morgan had harbored doubts about this dark side of Sophie—and he had—those doubts were dispelled by the look on the royal's face. It was not a look of shock, but one of being caught—a child with a hand in the cookie jar.

"She was," Caroline admitted. She let go of the saddle's strap she was tightening and stood upright. "She *was*," she said again, putting emphasis on the past tense.

Morgan shook his head. "A man killed himself last week, Your Highness. Private have been investigating his death, and we found evidence of blackmail. We believe Sophie is behind it."

"Sir Tony Lightwood," Princess Caroline said quietly.

"You knew him?"

"No. I . . . I read about it in the papers."

"He killed himself in shame over videos that we believe were, and still are, in Sophie's possession. And now she's missing. Did she do that to hide and protect herself, or has someone else made her disappear?"

"That's why I hired you, Mr. Morgan, to find these things out. The reasons aren't important. She just needs to be *found*."

In their stalls the horses began to twitch with nerves. Empathetic animals, they could sense the building charge of tension between the two people.

"The reasons are everything, Your Highness, and I need to know yours. Was Sophie blackmailing you?" Morgan asked bluntly.

"No!" she replied, offended.

"Then just what is your relationship with her?" he pressed, his gut telling him there was more. Much more.

"*Friendship*, Jack."

"There's enough horseshit in here already, Caroline. Please don't waste my time."

For a moment the Princess was silent. "Is it that you're

not used to conversing with royalty," she finally managed, "or that you just don't care about protocol?"

Morgan put a calming hand on the horse's nose. "I'm here to find Sophie, and I can't do that if I'm kept in the dark."

"I swear, Jack, Sophie was not blackmailing me."

"But if she was, it *would* suit you to have Sophie found, and silenced."

To Morgan's surprise, she let out a bark of laughter. "Half of my bodyguard are SAS, Jack, and they are devoted to me. If we lived in this fantasy where I want people silenced, don't you think I'd go to them?"

Morgan said nothing, and Caroline shook her head, the laughter gone. "Hurting Sophie is the last thing on my mind. I just want her found, Jack. Please, find her."

"I'll find her," Morgan promised. Then, as he walked from the stables and out beneath a gray sky, he made another promise to himself.

He would find out why Princess Caroline was lying.

Chapter 25

SHARON LEWIS WAS there to meet Morgan as he left the stables.

"Are you here to help me, or spy on me?" he asked.

Lewis simply gave a small shrug of her shoulders.

"Can you take me to Cook?" the American then asked.

"Of course," she replied. Morgan caught a trace of disapproval in her words. They found Cook at the kitchen table, where she was exchanging pleasantries with one of Princess Caroline's staff.

"Jane," Morgan said, "I need to talk with you. Alone."

Lewis half rolled her eyes as the pair left the room.

"She thinks we're..." Cook suggested as they found a quiet corner.

Morgan quickly changed the subject. "What are the rules of engagement for SAS operatives? Can they take out British citizens, on British soil?"

Cook shrugged. "They can. That's what Northern Ireland

was, wasn't it? But their operations are better hidden now than ever before. There are hundreds of would-be terrorists in the country, but only a few attacks a year."

"Taking out terrorists is one thing, but would they kill to silence a scandal? Would they kill for the Princess?"

Cook shook her head. "I really don't think so. The armed forces are furiously loyal to the Crown, but that would be flat-out murder. Soldiers are used to seeing politicians throw them to the wolves at the first hint of a rule being bent, even in combat, so I doubt volunteers would be lining up to commit such a high-profile crime, even for her."

Morgan wasn't so sure. "Maybe not when they're serving, but you and I saw what Aaron Shaw and Alex Waldron did for money," he told her, referring to the two former servicemen who had kidnapped Abbie Winchester two years earlier. "Shaw's record was exemplary while he was in the service."

"People can lose their way when they leave the forces," Cook acknowledged. "I'm sure there are more former soldiers like Shaw and Waldron out there—hired guns with no moral compass."

Jack Morgan had experienced enough of them in his time to know that such men were not in short supply.

"There's more to the Princess's relationship with Sophie than she'll admit. She's keeping secrets."

Cook's bright eyes narrowed. "You're thinking she'd hire someone to protect them?"

"No. She's lying about something, but not that." He shook his head. "You could see it in her eyes, Jane. She cares for Sophie, and she's worried. Very worried."

Cook placed a hand on Morgan's arm—the touch of it

sent a thrill through his body, though her words sent worry to his stomach.

Because they were a warning.

"She's a royal, Jack. She's been trained her whole life how to act, and how to lie. Out of all the people involved in this, she's the one we can trust the least."

Chapter 26

THE SKY ABOVE London was thick with cloud, the air muggy. On the roof of Private London's headquarters, Peter Knight looked at the city skyline, deep in thought.

The case of Sir Tony Lightwood troubled him. Now that there seemed to be an irrefutable link between Sir Tony and Sophie Edwards, Knight was trying to decide if there could be a reasonable explanation for why both people kept appearing within thirty minutes of each other at the same hotel. If not, were both of Private London's major cases actually one?

He shook his head, thinking it over from the beginning. Sir Tony was wealthy; Sir Tony stayed at the Mistral hotel on seven Wednesday nights; Sir Tony was blackmailed; Sir Tony killed himself.

Then there was Sophie. She graduated from LSE before becoming something of a party girl. She had arrived within thirty minutes of Sir Tony during each of his visits. She had been missing for days, but it was impossible to know exactly for how long—Private's canvassing of friends, family and social media could only make a vague estimate, which put it around the same time as Sir Tony's suicide.

If Sophie Edwards *was* Sir Tony's blackmailer, he could have killed her before taking his own life in remorse. That was possible, but why then the attempt on Morgan's life? Who could have arranged the hit on Sir Tony's behalf?

Then there was the question of why Sophie had turned to prostitution and blackmail, if indeed that was the case. At least Knight had been able to make some headway there: despite graduating as a promising student, Sophie had never stuck at any of the high-paying positions she had landed, her lifestyle getting in the way of doing the job. The salaries she'd been offered by companies had gradually diminished as she bounced from one hedge fund or financial institution to the next. As she'd become more and more embedded in London's high-society party scene, it was very likely that Sophie's expenditure had been outstripping her income. She wouldn't be the first smart girl to turn escort in the Big Smoke. She wouldn't be the first to get greedy, either, and find ways to exploit the men who paid thousands for a night with her— and would pay anything to keep that secret.

The humanist in Knight wished it wasn't that way, but the evidence was stacking up against the young girl. The CCTV footage had revealed Sophie leaving the Mistral hotel at eight every time she stayed. Sir Tony always left thirty minutes later. With some old-fashioned investigative backhanders to the hotel staff, Knight had discovered that there was nothing organized in the Mistral that would account for these regular timings—no backroom parties, poker games or secret clubs.

Knight rubbed at his face. He was tired. Tired physically, and tired of seeing good people turn bad. He was the rare kind of person with a clean soul, and the dishonesty that he witnessed on a daily basis weighed on him heavily. The only thing that could possibly weigh on him more would be doing nothing about it.

He would crack this case.

"You're not gonna jump, are you?" The familiar voice came from behind him.

"Depends on what you're here to tell me," Knight replied. Hooligan walked over to him from the rooftop's fire escape. "Did you finish the search of Sir Tony's emails?" Knight had ordered the tech expert to comb through the data once Eliza Lightwood had given her permission.

The redhead smiled. "I have."

"And?"

"Hold on to something, mate, because this one's gonna blow your socks off."

Chapter 27

JACK MORGAN WAS at the kitchen table with Lewis, looking over potential sites to lure out and trap his would-be assassins, when Peter Knight's call came in. The American stepped outside to take it.

Across the room, Jane Cook looked up from her laptop, her eyes following Morgan's every step until he was out of sight.

Sharon Lewis snorted.

Cook, frustrated by the case, couldn't ignore it. "What's your problem?"

"Women like you. You lot make it more difficult for those of us who aren't willing to sleep our way around the office to further our career."

Cook couldn't care less about Lewis's opinion, but the respect of her colleagues at Private mattered to her, and Lewis had touched a nerve, giving voice to what she feared others were thinking.

To avoid those thoughts she turned her attention back to the laptop in front of her, continuing her trawl through Sophie Edwards' social media. In particular, her Facebook photo albums. Most of the photos were of hedonistic parties where Sophie seemed to be the life and soul. Men came and went, but none appeared regularly enough to suggest a boyfriend. It all painted a picture of a party life that rarely left London.

With one exception.

Between the photos of popping champagne bottles and rooftop bars, one location continued to show up throughout the years since Sophie had left Brecon—a beautiful waterfall surrounded by forest. Sophie was posed in front of the cascading white water in several pictures, each one chronicling the effect that drugs and alcohol were taking on her body, her ageing accelerated by her damaging lifestyle.

"She went downhill fast," Lewis commented, looking over Cook's shoulder.

"Do you know this location?" Cook asked, pointing to the waterfall. "It could be somewhere around here that she knew from her childhood."

Lewis shook her head. "I don't. But print me a copy and I'll pass it around the team. A lot of the guys are into distance running and mountain bikes. Maybe they know it. If not, we can ask the farmers. You expect to find her there?"

Cook shook her head. "I doubt she's gone missing because of a hiking accident, but what else do we have? If it's close, it's worth investigating."

"You're right. I'll go get the printouts from the office."

Lewis had only been gone a moment when Morgan re-entered the room. Cook was about to tell him of her small lead, but something on the American's face told her that he had bigger news.

She wasn't wrong.

"Peter and Hooligan found the origin of the blackmail note: Eliza Lightwood's penthouse."

Chapter 28

PETER KNIGHT NEEDED to clear his thoughts. His mind was in the trees, and he needed to pull back to see the forest. If there was one thing that helped him see clearly, it was the faces of his children.

Knight's ten-year-old daughter accepted his video call. As always, the joy of seeing her was mixed with a pang of sadness and loss—she looked so like her mother.

"Hi, Isabel. Is your brother with you?"

Isabel called out for Luke, and her slightly younger sibling pushed his way onto the screen.

"Hi, Dad!" he bellowed.

"Hi, Luke. What have you guys been doing today? Did you have a good time at football?"

"No. We lost," Luke replied.

"Winning isn't everything," Knight told his son. "It's how hard you tried that counts."

"Is that what it's like in your job, Daddy?" Isabel asked.

Knight forced a smile, pretending he wasn't involved in

a career where losing often meant someone's life. "I try my best, Isabel."

And that was the truth—how could he do less? He loved his children with every ounce of his heart. They were growing fast—too fast—and soon they would be adults, unleashed into the big bad world. Peter Knight knew just *how* bad it could be, and he would do his utmost to make it safe for his own kids, and those of every other parent—no one should have to witness or suffer the kind of loss that he had seen.

"Are you OK, Dad?" Luke asked.

Knight smiled at his son's perceptiveness. "You'd make a great policeman."

"I want to be a stuntman!" Luke said instead.

"What happened to being a pilot?"

Luke thought on that. "A stunt pilot!" he declared.

I should just keep quiet, Knight said to himself. "I love you both," he told his children, signing off.

With their goodbyes in his ears, Knight walked from his office to Hooligan's lab. He saw Perkins, the royal liaison, napping on a couch in the shadows. Hooligan was, as usual, enraptured by the data on his screens.

"You look happy," Hooligan said, turning to Knight. "Call with the kids?" he guessed, knowing the man well.

Knight nodded, then got to business. "Find anything on Eliza?"

The East Ender shook his head. "Not a banana. The only link between her and the blackmail is that it was sent from her home."

"I can't think of any good reason why she would blackmail her own father," Knight mused.

"Well, maybe because she knew it would push him into suicide. She's an only child and next of kin. We've seen her dad's financials. She's about to be a very wealthy girl."

Knight shook his head. "She's already a wealthy girl, Jez. We've seen *her* financials. She's been making a killing since leaving university. And, more to the point," he added, "if she was blackmailing him, why would she hire us to investigate it?"

Hooligan looked over Eliza's bank statements again. Sir Tony's daughter had granted them full access in a move to show good faith and full cooperation. "Looks like Cambridge was the wrong choice for me." The man laughed. "Should have gone to LSE."

Knight stopped dead in his tracks.

"I said I should have gone to LSE," Hooligan repeated, thinking his joke had fallen on deaf ears. "*LSE*. Eliza's university. The London School of Economics."

Knight cursed himself for having taken so long to put the pieces together. "Eliza was at LSE?" he managed, trying to picture again the educational certificates that adorned the walls of her home.

"Yeah," Hooligan answered, wondering at Knight's exasperated expression. "Graduated in 2011. Why?"

Knight said nothing. He was too busy thinking over possibilities, plots, motivation, and murder.

Because Eliza Lightwood was not the only promising young lady to graduate from LSE in 2011.

There was another he knew of, and her name was Sophie Edwards.

Chapter 29

KNIGHT RAN FROM Private's building to Eliza Lightwood's home. The London traffic was heavy, and he wanted answers without delay. The gray clouds had finally delivered on their threat and rain was falling. Knight drew stares as he weaved between umbrella-carrying pedestrians.

He was soaked by the time he arrived at Eliza's apartment complex. There was no way in without a code, but Knight's disheveled state drew a compassionate look from the security guard who sat behind the building's glass frontage. The man got up and shuffled to the door.

"I've seen you enough times," he told Knight, opening the door. "So much for summer, right?"

"I know," Knight agreed, rewarding the kind gesture with a smile. "I appreciate this. Thank you."

The security guard smiled back, glad that he could do a little to help someone's day. Knight gave the man a parting wave and made his way to the elevators. After shaking his hair like a soaked dog, he knocked gently on Eliza's door.

There was no answer.

He knocked again and again. No answer.

Knight pulled out his phone. Eliza's number was a fixture in his recent calls list. He hit it. It went straight to voicemail.

He frowned. He tried again. Straight to voicemail.

Knight looked at the apartment door's lock. It was the Trilogy model that was popular in the homes of the wealthy. There was a slot for a key card, and then a pad for a code. He could only hope it wasn't set up to require both.

With nothing but intuition from his gut to guide him, Knight entered the birth date of Sir Tony Lightwood.

An LED flashed green, and the lock clicked open.

Chapter 30

THE RANGE ROVER made easy work of the forest tracks as Jane Cook drove them toward the location of Sophie Edwards' waterfall photos. One of the royal residence's cleaners, a Brecon Beacons local her entire life, had identified the spot, and now Jack Morgan guided them there with the use of an Ordnance Survey map.

"Take this," he told Lewis, seeing a call from Knight coming through and taking it on a headset. "Peter?"

"Can I be overheard?" Knight asked.

"No," Morgan replied.

His brow creased as Knight revealed that Sophie and Eliza had both attended the same university and graduated in the same year.

"It's not a big school, Jack. There's a good chance they could have known each other."

"Is she with you?" Morgan asked.

"No. Her phone's going straight to voicemail. I've tried her offices, and she's not there either."

Morgan ran a hand through his hair as he worked through it. "Sophie and Eliza were blackmailing him together," Morgan concluded. "Where do you think she is now, Peter?"

But there was no answer.

The line was dead.

"Dammit," Morgan cursed, looking at his phone screen. "I've lost all service. Do you have anything on yours?" he asked the two women with him in the Range Rover.

"Nothing," Lewis replied. "We're deep in the forest now, Morgan. Not LA."

Morgan held his reply.

"I don't know what you're expecting to find here," the Welshwoman said to no one in particular. "Needle in a bloody haystack."

"You could have stayed behind," Cook answered, getting frustrated with the other woman's negativity. "Or I can stop the car, and you can walk back?"

"Someone has to look after you."

Something in Lewis's reply put Morgan on edge. Unconsciously, he checked the knife that still resided in his boot, working it upward a little so that it was loose. It would take a second to draw it, and another second to use it. He wondered how fast Sharon Lewis was with the pistol, and if she had a round already chambered. If she was forced to draw back on the pistol's top-slide first, he was certain that split second would cost the officer the fight.

"We're almost there," Lewis said. "Pull up in that clearing."

Cook did as she was told, then opened the door. The sound of rushing water was stark against the otherwise still forest, and the ticking of the Range Rover's cooling engine. As they exited the vehicle, Morgan made sure he mirrored Lewis's movements, sliding from the back seat on the passenger side so that he was behind her, and close. Outside the car, the smell in the air was thick with the scent of damp earth.

"Bloody perfect timing," Lewis complained as thick blobs of rain began to penetrate the forest's canopy. "Let's get this over with before we get soaked."

"You've got the map," Cook told her. "Lead on."

The police officer sighed, and made her way across the clearing to where a worn pathway led through the trees.

The roar of water was growing louder. The sound of the waterfall was the only waypoint needed now.

"I bloody hate the rain," Lewis grumbled as she folded the map away, placing it inside her jacket. The shower had become a downpour, the rain bouncing from the forest floor and slapping at the leaves. What had been a quiet haven was fast becoming a cacophony—the rain even drowned out the sound of the waterfall. It made it hard for Morgan to gauge how close they were drawing, and so the cascading white waters were almost something of a surprise as they turned a corner of rocks and shrubs and saw nature's marvel revealed ahead of them.

But Jack Morgan was not looking at the waterfall, no matter how beautiful.

He was looking at the body that was hanged beside it.

Chapter 31

SOPHIE EDWARDS' BODY hung bloated and purple from a rope tied to a tree branch.

"That's her," Lewis confirmed, without having been asked. "Looks like her tricks caught up with her."

Morgan turned to look at the police officer. "Her tricks?" he said evenly. "So you did know who she was, and what she was doing?"

"Of course I did."

"And Sir Tony?"

"Who?" the woman asked, her look convincing Morgan that she was either ignorant of the man and his connection to Sophie Edwards, or that she was an excellent liar.

Cook was about to walk forward when Morgan gently grasped her elbow. "We need to leave the police a good crime scene. Or whatever's left of one after this rain."

Cook nodded, understanding. "Such a waste," she said, shaking her head. "She had so much going for her."

Morgan looked to his phone: there was no reception.

"We should go back to the car," Cook suggested. "Head back down the track until we get service."

"You go and call this in," Morgan told her. "I'll watch over the body."

But as Cook turned to go back up the trail, the crack of bullets crashed through the trees.

Chapter 32

MORGAN, COOK AND Lewis threw themselves to the ground within a half second of hearing the first round crack by. By the sound of the round's low buzz, Morgan knew that the bullets were subsonic, and from a pistol. The fire was accurate, and so the firer must be extremely lucky, or within fifty meters.

No—firers, Morgan corrected himself, hearing overlapping shots as broken branches and splinters fell down onto his head.

"They're over there!" Morgan said, calculating the location by observing the strike marks as the bullets thwacked into the trees.

Lewis sprang up and half stumbled behind a small boulder, her feet slipping on the wet soil. The shooters saw her move and sparks flew up from the rock as rounds ricocheted from its surface.

Morgan watched, heart in mouth, as Lewis raised herself

into that fire and began to shoot double taps at their assail-
ants. Thinking that her fire would distract them, he took the
chance to bound into better cover, grabbing Cook by her
jacket and pulling her with him as she scrabbled along on her
hands.

"Are you hit?" Morgan asked her.

"I'm good," she told him. Morgan felt his chest sag in relief.

"Change position!" he shouted to Lewis, and the police
officer ducked. Sure enough, a few rounds smacked just
behind where her head had been.

"Give me the gun!" Morgan called to her, crawling
forward.

"Fuck off!" Lewis snarled back, rising from her new cover
to deliver two double taps, before dropping down again and
scuttling into a new position. "This isn't Hollywood—I don't
need the Americans to save me."

"Christ, she's enjoying this." Cook shook her head, crawling beside Morgan—without a weapon herself, the former
soldier had never felt more vulnerable, or useless.

"Bloody right I am!" Lewis shouted. "Fuck off back home!"
she shouted over the rocks at the attackers.

And perhaps they listened, because the echo of gunshots
through the trees was steadily giving way to the hammer of
the rain. Morgan looked through a hand-width gap between
rocks and saw two silhouettes moving a hundred meters
away through the foliage. They were not firing now, but one
shape moved as the other held position and took aim. *Either
they're military*, Morgan thought, *or they took the time to learn a
killer's profession.*

Lewis was looking over the sights of her pistol as Morgan
reached her side.

"This is gonna be a lot of bloody paperwork," the police officer said, panting for breath.

"Thank you," Morgan told her, feeling guilty that he had ever doubted the woman. "And now, if it's all right with you, officer, I'd like to go get these bastards."

Chapter 33

JACK MORGAN'S BOOTS thumped into the wet dirt of the path as he ran back to the Range Rover. He was wary of an ambush, but the shooters had moved off in a different direction—Morgan reasoned that the angle meant they would reach the vehicle first. Cook was warning him that there could be a second group of shooters waiting at the vehicle, but Morgan was willing to take that risk—he had to. He had made sure that he was at the front, ahead of the only armed person in their team—if Morgan was wrong and there was a second ambush, then he would be the first one into it. It was a gamble, but every second bought the shooters time to escape.

He saw the Range Rover through the trees and motioned for Lewis and Cook to stop as he ran on alone. Drawing closer, he could see that the vehicle's tires had been slashed, but that fact gave him no concern—he had insisted that the Range Rover come with run-flats. Jack Morgan had learned the hard way how vulnerable tires can be, and how useless the rest of the vehicle becomes without them.

"Come on!" he called, happy that the coast was clear.

"Over there!" Cook pointed as she sprinted.

Morgan turned to follow her indication, and spotting the blurred shape of a four-by-four moving two hundred yards to his right.

"Get in! Let's go!" he urged, jumping behind the wheel himself. Lewis piled into the passenger seat and Cook the rear. They had barely touched the seats before Morgan was gunning the engine and slewing forward through the wet muck of the clearing.

"Jane, keep trying the phones!" Morgan instructed as he blasted the Range Rover through the narrow track between the trees. "Lewis, what's your ammo count?"

"Magazine and a half," she told him. "Twenty-five rounds."

It would have to do. Ahead of them, on a parallel track, Morgan could see a black Land Rover Defender whipping through the branches. In that vehicle were at least two shooters—what was *their* ammo count?

"Still nothing on the phones," Cook announced, cursing as they hit a hard bump and her head bounced off Lewis's headrest.

"The tracks merge soon!" Lewis shouted, the Ordnance Survey map spread on her lap. "No more than half a K!"

"We'll let them get out in front," Morgan told her. "We need to trap them, but we can't do it until we've got help on the way."

"No telling how much ammo they've got," Lewis agreed.

Up ahead, Morgan saw a figure loom large in the window of the Defender's passenger seat.

"Down!" he shouted as a pistol's muzzle flashed and the

first of three shots thumped like a hammer strike against the Range Rover's hood.

"Down!" he ordered again, this time because Lewis was making to stand up on her chair, pushing upward as she retracted the Range Rover's sunroof.

Two more shots cracked. The driver's-side mirror shattered, its electrics hanging like spilled guts as a warning to Morgan.

"Lewis! Get back in here!" he shouted, but the police markswoman was already firing steady single shots, Morgan chancing to look from the track as sparks flew from the Defender's metal.

Lewis's fourth shot smashed into the passenger window.

"I think I got him!" she shouted, her triumph cut short as Morgan pulled hard on her belt, yanking her down savagely as a low branch swiped hard across the Range Rover's roof.

"Thanks." She grinned, knowing that she had been a second from death.

"I think you did get him," Morgan replied—no more fire was coming from the Land Rover, and it pulled ahead of Morgan, both four-by-fours now on the same narrow track. Outside, the rain began to pour harder, cascading through the Range Rover's open roof and lashing against its windshield.

"Can you get a plate?" Morgan asked the officer.

"I can't. I can't see a bloody thing."

He was about to say that it was likely covered up anyway, when Cook's voice came from the back seat—she had found a signal. She was straight onto Private London, coordinating the police's response. "Pass me the map," she told Lewis, who retrieved it from the dirty footwell. "I need to send them grid references."

Confident that there were reinforcements on the way, Morgan knew it was time to play the endgame.

"Next time the track splits, we get ahead of them and box them in."

"Can't we just follow them out to the main roads?" Lewis asked. "Let the uniforms take over?"

Morgan shook his head. "They're armed, and the last thing these roads can handle is a high-speed pursuit. People will get hurt."

Lewis nodded her head, understanding. Those people would be innocent, unwitting of the game they had been caught up in. Their families would lose loved ones, and never understand the reasons why.

Not so Morgan, Lewis and Cook. Each had made a decision to serve, be it the Marine Corps, police force or army. Each had chosen a life that put others' needs before their own. Each had chosen a job where the possibility of sacrificing yourself for the good of strangers was a well-known requirement. Cook and Morgan were out of uniform now, but such things were embedded in their characters.

"We'll keep them bottled up until the cavalry gets here," Lewis said, accepting what could happen to them in that attempt.

"The next break in the track," Morgan confirmed.

"They're scrambling the police helicopter," Cook told them from the back, the map in her hand. "Jack, the track breaks left in a hundred meters."

Through the rain and the dirt kicked up by the speeding Defender's tires, Morgan saw it. He let the shooters pull further ahead, waiting for them to choose their path. They stuck to the trail, so Morgan gunned the engine hard and turned up onto the parallel track. Within moments, they were pulling abreast, separated by nothing but trees and rain.

"Shoot across me!" Morgan commanded.

Lewis pushed the weapon out in front of the American, snapping a double tap, the empty cases hitting Morgan's jaw. He had no idea what impact Lewis's shooting was having, but the passenger in the Defender showed themself to be alive, rounds beating the Range Rover's skin like a drum. Cook barely covered her eyes in time as shards of glass shattered inward.

"Get ahead, Jack, get ahead!" she shouted, and Morgan pushed the Range Rover harder, throwing a backward glance at the Land Rover, desperate to see the faces of the shooters—the faces of the people that wanted him dead.

"Jack!" Cook cried.

"Are you hit?" he called.

But his eyes saw the reason for her shout as his eyes turned back to the track, and the piled logs that lay across it.

"Jack!" Cook shouted again as Morgan hit the brakes hard. The Range Rover slid forward into the wood. Timber went bouncing and breaking into the air as Morgan and his team were slammed into the steering wheel, dashboard and seats.

Morgan's first instinct was to bail out of the car, certain that at any second bullets would begin to rip into his flesh as the shooters stopped to finish the job.

But the danger passed by them—the shooters were not firing, and the Land Rover was gone.

Chapter 34

FURIOUS THAT THE shooters had escaped, Morgan thumped his fist against the Range Rover's mud-splattered bonnet. "What's the ETA on the police helicopter?"

"It will get to the point where the main road meets the forest track in ten minutes," Cook told him.

Morgan shook his head. "Not fast enough. They'll hit it in less than five, and that's if they use the same point into the forest that we did. There could be others. They could even dump the vehicle and make it out on foot."

"They could," Cook agreed, downcast.

Rain pattered from Morgan's shadowed face as he made his decision. "You two will go back in the Range Rover and secure the scene until the police arrive."

"We can't split up, Jack," Cook pleaded. "They could still be out here, setting up a second ambush."

"All the more reason for me to be on foot," he replied. "I can stay off the tracks. It's not thick forest. I'll make quick time."

"But—"

"Jane, thank you, but remember who we are and what the hierarchy is. This is my call."

"Of course," she managed, taking a half-step backward.

"She's right though, Morgan," Lewis added from the passenger seat. "No offence to the girl, but Sophie doesn't know if she has company or not. Don't risk the living for the dead."

"The crime scene needs preserving," Morgan insisted, pulling tight his laces.

Lewis put her hand out of the window and into the pouring rain. "The crime scene is bollocksed, and the local bobbies will be here in well under an hour."

"We should stick together, Jack," Cook ventured again.

It was her eyes more than her words that convinced Morgan. It had nothing to do with tactics, he admitted to himself, and everything to do with not wanting her to be out of his sight.

"OK," he conceded. "Find us a new route out of here, Jane, just in case there's another surprise on the route that we came in on."

"Where are we going?" she asked.

"The Princess hired us to find Sophie," Morgan said, grim-faced. "We need to be the ones to tell her what happened to her."

Cook nodded solemnly. "And then what?"

It was a moment before Morgan answered. He was prying something out from the shattered windshield with his fingers. "And then," he told Cook, holding up the dull shape of a flattened bullet, "then we find the connection to two bodies. We find Eliza Lightwood."

Chapter 35

PETER KNIGHT STOOD in his office, hands on his head, his eyes burning into a map of the United Kingdom that he had taped to the office wall. Brightly colored pins had been jabbed into various towns and villages with Post-it notes attached. These were places with known connections to Eliza Lightwood—grandparents, cousins, ex-boyfriends, favorite getaway locations. Hooligan had laughed out loud at Knight's low-tech methods, but Knight was a man who liked something tangible to work with, and in front of him was the map of what his Private employees had been able to piece together through Eliza's records, social media and character profiling.

She could be anywhere, he thought, staring at the array of pins that stretched across the map.

But she was not.

"Peter," a familiar voice said at the door, with a gentle knock.

Knight turned. His hands dropped from his head. His jaw dropped to the floor.

"Eliza," he gasped.

"I heard you've been looking for me. I went to the coast to think," she explained, taking the chair Knight offered her.

"You went to the coast?" he gently pushed.

"Just to drive, and think. There's been so much bloody noise since my dad died. Some of it of my own creation, but then there's his businesses, bloody lawyers, relatives who want a handout. He's not even in his grave and they're after his money."

"That must be hard."

"It is hard. I just needed a break from it. I just wanted to drive and listen to music. No phone. No arseholes trying to call me. Present company excepted, of course." She gave a weak smile.

"There were some things I needed to talk with you about." He spoke gently, finding himself convinced by Eliza's words and manner. "Do you know a woman by the name of Sophie Edwards?"

A look of bewilderment passed over her face. "I know *a* Sophie Edwards," she explained. "But I imagine there would be more than a few people by that name in London."

"This Sophie was at LSE with you."

"Then yes. Why are you asking?"

"Actually," Knight smiled, anxious that Eliza was becoming too defensive, "it's for another case Private is working. I saw your name on her class records."

"Oh." Eliza relaxed a little. "Small world, isn't it? But yes, we were in the same class at LSE. We kept in touch, but we aren't particularly close."

"When was the last time you saw her?"

"The weekend before last. She came to one of my bigger dinner parties with her boyfriend."

"She has a boyfriend?" Knight asked, hiding his surprise.

"Sort of. I don't know how serious they are exactly, but it's London. His name's Mayoor Patel; he's a hedge fund manager that I work with pretty often. Great guy. Very funny."

"Does he come to all of your dinner parties?"

It was a moment before Eliza replied. "No."

"Why?"

"Because he brings Sophie," she admitted, breaking her gaze from Peter.

"And Sophie had a thing for your father?" Knight guessed, seeing his torpedo strike.

"Two types of people go to LSE, Peter. Those who want to make money, and those who want to take it."

"And which one was Sophie?"

Eliza smiled, but there was no happiness in it. Only malice and resentment. "She looked at my dad like he was a five-star meal ticket. Why are you asking me all this, Peter? And don't bullshit me about other investigations. I'm not stupid, so spit it out."

Private's agent met her wild stare. "I think Sophie Edwards was the one blackmailing your father."

Chapter 36

THE STATE OF the battered and shot-up Range Rover drew stares from the two plain-clothed guards at Llwynywermod's gate, the two men emerging from a four-by-four of their own and into the rain. "Are you all right?" they asked their colleague Lewis.

"I'm good," she beamed. "Got one of them through a passenger window."

"You ally bastard," one of the guards grinned. Jane Cook recognized the army slang for "cool."

"We need to see the Princess," Lewis followed up. "Like, now."

"She's not here, mate." The evident soldier shook his head. "Chopper took her out earlier. Got an event on in London."

"Opening a school, I think it was," his partner added.

"Shit," Lewis sighed.

Jack Morgan was not so deflated—Princess Caroline wasn't the only one with access to helicopters, and on Morgan's instructions, Private dispatched one to Wales.

"Go on up," one of the armed men told Lewis. "And enjoy your paperwork."

"Piss off." She laughed as Morgan put the vehicle into gear, and they wound their way up to the royal residence.

"He's right though." The police officer shook her head. "If you survive a shooting they just try and drown you in paperwork instead. I'd better get inside and put in an after-action report. I'm afraid I'll be no use to you now, either."

"What do you mean?" Morgan asked.

"I mean I've got to hand in my weapon once I report this shooting. Then I'll be placed on leave, pending the results of the investigation."

"You've got to be kidding me," the American gasped.

"That's ridiculous!" Cook exclaimed from the back seat.

Lewis shrugged her shoulders. "Well, there it is. I got to do what I always wanted to do. Now I've got to take it in the arse from the desk jockeys." She gathered her few possessions from the Range Rover and made to leave. "I enjoyed working with you guys."

Morgan smiled. He knew that sentiment was a lie, at least for the most part, but there was nothing like the shared danger of being shot at to bring a team together.

"Thank you, Lewis." Cook put out her hand. "Without you we'd be dead."

"We would," Morgan agreed. "You ever need anything, you call me."

"We'll see each other again," Lewis promised. "In court, probably."

"Goodbye, Lewis." Morgan watched the brave woman he'd once suspected as his would-be assassin walk through the rain and into the residence.

"I got to like her," Cook admitted. "Some balls on her."

"Brass ones," Morgan agreed.

"So we'll go back to London?" she asked.

There was a second's delay before Morgan replied, "I will." He saw the slightest slump in Cook's shoulders, unable to hide her disappointment.

"Lewis is right," he explained. "There's going to be a paperwork circus after today. I've sent for our legal team, but until they get here, I need you to hold the fort. Make sure the transition to the police goes smoothly."

"I can do that," she told him, professionalism overcoming her desire to be close to Jack Morgan. "Will I see you back in London?" she asked.

Something in her eyes, something in her words, made the investigator in Morgan question what he had been told.

"You're not in a relationship, are you, Jane?" he asked her.

"I'm not," she confessed.

"Then why—"

"Because I didn't want to be the woman sleeping with the boss," Cook blurted out. "I didn't want people talking behind my back. But more than that, I needed to know how Jack Morgan would treat me if we were colleagues, and not lovers."

Morgan let the words sink in. "Well, now you know." He stepped in closer, less than a foot between the two of them as the rain pattered against Cook's upturned face.

"Now I know," she agreed.

He put out his hands, and pushed back the wet hair from her face, tucking it behind her ears. She was beautiful. No matter how he had tried to suppress his feelings, they had not diminished. Now Morgan looked deeply into Cook's eyes.

"We're close to finishing this," he promised.

She understood that he meant their absence as lovers as well as the case.

"And when we are, we'll go away. No work. No cases. Just us."

"Sounds perfect." Cook smiled. "Where?"

"Hawaii," Morgan told her, picturing the blissful image of big waves, blue skies and Jane in his arms. Despite the cold Welsh rain, he felt as though he was already there. Only the sound of helicopter blades broke him from his reverie.

"You have to go," she almost whispered.

"I'll send it back for you," he promised. "Hand over to the legal team, and I'll take care of the Princess." Morgan turned to watch as the helicopter touched down a hundred yards from the house, the mountains behind it ominous and dark beneath the thick cloud.

It was time for Morgan to leave Wales. There was only one more thing for him to do.

He took Cook's hands in his, the touch full of the spark and promise of what was to come. "I'll see you in London."

And then he kissed her.

Chapter 37

PETER KNIGHT LOOKED at what had become of his office. His map of the United Kingdom and the carefully placed pins lay crumpled and torn on the floor. A chair lay on its side by the door. The pens, photos and paperwork from his desk had been tossed like confetti.

"Are you calm now?" he asked the woman who had trashed his office. Fearing for Eliza Lightwood's safety more than his own, Knight had taken her down with a self-defense move and was now sitting on top of her, exerting just enough pressure to keep the woman pinned.

"I'm sorry," Eliza wheezed out.

"I know you've had a shock, Eliza, but I can't let you up if you're going to do that again."

"I'm good, Peter, honestly. I'm sorry. That just all came as a shock. It...it really threw me. I'm sorry. I just lost it for a moment."

Knight could understand why: hearing that your friend was responsible for blackmailing your father into suicide was not something that could be taken lightly. Still, it gave Knight pause for thought. If Eliza's temper was as violent as this...

He hadn't revealed to her that Sophie's body had been found, but could Eliza already know that the blackmailer was hanging in a Welsh forest? Could she have been the one to put her there, during her absence that she claimed was a drive to the south coast?

He had more questions than answers. He expected he wouldn't learn much more by keeping Eliza pinned to his office floor.

He stood.

She got up slowly, red with embarrassment and exertion as she took in the devastation she had caused. "My God, Peter...Send me the bill. Whatever it is. Redecorate the entire floor of this building and I'll pay for it. I'm so, so sorry."

"That won't be necessary, Eliza. You've had a rough time recently. It's perfectly understandable."

"Thank you, Peter." She sighed. "You've been so amazing throughout all this...Do you have a bathroom I could use? I'd like to clean myself up before I go."

"Of course." Knight smiled, and showed her the way.

As soon as she was out of sight, he pulled out his phone and wrote a text message to Hooligan:

Look deeper into Eliza. Could she have put contract killers onto Sophie? Or killed her herself? Possible she could have got to Wales and back in time to dump body? Try to discover her movements in the past three days.

Private London's tech guru replied a second later.

OK. What will you be doing?

Peter looked toward the bathroom before he replied.

Old-fashioned stuff.

"Thanks for waiting, Peter." Eliza smiled as she emerged from the bathroom.

"No problem." He smiled back, walking her out to the front of Private's building and waving her goodbye.

Then, as Eliza opened her umbrella and blended into the pedestrian traffic of London, Knight began his tail.

Chapter 38

KNIGHT WASN'T SURE where he expected Eliza Lightwood to go when she left Private headquarters, so he wasn't caught by surprise when her distinctive red umbrella marked her as taking a detour from the shortest route to her home, instead joining dozens of other Londoners as they bustled into an Underground station, umbrellas snapping closed with sighs of relief as they found sanctuary from the rain.

Like any investigator or law enforcement agent, Peter Knight hated the London Underground. It made what was an already difficult job so much harder—a sprawling warren of tunnels, staircases, barriers, carriages, escalators and lifts, not to mention the thousands of people that could be inside the busier stations. Each one of these factors was an obstacle that had to be overcome again and again. Get too close, and the target of the tail would see you—in this case, shattering any trust that Eliza had in Knight should she be innocent. If she was guilty, well... then Knight knew that any chance of Eliza slipping up would be gone—she was too intelligent to make mistakes twice.

He pushed back the hood of his jacket as he entered the station and replaced it with a cap he kept in its pocket—the "disguise" wouldn't save him from a direct look, but on the crowded levels of the Underground, it was enough to protect against a target's peripheral vision, or sweeping gaze as they sought out platforms, lines and train times.

There were no such looks from Eliza. She cut through the station like a missile, leaving in her wake a trail of angry looks and muttered curses. It made Knight's work as a tail a hundred times easier, but there was always the chance that Eliza could stop and turn quickly, catching him out and ending a game in which Knight hoped he was the only witting player. To counter this, he had a plan.

In fact, he had a plan years ago, and he had been working on it ever since. Like any true professional, Peter Knight had prepared and he had practiced. Every member of Private London's staff had taken turns trying to lose their co-workers in London. The Underground was a particular favorite place to do this, and Knight had made it a priority that he and Private's agents honed their tracking skills whenever their investigations allowed. Seeing the Underground as one great maze to be understood and mastered had led to great competition developing amongst Knight and his agents, and it became impossible for Knight to take even the shortest trip with his family without finding himself seeking out the best vantage points, the quickest turnstiles and the most covered approaches.

He used this accumulated knowledge of the system now as he passed through the other travelers with as little fuss as possible. Peter Knight was a much bigger person than Eliza Lightwood, and he would not be able to get away with the same kind of barging approach that the petite woman had—while Eliza's behavior had drawn shaking heads and disgusted looks from some men, it could mean a punch for the six-foot man.

Knight held back as Eliza neared the top of an escalator. He was not surprised at all to see that she went straight to the left, and shuffled down the moving stairway quickly. Knight loitered at the top and watched until she was almost at the bottom—he would make up the gap soon enough.

Eliza cleared the escalator, and broke left. Knight followed, offering hushed apologies as he squeezed by commuters and tourists. He checked his speed at the bottom, moving the opposite way to the route of most tourists—he knew from his training exercises that the only route left then turned right onto a platform. He could bypass the left turn by going right, along that platform, and then use an adjoining foot tunnel that connected the two platforms at their heads. Then he could work his way closer to Eliza. Close enough to keep his eye on her, at least.

Of course, all this had to be done before Eliza had a chance to board a train. Knight remembered the average time between them at this station to be about three minutes. Watching on the escalator, he had not seen the hurried sprints and shuffles of passengers as they rushed to catch the closing doors, so he figured that at least a minute had gone by since the last, giving him two minutes at best to find Eliza. He ran the length of the platform on his right, sidestepping a wide-eyed old man who was also taking the least busy route—Knight wasn't the only one who had spent time on the Underground and knew its shortcuts.

Exiting the short connecting foot tunnel onto Eliza's platform, Knight saw that it was busy but not crowded. Looking up, he also saw from the information board that the next train was now due in.

He had less than one minute to find her, but the moment for rushing and recklessness had gone. Instead, like dozens of others on the platform, Knight pulled his phone from his pocket. With his head down, but eyes up, he began to work his way along the back wall.

Eliza's red umbrella was the first thing to catch his eye, its color picking it out amongst the black trousers and boots of other passengers as she held it down by her side. Knight chanced a look at her face and saw that she was staring across the empty tracks with a fixed look of single-minded purpose. As the train came in, she was the first to enter a carriage. He noticed that she took no seat, instead standing by the open door. Knight stepped onto the train in the next carriage along, his height allowing him to make out the top of Eliza's head through the windows. He prepared himself to clear the closing doors quickly should it all be a ruse to send him off her path, but Eliza's head was motionless as the doors slid into place and the train heaved its way from the station.

Chapter 39

IT WAS AT the third stop that Eliza disembarked. Knight followed, happy to see that there were other passengers emerging who could cloak him.

He needn't have worried. Eliza's focus was on moving forward, and in no time they were out of the station and onto the streets of Kensington. The rain had weakened, but was still heavy enough to justify Knight pulling the hood of his jacket back over his head. From beneath the brim of his cap, he saw Eliza walk inside a Tesco supermarket. He watched the entrance, waiting for her to reappear. He made use of the opportunity to call in to Private HQ and update them on his intention and location.

When Eliza emerged onto the pavement, Knight hung back as she paced along Kensington's long streets, confident that he could hold his tail from a distance. It was only when she turned and walked up the steps of a beautiful brick town house that he pressed closer, using the parked luxury cars that lined the road as cover.

From thirty meters away, he watched as the small woman rapped her left fist against the cream-painted wood of the door, her umbrella clutched unopened in her right hand. She knocked on the door again, and again, and again.

An Indian man opened the door, and his handsome face twisted in bewilderment.

Eliza had let go of the umbrella and was left clutching something else in her right hand.

It was a knife.

"Where is she?" she screamed at the top of her lungs. "Where is she?"

The man at the door was shocked into stillness at first, but then his survival instincts kicked into life and offered him the choice of fight or flight.

He chose flight and ran back into the house.

"Where is she?" Eliza screamed again, running in after him.

Knight was already across the road and nearing the steps to the house at a sprint. He ran up the steps and into the shouts, screams and crashes coming from inside the beautiful Kensington home.

He followed the noises to a living room, where the terrified man had taken refuge behind a sofa and was trying to keep Eliza at bay by hurling at her books, vases, ornaments and anything else within reach. One heavy leather-bound tome connected with her face and blood poured from her nose.

"Where is she, Mayoor?" Eliza screamed at the man again, oblivious to Knight behind her. "Where is that bitch? Where is she?"

Knight knew he could take no chances. For the sake of all three lives, he had to act swiftly and decisively.

"Help me!" Mayoor called, catching sight of Knight in the doorway. "Please!"

Eliza turned to see where Sophie's boyfriend's panicked eyes were looking. Her own barely registered the look of remorse on Knight's face as he threw the punch and knocked Eliza Lightwood into unconsciousness.

Chapter 40

JACK MORGAN LOOKED out of the helicopter's windows and over the gray landscape of a rain-sodden east London, his destination clearly marked by the second helicopter that was landed on a school's football field. It was Princess Caroline's helicopter, and Morgan had come alone to tell her that Sophie Edwards was dead.

The chopper's skids touched down on the grass, and Morgan thanked the pilot before handing him his next orders—to head back to Wales and bring Cook to London as soon as Private's legal representatives arrived to deal with the fallout of the case. With that, he opened the door and stepped onto the field's wet grass.

A man was waiting to meet him. The face was familiar but the clothes were not—Colonel Marcus De Villiers was wearing civilian clothing, a green Barbour jacket over corduroy trousers. Even out of uniform, the man stood out as a military officer.

The Englishman put out his hand to greet him. "Morgan, I've spoken to PC Lewis. She said that you saved her life."

"She saved mine," Morgan replied, accepting the hand-shake.

"Regardless, you have my thanks. Lewis is a good woman, and fiercely loyal. She's one of my favorites on the protection teams," the Colonel admitted, and for the first time, Morgan saw a second side to De Villiers. One which was, perhaps, just as fiercely loyal to his team as Lewis was to her superiors.

"I'll be putting her forward for an award," De Villiers told Morgan as they walked across the sports field and toward the school. "Because of the reasons why she was in that situation in the first place, it will never pass, but at least she'll know that I recognize her bravery."

The pair paced in silence for a few seconds before De Villiers addressed the reason behind Morgan's arrival. "She's going to be upset about Sophie." There was no trace of sadness in his words.

Morgan pulled up, and the Guards officer stopped and turned to him. "What is it?" De Villiers asked.

"Did the Princess hire Private to find Sophie, or bury a secret?"

"I'm not sure which particular secret of Sophie's you're talking about. She had many—"

"I'm not talking about Sophie's secrets. I'm talking about the Princess's secret, Colonel. The secret that she and Sophie Edwards were lovers."

Chapter 41

DE VILLIERS SAID nothing.

"Don't tell me you didn't know," Morgan insisted.

"I did," the Colonel admitted. "Her security personnel and staff give their loyalty to her first and foremost, and they kept it from me, but certain things you can't hide. When they were together? Well, you'd have to be a bloody fool not to see it."

For a moment, Morgan thought about the attraction between himself and Jane Cook. The Englishman was right—some things could not be hidden.

At least, not while those people were alive.

"Someone killed Sophie to hide this secret and prevent a scandal," Morgan declared.

"Impossible!"

"Quite possible, Colonel. Not only is Sophie dead, but three of us only just escaped joining her that way in the forest. Someone didn't want us to find her. To avoid secrets finding the light."

"Are you suggesting the Princess had Sophie killed?" The

Colonel shook his head. "If the Princess murdered Sophie to hide the secret of their relationship, then why would she hire you to find her?"

"I don't believe for one second that the Princess would harm Sophie. I think that whoever wants this secret buried works for the royal family. They knew where we'd be, and they wanted us stopped."

It took the Colonel a moment to form his reply, which came out in a forced tone that barely concealed his anger. "I will not stand for accusations like this being thrown at my people, Morgan. We keep very close control over our firearms and their use.

"Send your experts to our facilities, and I'll give them full access to our armory and records so that you can run ballistic tests against them and the ones recovered from your hotel and Range Rover. You can have that and anything else you need to put this wild theory to bed.

"Well? Is that good enough for you? Morgan?"

But Jack Morgan wasn't listening. He was watching as a group of people emerged from the school and made their way toward the helicopter. Princess Caroline was at their head, and Morgan could almost feel the frustration emanating from her as she saw him but resisted the urge to run toward him.

Once she had reached them, she wasted no time in asking the question: "You found her?"

"I did."

A solitary tear made its way slowly to Princess Caroline's cheekbone. There it was flicked away as if it were an errant eyelash, the movement hiding the flash of vulnerability from all but Morgan—looking into her eyes, he could see that a tidal wave of emotion was building inside her, threatening to break through.

"I'd like to talk to the Princess inside, and in private," said Morgan.

"Of course," replied De Villiers, quickly showing them back inside the building to rooms that had been cleared and guarded for the use of the royal visitor and her team. Crayoned pictures of families, sunshine and pets covered the walls of the classroom. *Life begins so happily*, Morgan thought to himself.

"Sophie's dead, Your Highness," he said simply. "I'm so very sorry."

"I knew it as soon as you spoke outside," she replied.

Morgan watched as Princess Caroline cast her eyes over the children's pictures, no doubt thinking the same thoughts as Morgan.

"At what point does it go wrong?" she asked, almost to herself.

Morgan didn't reply. If he allowed Caroline to talk, perhaps she would shed some detail on Sophie that was a thread Morgan could pull at to unravel the mystery surrounding her connection to Sir Tony Lightwood.

"Have you ever been in love?" she asked.

The question surprised Morgan. "I have," he admitted after a moment, the image of Cook's face floating in his mind. He could almost feel her, if he closed his eyes.

"I can see it." Princess Caroline half smiled. "You'd do anything for her?"

"Of course."

"You'd lay down your life for a stranger, or a case?" She thought it over. "I suppose there's no end to what you'd do for someone you loved . . ."

Her words trailed away, and Morgan let them go, waiting for her to come to her point.

"I'm sure you've worked out that Sophie was more than a friend to me. I don't know if what we had was a relationship, but I know that it was love. You see, Jack, I didn't care about her past, but we knew that we couldn't think about a future. It was impossible. Can you see that?"

Morgan nodded. "She was the one with secrets, but you're the one who couldn't carry them."

"She was everything to me, and yet we couldn't ever be *anything*. Times have changed and society has moved forwards, but the support of the royal family is a conservative base, Jack. A lesbian princess? I hope, soon, that this is something Britain can embrace."

"But not when her partner has a history of prostitution and blackmail," Morgan finished, as delicately as was possible for such a statement.

"Even when you say it kindly it sounds terrible, doesn't it? I swear to you, Jack, those days were behind her, but we both knew... we both knew that you can never be free of the things you do and the mistakes you made, no matter how long ago."

A heavy silence filled the room.

"How did she die?" Caroline asked eventually.

"I don't think you want to—"

"Jack, please. Just tell me how."

"We found her hanged. It was by a waterfall, in a forest."

"Sounds like a beautiful place," she managed, doubtless trying to push away the image of Sophie's body.

"It was."

Princess Caroline sat. Morgan knew the woman's next question was the one that was eating at her soul. "Did she kill herself, Jack?"

Morgan shook his head. "I don't think so. I think it was staged to make it look that way."

"Then find whoever staged it, Jack," she begged, taking his hand in a grip like steel. "Find them. Find them, and bring them to justice."

Chapter 42

PETER KNIGHT WATCHED from the Kensington home's doorway as Eliza Lightwood's stretcher was loaded onto the back of an ambulance. Though he had prevented a stabbing, and possibly murder, Knight felt awful—he had been raised never to hit women. At moments like this, he wondered what his beloved wife would think of him.

"Everything all right?" a police officer asked, seeing Knight's melancholy.

"All good," he lied.

"Look, doesn't sound like there was any other choice," the officer comforted the Private agent, empathizing with him. "I just finished interviewing your man in there, and he says that you saved his life."

"Still..."

"No one said our jobs are easy." The policeman shrugged. "He's all yours if you want to talk to him."

Knight gave his thanks to the officer, took one last look at the ambulance and walked back into the house. He found

Mayoor Patel in the kitchen, the tea in his hand almost sent spilling as he got to his feet quickly at the sight of Knight.

"Mate, thank you so much, yeah." Mayoor Patel spoke with an energized London accent. "You saved my life, mate. Listen. If there's anything I can ever do for you, you've got it. Anything, yeah."

"Thanks. I'm Peter Knight."

"Mayoor Patel."

"Do you mind if I sit down with you, Mayoor?"

"Course not. You want a tea? Or a beer? We could go out for a drink if you want, yeah? I owe you my life, mate."

"Tea will be good, thanks."

Knight watched as Patel quickly fussed over the brew and brought it to the table. "I'm all out of biscuits, mate," Patel apologized, sitting down.

"That's OK. I just want to ask you a few things, if that's OK?"

"What, like questions?"

Knight nodded, and a frown grew on Patel's face. "I already spoke with the police."

"I'm a private investigator," Knight explained. "I was following Eliza when she attacked you. Anything you could help me learn about her would help."

"Oh...well, yeah. Happy to help."

"So how do you know each other?"

"We work together, yeah. Sometimes, anyway. I'm at a hedge fund, and we have some mutual interests."

"Would one of those mutual interests be Sophie Edwards?" Knight asked, leaning back into his chair.

For a moment Patel said nothing. Knight tried to decide if his wide eyes were a symptom of confusion, or fear.

"Sophie?" the man managed after a moment.

Knight nodded.

"She's my girlfriend," Patel explained. "What's she got to do with Eliza?"

"They were at LSE together."

"So were a lot of the City," he shrugged, referring to London's financial sector.

"That's true. But Eliza came to your house with a knife and was screaming 'where is she?' Is she talking about Sophie?"

"If you're not police, I don't have to talk to you, do I?"

"You don't. But I can ask them to come back in if you like?"

Patel said nothing.

"I saved your life, Mayoor," Knight went on. "Why would I do that if I wasn't on your side?"

The man thought that over. "Listen, yeah. Soph is a free spirit. She comes when she wants, she goes when she wants. I don't know where she is now, and I definitely have no fucking idea why that information is worth stabbing me for."

"When was the last time you heard from Sophie?"

"Couple days ago." Patel shrugged again. "Like I said, she's a free spirit. Can I use the bathroom before we keep going with this? I've had two teas now and I was already close to pissing myself when she pulled that knife."

Knight's eyes narrowed a little in suspicion.

"It's right there." Patel pointed to a door adjoining the kitchen, and Knight was able to see that it was central to the house.

"It's your home."

Knight watched as the man opened the door, a quick look satisfying him that it was a small bathroom and nothing else.

"Peter," the policeman said, poking his head inside the kitchen. "We're going to leave now if you don't need us."

"All good." Both men tried not to laugh as the sound of loose bowels emanated from the bathroom.

"Can't really blame him," the officer said. "It was a big knife. See you soon, Peter."

Knight said his goodbyes. Looking for a distraction from the noises coming from the bathroom, he got to his feet and began to pace the kitchen. There were photos of Sophie Edwards and Mayoor Patel dotted about, some stuck to the fridge with magnets, others framed and placed on work surfaces.

He noticed that one of the framed photos was turned facedown. He lifted it and saw a smiling Patel and Sophie standing beside a waterfall. The picture was so calm and idyllic that for a moment, Knight swore he could hear running water.

And then he remembered Jack's description of where Sophie's body had been found.

He turned toward the bathroom, but it was too late. The door was open and Mayoor Patel was a half-step away from him—and there was something in his hands.

Then, for Knight, there was darkness.

Chapter 43

LIGHT BEGAN TO seep beneath struggling eyelids. It pained Peter Knight to open his eyes, but a voice in his head told him—screamed at him—to get up. He was alive, but he could still be in danger. He had to wake up, get up, and be ready to defend himself.

He rolled onto his front and felt a mouthful of hot blood gush over his lips and onto the floor. With his eyes open, he could see that he had been knocked to the ground of Mayoor Patel's kitchen, but of the man there was no sign. Two broken pieces of ceramic lay beside him—the toilet's cistern lid that must have been Patel's weapon—and Knight knew he was lucky to be alive.

His head throbbing and mouth aching, he pushed himself up onto his knees, feeling his pockets. His phone was still there. The fact that Patel had left it suggested to Knight that he was out of his depth, acting on terrified instinct rather than cold-planned killing.

Knight hit his speed dial.

"Jack," he croaked, wiping away blood with the back of his hand.

"Peter, are you OK?"

"Patel knocked me out," Knight admitted, shame burning every inch of his skin. "I'm sorry, Jack. He got away."

"Why would he attack you?" Jack Morgan asked.

Knight picked up the photograph of Sophie and Patel in front of the waterfall. "I think he killed Sophie. There was a photo of them together where you found her. It was turned facedown."

"He couldn't look at it," Morgan guessed. "But why keep it?"

"Maybe because he didn't want her friends to be suspicious if they came by?" Knight suggested. "Or he kept it because to hide the evidence would be an admission of his guilt he wasn't willing to make, even to himself. He doesn't seem like a cold-blooded killer, Jack. I think he killed Sophie, but I'm almost certain it was a crime of passion. When I saw him cornered by Eliza, there wasn't an ounce of aggression in him. He was terrified."

"Don't sleep on this guy, Peter. For all we know, he thought you were dead when he put you down. We need to find this bastard, and soon."

Knight knew the same, and began a frantic search of Patel's home for clues. "Stay on the line while I take a look around," he told Morgan.

"Go to his office, or whatever he has that passes as one," Morgan instructed. "Look for a passport. We need to know if he's trying to jump the country."

Knight found the office at the top of the stairs. He began pulling out the drawers of Patel's desk, dumping their contents out on the floor and searching through. "No sign of a passport."

"Check his closet," Morgan suggested, and Knight ran to the bedroom, flinging open a door to a walk-in wardrobe—there was a large section of clothes missing in a chunk from the railing, and more on the floor.

"He grabbed a load of clothes in a hurry," Knight informed Morgan. "He's not coming back. Can we stop him at the airports?"

"Not a chance. He's only a suspect to us, not to the law. Either we stop him, Peter, or no one does."

There was silence on the line as both men contemplated that likely and sickening possibility.

It was Knight who broke it.

"I've got an idea."

Chapter 44

JACK MORGAN PACED outside the school with the phone held to his ear. The line had been silent for almost five minutes while Knight carried out his plan. Morgan thought it was a long shot at best and was readying himself for the news that Knight had come up empty-handed from his inglorious task—Knight had emptied the contents of Patel's trash on the pavement and was rummaging through it for clues. Knight's reasoning was that Sophie's death had occurred within days and that the bins were full. They probably hadn't been emptied since it happened. Knight didn't expect he'd find evidence of a murder in such a place, but there might be a suggestion as to the destination Patel could be looking to escape to.

"I've got it!" Knight shouted victoriously down the line. "I've got something, Jack!"

"What is it?"

"It's a torn-up letter. I found all three pieces. It's thanking Patel for opening a safety deposit box at a bank in Staines."

"Staines?" the American asked.

"It's close to Heathrow!"

Morgan understood the implications at once—a safety deposit box opened within days of the murder of Sophie Edwards, a few minutes from one of the world's busiest airports.

"How long to get there from where you are?" Morgan asked, feeling his pulse quicken.

"No more than ninety minutes," Knight replied. "He's got at least an hour's head start on us, Jack."

"OK, send me the address and I'll head there too...And Peter, contact your sister-in-law at the Met. Beg her, lie to her, do whatever, but we need surveillance at every train station within a three-mile radius of that bank, and the bank itself."

"I'll do my best," Knight promised. "Why three miles?"

"Patel hasn't planned any of this well, but he may be smart enough to not get off at the nearest station."

"But what if he gets a cab, or a bus?" Knight asked.

"There's nothing we can do about that. I'm sending Cook to your location. She's too far out to make it to the bank ahead of us, but she can secure Patel's place ready for the police investigation."

"OK, Jack. I'm running to the nearest station now. I'll lose signal on the Tube, so I guess I'll see you there."

Morgan hung up and walked back inside the school. He found De Villiers waiting for him by the entrance.

"Trouble?" the Colonel guessed.

"Not for long," Morgan replied. "I need to use the Princess's helicopter."

"That's impossible."

Morgan shook his head. "It's totally possible, Colonel. And it's going to happen."

"It is?" De Villiers snorted.

"It is." Morgan smiled. "Or you can explain to the Princess why Sophie's killer escaped."

Chapter 45

MAYOOR PATEL ENTERED the bank less than ten minutes after Jack Morgan had ended his call with Peter Knight. He was inside for twenty minutes more, during which time he collected his passport and money that he had deposited there should he be forced into fleeing the country. That eventuality was now a reality, and Patel had surprised himself at the level of calm he had shown since it had become apparent that London could no longer be his home.

It hadn't begun that way. When the private investigator had questioned him regarding Sophie's whereabouts, it was all Patel could do not to lose control of his bowels right there and then at the kitchen table. Having locked himself in the bathroom, he had been afforded some moments to think, and the answer to his problem had been both obvious and terrifying: he had to kill the investigator, and escape.

That was easier said than done. Patel had had no weapon and he was certainly no fighter. It was only after a thorough search of the bathroom that he'd settled upon the cistern's ceramic lid, and even then Patel had almost scuffed the plan, his sweaty hands barely able to hold the shiny porcelain.

But then he had thought of the alternative to carrying through his attack: prison. Mayoor Patel was self-aware enough to know that he was not a hard man, nor could he ever become one. Prison for him would be a series of beatings and rapes. He knew that he would kill himself before his first year was served. The only way to avoid that fate was to kill one more person.

He had been crying when he swung the ceramic at Knight's head. They were tears of fear, anger and frustration. When Knight had crumpled to the floor, Patel had laughed in relief. The man was unconscious, but alive! He would not have the investigator's blood on his hands, and that was part of the reason he felt so calm. The other was that he knew he could not be stopped. By the time the investigator regained consciousness, it would be too late. Patel would be on his way. His first stop would be India, where any man could lose himself and buy a new identity. Then perhaps the Maldives. God knows he needed a place where his mind and soul could recover.

With the thought of white sandy beaches and clear blue ocean in mind, Patel did not pay much attention to the man who dropped his credit card as he walked toward the bank's ATM and crouched to pick it up. In fact, the first time he really became aware of the figure was when that man sprang forward from his kneeling position and barreled into him, picking up Patel in a double-leg takedown and driving him into the pavement.

"Help!" Patel shouted as he was rolled onto his front and his arms were pulled up sharply behind his back. "I'm being robbed! Help me!"

And help did come. It came from a tall man who ran across the street, his gaunt face drawn into a grim expression.

But Patel's stomach dropped when his attacker turned to address the tall man.

"Good of you to join me, De Villiers," the attacker said.

"Is this him, Jack?" De Villiers asked.

"It is," said the man pinning Patel to the ground.

De Villiers waved and two men came running to join them.

"Arrest this man for the assault of Peter Knight."

Chapter 46

ALL WAS QUIET in interview room number four of the Staines police station. Mayoor Patel sat on one side of the cheap metal table, Jack Morgan on the other. In the room's corner stood the stern-faced police officer who had placed Patel under arrest.

"I'm charged with assault?" Patel addressed the officer, who only nodded back. "Nothing else?"

"Nothing else," the officer confirmed.

"Then I think I want my—"

Morgan's fist slammed onto the table to cut off Patel's request for a lawyer, the violence sending the Londoner shooting back in his seat.

"Before that, I have a few things for you to consider."

Patel swallowed what seemed to be a football in his throat. Morgan's face was a blank mask, but his eyes burned into Patel's like dry ice.

"Who are you?" the arrested man finally managed.

"My name is Jack Morgan. I'm a private investigator."

"You're here because I hit your friend," Patel mumbled.

"I'm here because you killed Sophie Edwards," Morgan corrected him. "And I need to know why."

Patel's eyes widened and he quickly looked to the officer in the corner of the room, then back to Morgan, but said nothing.

"You see, Mayoor, you're in here because you were arrested for the assault of Peter Knight, my colleague. Nothing else. There are no other witnesses, so if Peter drops his charges against you you'll be a free man. Free to go. Free to walk the streets, where bad things can happen."

"You're threatening me," Patel managed, beginning to sweat.

"I'm just telling you how things are out there." Morgan shrugged. "Bad things happen to good people." He smiled. "And really bad things happen to bad people."

"What do you want?" Patel almost whimpered.

"What happened to Sophie?" Morgan asked, his voice as calm as a dead sea. "You'll be charged with her murder, Patel, but prison can be a safe place with the right people looking out for you. Or prison can be a very, very unsafe place."

It was too much for Patel. He was an intelligent man, and he could see he was out of choices. He burst into tears.

"What . . . what happens if I tell you?" he muttered between sobs.

"That's up to the system, not me," Morgan told him. "The truth is all I want. Tell me what happened, Mayoor. Take the easy way out of this, and talk."

"I'll talk," Patel promised.

And he did.

He told Morgan how he had met Sophie, the life and soul of the party. He told him how he had fallen for her, and the pair had begun to see each other outside of house parties and clubs. The rules of their relationship were looser than most, but it was London in 2018, and Mayoor Patel enjoyed his own freedoms.

"I didn't have a problem sharing her physically," the man admitted. "It's just sex, yeah? But when I thought she was seeing someone else. When I thought it was emotional..."

"You got jealous?"

Patel had, and had begun to trail Sophie, eventually leading him to Sir Tony Lightwood and the Mistral hotel.

"Soph told me that it was strictly business. The truth is, the fact that she was an escort hurt me a lot less than if she was in love with someone else."

"But you needed to make sure?" Morgan pushed. "You needed to know she was loyal only to you."

"The blackmail was my idea," Patel admitted, his head hanging on his chest. "I didn't need the money, I just needed to know she would do it for me. That she was mine where it mattered," he said, touching his heart, "and no one else's."

"But she wasn't, was she?"

For a moment there was only the sound of crying. Then Patel looked into Morgan's face, tears thick in his red eyes.

"A fucking princess, yeah?" He shook his head. "At first I thought Soph was a genius. How much would they pay to cover that up? But then she...she..."

"She wouldn't blackmail her," Morgan finished for him.

"She was in love!" Patel screamed out. "With a fucking woman! Not me!"

"So you killed her," Morgan said gently. "You got angry because she loved someone else, and you killed her."

"I did." Patel sobbed. "I didn't mean too, believe me! I think her neck broke."

"Is that why you tried to stage the hanging?"

"Yes," the man admitted, wiping tears from his face. "I knew that she always loved that place. I didn't want to kill her, please believe me. I just wanted her to be mine. I wanted her to love me like she loved *her*."

Morgan had heard enough. He looked back over his shoulder to the officer in the corner of the room. The man nodded.

"Where's he going?" Patel asked as the officer left the room. "Where's he going?"

"This conversation is just for us." Morgan sat unmoved in his chair. "You're going to tell me who you hired to kill me and my team."

Morgan watched as confusion replaced the fear and guilt that had been etched into Patel's face. "What are you talking about?" he managed.

"You hired shooters to take out my team and stop us finding Sophie. Who are they?"

"I have no idea!" Patel cried.

With disappointment Morgan realized that he believed him. "You didn't hire anyone to come after us?"

"No!" Patel begged. "I'm a hedge fund manager, not a gangster! I wouldn't even know where to find those people!"

Morgan swore under his breath. Then who would?

And why?

Chapter 47

POLICE CONSTABLE SHARON Lewis looked at the sticky pool of blood on the kitchen floor.

"It's Knight's," Cook told her, pointing out the broken pieces of porcelain that lay close by. "Can you imagine getting hit with that?"

"I took a frying pan to the head once."

Cook looked at her with surprise.

"My dad," Lewis explained.

"Is that why you became an officer?" Cook guessed.

"You should have been a shrink," Lewis smirked sarcastically. "If you play the punchbag enough times, it's a nice feeling to be the fist. I don't tell people that, though. Most of the blokes already assume that any woman in uniform has daddy issues."

Having been an army officer, Jane Cook knew something about that. "I was lucky—I didn't have any issues with my dad."

"Then what made you join?"

"I grew up on a farm and my dad taught me to love the outdoors. As I got older I wanted to see more of the world. My family didn't have the money to fund that kind of thing ourselves, so I joined the army."

"And you liked it?"

"Loved it. You?"

"It's my life," Lewis admitted. "I don't know what I'll do when I leave."

"I thought the same," Cook confided. "But now I have new teammates and new challenges. It's all I want."

"And the boss, too," Lewis needled.

"It's not like that."

"I know. I'm only teasing you. To be honest, when I first met you, I didn't like you. I thought you were another pretty girl shagging her way up the ranks."

"I'm not," Cook said stiffly.

"I know that now." Lewis smirked. "I was wrong. I didn't realize it was love."

"I didn't say it was that either." Cook smiled, thinking of Jack Morgan, and how they would soon be free to find out exactly what it was.

"You didn't have to." Lewis smiled back. "I'm sorry we didn't get off to a good start, Cook. You and me have both come up in organizations dominated by men. At first I thought you were the kind that held women back, but now I see why you've got to where you are, and I hope we can stay in touch after this."

"We will," Cook promised. "There aren't many people I can say have saved my life. The least I owe you is a spot on the Christmas card list."

"Bloody hell, what an honor!" The police officer laughed. "You want a brew or what?"

But before Cook could reply, she heard a sound in the doorway.

She was about to greet the expected police officers. Instead, the words died in her throat.

Jane Cook was staring down the barrel of a gun.

Chapter 48

"MOVE AND I blow her brains out," the masked gunman barked at Lewis.

"I'm a police officer," she replied evenly.

"I know who you are."

"Then you know you're fucked if you hurt us."

"Keep your mouth shut, pig," the man replied. "And put your phone down on the floor. One wrong move and your mate's brains go on the wall."

"Don't do anything stupid," Lewis urged, wishing she had her pistol, now handed in as part of the investigation into the forest shooting. "I'll do as you say."

"Bollocks to that," Cook hissed through gritted teeth. "Run, Lewis."

"You shut up," the gunman growled.

"Run," Cook urged.

But Lewis would not. Instead she placed her phone onto the floor.

"Kick it away," the gunman demanded.

Lewis did as she was bid.

"Now take out hers," the man ordered, a slight twitch of his gun gesturing to Cook.

"Just run, Lewis," Cook tried again, but the officer would not abandon her, and Cook's phone joined Lewis's on the floor.

"Now both on your knees." The man spoke through the fabric of his mask. "Hands on your head. Interlocked fingers."

The women complied, the pistol's muzzle tracking Cook's forehead through every inch.

"Who are you?" Cook asked.

"I think you can guess." The unexpected reply came from behind the gunman as a second man entered the room. Though the newcomer's face was also hidden behind the black mesh of a balaclava, Cook instantly recognized the voice and her skin crawled at the terrifying revelation.

Because she knew she was a dead woman.

Chapter 49

PETER KNIGHT WAS helping himself to coffee in the station's cafeteria when Jack Morgan approached.

"You got the confession?" Knight asked.

"I did," Morgan confirmed.

"Then what's up?" Knight could read his friend's expression.

"Something isn't right." Before Morgan could elaborate further, his phone began to buzz urgently in his pocket.

"FaceTime from Cook," he told Knight, his pulse quickening at the prospect of seeing her, even just on a screen. "I'll tell her and Lewis to stand down as soon as the police arrive."

"OK. I'll pour you a coffee."

"Thanks," Morgan replied, moving outside in the corridor and hitting answer. "Hi, Jane . . ." he began.

But the smile died on his lips as the picture's quality cleared, and he found himself looking not at the face of the woman he loved, but at the figure of a masked gunman who held a pistol to her head.

Chapter 50

MICHAEL "FLEX" GIBBON had waited years for this moment, and the picture of Morgan's anguish made every second worthwhile.

"Hello, Morgan. Shame we couldn't do this in person, but good to see you again."

Morgan recognized the voice of the muscle-bound maniac with his gun held to Cook's head.

"Whatever it is you want," Morgan tried, "you can have it. I will sell Private, and you can have every dime."

"This isn't about money, Jack!" Flex shouted at the phone, his rage boiling over. "This is about honor! This is about righting a wrong! You don't walk into my town and insult me! You don't come onto my turf and sucker-punch me in my own gym!"

"Sucker-punch?" Cook laughed at Flex's feet. "He beat the shit out of you!"

"Shut the fuck up!" Flex snarled, pistol-whipping his captive with such force that her head snapped back and blood gushed from her nose.

"Jane! Please, Flex," Morgan pleaded, "I'll do anything." He meant every word.

"Anything?"

"Yes. Anything. Anything!"

"Good." Flex lowered the pistol and ran his hand through Cook's hair. "So shall I tell you what I want, Jack?"

"Yes! Just tell me! Tell me and you'll have it!"

"I've already got it, you prick," Flex laughed. "All I want, Jack, is for you to watch."

Then he lifted the gun and pulled the trigger.

Chapter 51

JACK MORGAN SANK to his knees. The phone fell from his hand and bounced across the floor. As he brought his hands to his face, he could hear Lewis's anguished screams coming from the phone's tiny speaker.

"Jack!" Knight shouted, running to his friend's side. "What is it?"

What was it?

It was witnessing the cold-blooded murder of a colleague. More than a colleague. *It* was being helpless to prevent it. *It* was a sense of the deepest revulsion, and the fast-growing tide of anger.

It was the loss of someone Morgan loved, and would never hold again.

"He killed Jane."

"What?" Knight mumbled, unable to comprehend the words. "What...?"

"He killed Jane!" Morgan said again, the anger beginning to take over every other emotion. "I'll kill him," he growled in the back of his throat as he pushed himself up and picked up his phone.

The call had ended.

"Jack? Tell me what's happened. Talk to me, mate."

"Flex executed Jane. He's still got Lewis. I'm going to find him, Peter," Morgan promised, his eyes like burning embers. "I'm going to find Flex Gibbon, and then I'm going to kill him."

Chapter 52

MICHAEL GIBBON LOOKED down at the body that lay in front of him. What had been a beautiful woman was reduced now to a body of useless meat. It was a waste, really. Still, the bitch who had attacked him at his gym was dead, and Morgan had seen her die. That gave Flex some solace, but it did not fill him with satisfaction. That wouldn't come until Jack Morgan had suffered still more, and then finally died in agony himself.

"You fucking coward," Flex then heard, breaking him from his thoughts.

He turned his masked head to look at the police officer, Lewis. She was on her knees and trembling, but her face was hard and defiant.

"You're a copper," Flex stated.

"I am," Lewis answered, with a proud jut of her chin.

"Look at her. Go on. Look at her," Flex urged with a wave of his pistol.

Willing herself to be stoic, Lewis obeyed and turned her eyes to Cook's body on the floor.

"This woman was a traitor," Flex declared, lifting up Cook's head by her hair so that her dead eyes looked at Lewis. "She was a traitor, and so she got treated like one."

"She wasn't a traitor, you fucking murderer!" Lewis shouted, hoping that she could face death with the same tenacity that Cook had.

"She was," Flex stated coldly, dropping Cook's head so that it hit hard on the floor. "She's been working with that American bastard to undermine British security. She's been working to undermine the army, and the police. *Your* team, Lewis. She's been out to fuck *your* team."

"Bollocks!" Lewis spat. "Just shoot me and get it over with, you fat bastard! I don't want to hear your crap!"

Flex's accomplice hit her hard in the face. The police officer tasted blood, and braced herself as she saw a boot coming in at her stomach.

Being ready wasn't enough. Lewis doubled over in pain as she felt one of her lower ribs crack.

"I've got nothing against you, Lewis," Flex explained. "But I've had nothing against a lot of people I've killed, so don't let yourself think that will stop me. Now," he asked, bringing up the silencer of his pistol to brush against his captive's forehead, "are you gonna help me, or are you gonna die?"

Chapter 53

JACK MORGAN SPRINTED out of the police station, Peter Knight on his heels, and a series of clattering doors and bewildered faces left in their wake.

"Jack!" Knight shouted at his friend's back. "We can't rush into this alone! We don't have weapons! We need the police!"

Morgan ignored Knight's calls until the men stood in a wide stretch of empty car park. The American came to a stop and turned to face Knight.

"No police," Morgan declared, his voice guarded and lethal like a holstered pistol. "If Flex sees police, Lewis will die too. I've already had HQ call off the uniforms who were supposed to take over Patel's crime scene."

"But—"

"No police, Peter! These are our people, and it's up to us to save them!"

Knight didn't point out that Private's own agent was beyond help. "Lewis is police. Her own people deserve to know what's happening."

Morgan shook his head. "I'm getting her out of this."

Knight could see that the shock of Cook's death was clouding Morgan's judgment. The American had pulled off so many daring feats that Knight had lost count, but now that record was pushing Morgan into making rash decisions that would not only cost Lewis her life, but likely Jack Morgan his own.

"This is what he wants, Jack," Knight argued. "He wants you to run in there with no plan."

"I have a plan," Morgan protested. "I'm going to kill him."

Knight reached out and grabbed his friend by the shoulders. "Jack. Mate. Please. Reconsider this. Getting yourself killed will not bring her back."

But there was no reply for Knight, nor recognition that his words had even been heard. Instead Morgan looked to the sky. "Chopper's here."

Chapter 54

FLEX STOOD BACK as his accomplice delivered a kick into Lewis's side. The air was driven from her, red-hot pain shooting through the woman's body as the ends of her broken rib grated against one another.

"Here's something for you to think about," Flex growled through his mask. "Don't you think it's funny that Jack Morgan and Private keep turning up around the world just as shit is about to hit the fan? Look at London. Who was here to save the day at the Olympics? Who was here for Trooping the Color? It's always that bastard Morgan. He sets these things up so that his company profits from them! Can you not see that?"

"All I see," Lewis groaned, "is a fat boy with a man-crush. You should just get it over with and admit you want to fu—"

Flex's boot drove the last words from her lungs as a wheeze.

"You stupid bitch! What money are you on as a copper? Thirty grand a year? Morgan is making millions a year!

Millions! And he's making it by having others die for him. You think this sack of shit on the floor is the first one who's died to make Jack Morgan richer?"

"She died," Lewis spat, "because you killed her!"

"She died because she was a disposable asset!" Flex shot back. "Disposable to Jack Morgan, so that he can continue to live his life of beach houses and private jets!"

"You jealous bastard," Lewis laughed. "Is that all this is? You're going to kill me because you want Morgan's life?"

Flex told his accomplice to deliver another kick to Lewis's broken ribs, but it did not stop Lewis from finishing. "No wonder you're wearing that mask. Morgan is a good-looking bloke. I bet you've got a face like a cheese toastie."

She laughed at her own insult. Then, to her surprise, she heard Flex join in.

"You really don't think I'll kill you, do you, copper?"

"I don't think you've got the balls. Probably vanished from all that juice you've been doing." She snorted, taking in the man's steroid-inflated size. "You're a coward. And a small man in all the ways that count."

"A coward?" Flex laughed. "Well, maybe I am. But you don't have to be a brave man to do this."

Flex shoved the barrel of his gun inside Lewis's mouth.

She tried to speak, but the words were muffled by the barrel and came out as an angry gurgle.

"I want you to know," Flex said from above, "that you're gonna die to make Jack Morgan richer. Think about that as your last thought."

Flex laughed, and then he pulled the trigger.

Chapter 55

THE BUILDINGS OF London were a blur beneath the helicopter as it belted across the city, green parks just a flash as Morgan and Knight raced to Kensington, and to Sharon Lewis.

Morgan had been silent for the first two minutes of the flight, but now he pulled his phone and dialed into Private London's HQ.

"Put me through to Hooligan," he commanded the watch manager.

"Hooligan left once Patel was taken into custody," the watch manager explained. "I'll put you through to Denise."

"Who's Denise?" Morgan asked Knight as the call went through.

"We recruited her last year straight from Cambridge. Hooligan hand-picked her. She's quite brilliant, really."

"Denise, this is Jack Morgan. Are you OK with breaking the law?"

"I am if it's for a good cause," the young woman answered without hesitation.

"I need you to hack into any and all CCTV systems within five hundred yards of Mayoor Patel's home, and then feed them to me. Can you do that?"

"I can."

Morgan hung up the call.

"Why the hell isn't Hooligan there?" he asked Knight.

"Jack, he's been working non-stop. As far as he was concerned, our cases both wrapped up once we took Patel into custody. He couldn't have foreseen... *this*."

"Private isn't a part-time gig." Morgan spoke through clenched teeth. "If this new girl is as good as you say she is, then Hooligan's gone."

"Gone?" Knight stammered, flabbergasted. "He's a lynchpin in Private London, Jack. I know things are not great right now but—"

"Not great?" Morgan cut him off, seething. "Jane is *dead*, and my people are not where they should be."

"He didn't *know*," Knight pressed.

"And whose fault is that?" Morgan shot back, his eyes burning into Knight. "*You* are the head of Private London, Peter, and Flex is on your turf. If he was planning this, you should have known about it."

Knight didn't know what to say.

"Cook is dead because Private London didn't see this coming," Morgan warned. "Hooligan isn't the only one that's replaceable."

Chapter 56

INSIDE THE HELICOPTER was tense, and silent. Beside Knight, Morgan sat like a coiled spring. Then, without warning, the American's body sagged into his seat.

"I'm sorry, Peter," Morgan sighed.

"You don't have anything to be sorry about."

"I'm the head of Private, and all mistakes belong to me. If anyone killed Jane, then it was me."

Knight turned in the helicopter's tight confines so that he could look directly into Morgan's face. "*Flex* killed Jane. Don't forget that, Jack. Nobody else. *Flex.*"

After a moment Morgan grudgingly nodded. "I should have seen this coming, though, Peter. We beat him down when we were searching for Abbie Winchester. We kicked his ass. Reputation is everything in the security business, and Flex must have lost his when he took that beating."

"Not everyone kills over a reputation."

"But Flex would," Morgan countered. "I should have known that. I should have seen it. I came into this situation with blinkers on, and led us into one trap after another. Jane's dead because of me."

"Bollocks, Jack!" Knight grabbed his friend's shoulder. "She's dead because of that bastard!"

"She's dead because of me. And Lewis too. Flex won't take prisoners."

Chapter 57

FLEX PULLED HIS gun from Sharon Lewis's mouth and looked down at the policewoman.

He smiled.

"What are you looking at?" Lewis growled, fighting to control her shaking body.

"I'm impressed," Flex grunted. "I've seen SAS soldiers piss themselves when they've gone through that."

"That's because you're all a bunch of pussies!" Lewis braced herself against the expected reprisal.

None came.

"I need you alive," Flex explained. "I need you to deliver a message to Jack Morgan."

"What is it?" she asked cautiously.

"This."

And then the punch did come.

Chapter 58

"I'M PUTTING HER down," the pilot announced over the helicopter's internal comms, pointing to a patch of green amidst the city below them—it was Holland Park, the nearest clearing to Patel's Kensington home.

"Anything from the CCTV taps?" Knight asked Morgan as they dropped toward the ground, their stomachs lifting.

"Nothing useful."

"So what's our plan?"

Morgan didn't answer. Instead, as the helicopter's skids touched down onto the grass, Morgan threw back the door and ran.

Knight tried to stay on his heels, but the American was faster, the desire for revenge driving him on to a pace that Knight simply couldn't match. As their shoes beat the tarmac of Kensington's pavements, Knight began to fall behind. Only Morgan's occasional slowing to check his phone's map allowed Private London's leader to keep him in sight. Knight had no need for his own map—he recognized the area by sight. He knew they were drawing closer, and was relieved to see Morgan pull up short of Patel's street.

"We can't just sprint in there, Jack," Knight panted as he caught up. "They'll kill Lewis, and then us."

"We're not going in anywhere." Morgan looked down the street.

Knight followed the direction of Morgan's gaze, and he saw the reason why.

Patel's home was surrounded by police.

Chapter 59

"I TOLD YOU not to call the police!" Morgan shouted at Knight, seeing their chance to slip inside and rescue Lewis disappear.

"I didn't," Knight protested. "Honestly, Jack, this wasn't me. But look, the way that they're set up. This isn't a siege."

Morgan looked to the police cordon. The uniformed officers were facing outward, not in.

"None of them are in cover," Morgan realized. "They're not afraid of getting shot."

"Flex is gone," Knight said, the words barely out of his mouth before Morgan was again sprinting, this time toward the police.

"Who's in charge?" he called to the nearest uniform, the officer raising an eyebrow at Morgan's American accent.

"Please stay away from the cordon, sir," the young PC said in reply.

"I need to know who's in charge!" Morgan asserted. "My people were inside that house! I need to get in there!"

"Sir, please stay calm."

"I am calm! And I need to get inside!"

The sound of raised voices drew the attention of a police sergeant. As a veteran officer, she had seen enough grief to recognize it in Morgan.

"Sir," she said in a calm, controlled voice, "you say you know whose house this is?"

"It belongs to Mayoor Patel," Knight cut in before Morgan could speak. "But the two women here are Sharon Lewis and Jane Cook. One is a police officer and the other is an investigator for Private."

"They are *my* people," Morgan seethed. "And I need to see them."

The police sergeant thought over Knight's words, then looked back to the house.

"Have you been inside?" Knight begged. "Please, we need to know."

The sergeant held her tongue as she gestured for the young officer beside her to move away and give them privacy.

"The paramedics are stabilizing one woman who's been badly beaten," she told the men, looking straight into their eyes. "I'm afraid that one of the women . . . has passed away."

"Can we see them?" Knight asked.

Morgan opened his mouth but found himself unable to speak.

"This is Jack Morgan, head of Private. My name's Peter Knight, and I'm head of the London branch. If you call my sister-in-law at the Met, Elaine Pottersfield, she will confirm for you who we are."

"I'm sorry, sirs, but your identity is not the issue. No one but the police and paramedics can cross this boundary. If you will wait here, I'll go and find out which hospital they're taking her to."

"Thank you," Knight said, defeated. Beside him, Jack Morgan was white with rage.

"This is Flex's doing," he hissed between clenched teeth. "He called the police himself, to keep me from Jane."

The truth of that hit Knight like a blow. Then, in the same moment, he realized what other motivation a former SAS soldier could have for keeping them at the cordon.

"We're sitting ducks out here, Jack," Knight warned. "There are hundreds of windows on this street, and Flex could be in any one of them. Let's get clear and into some cover," he urged.

But Morgan stood firm. Knight considered how he could drag Morgan from the street and to safety. Thankfully, he was saved the ordeal by the reappearance of the sergeant.

"I gave your names to the lady in the ambulance," the police officer told them. "She wants to see you."

Chapter 60

MORGAN AND KNIGHT ducked under the police tape and followed the police sergeant quickly to the back of the ambulance. Knight threw a look Morgan's way, worried at the intensity he saw coming from his friend and boss. There was no knowing what kind of state Sharon Lewis was in emotionally, or physically. Knight had never met the woman, but his guess was that the last thing she would need would be Morgan going in bullheaded and demanding answers.

He needn't have worried.

"Lewis, I'm so glad you're alive," Morgan said gently. Knight could have sworn there were tears in the man's eyes.

And why not? Lewis was strapped to a gurney, her arms splinted to immobilize around the fractures she had suffered at the hands of Flex.

"What the hell have they done to you?" Morgan whispered.

The answer to that question was obvious—Lewis had been savagely beaten from head to toe. Her skin was already turning a mottled purple, her neck held firmly in place by

166 • James Patterson

a plastic brace. Her right eye was fully closed; her left was focused loosely on the two men who stood silhouetted against the ambulance's door.

"Morgan," she whispered. "Morgan."

"I'm here," he told her, placing his hand on hers. "I'm so glad to see you, Lewis."

"Like this?" She tried to smile.

"Not like this," he said softly, and Lewis's open eye shed a tear. They both knew what Morgan meant. He was glad to see her *alive*.

"I couldn't stop them," she said, the single tear followed by several others. "I'm sorry, Morgan. I couldn't stop them."

"Don't think about it, Lewis. Don't even think about it."

But of course it was all she could think about. The image of Cook on her knees with the barrel pointed at her head. The soft *psst* sound of the silenced pistol firing. The sight of Cook's body slumping to the floor.

"You need to rest, Lewis."

"I don't want to close my eyes," she whimpered. "It's all I see."

From long experience of violent memories, Morgan knew of one way to escape the emotional pain.

"Watch her, Peter."

Morgan slipped out the rear of the ambulance and returned a moment later with the paramedic. Without a word, the first responder took a syringe and fed morphine into the cannula in Lewis's wrist.

"He's given you something for it. You'll sleep, Lewis, and you won't feel the pain. You won't *see* the pain."

Lewis tried to blink tears away, but gravity held them on her eye. Morgan took a tissue from one of the ambulance's shelves and delicately dabbed them.

"You're one of the bravest people I've ever seen. I'm going to come with you to the hospital."

"No," she said, fighting against the drug that now began to overtake her. "No hospital, Morgan."

He had to hunch over to catch the rest of her words, which were lost to Knight. Finally, Lewis's lips stopped moving, the slow rise and fall of her chest showing the signs of a woman in a deep, drug-fueled delirium.

"What did she say?" Knight asked Morgan.

When the American turned to face him, his eyes reminded Knight of an impending storm. There was calm now, but soon all would be destruction and violence.

"That we finish this."

Chapter 61

JACK MORGAN AND Peter Knight stepped from the ambulance, the paramedic pulling the doors closed behind them. The vehicle's lights and siren started up and police officers hurriedly cleared a lane for it to pull away. Given the severity and nature of the attack, a police car followed in the ambulance's wake to ride shotgun. Morgan noticed the precaution, and gave his thanks to the police sergeant.

"She's one of ours," the woman said.

"She saved my life," Morgan told her. "Please look after her."

"We will," the sergeant promised. "I'm sorry that we can't let you inside. If it was up to me..."

"You've done enough," he assured her. In truth, it killed him that he could not run to Cook's side, even in death, but if he was to be denied that proximity to the woman he loved, then he would take himself where he was needed. He would take himself to where her killer was hiding, and there, he would deliver justice.

"We need to go," he told Knight.

"Our car will be here any second," said Knight, and sure enough, a black Range Rover appeared in that moment at the end of the street. "But that's not ours," Knight wondered, ready at any moment to shove Morgan into cover should the occupants prove hostile.

At the behest of a waving officer, the vehicle slowed to a stop ten meters short of the cordon. There the passenger door opened, and Knight felt his body relax as a familiar figure stepped into the street and beckoned toward them.

"Over here!" Colonel Marcus De Villiers waved, and after a final thank you to the police sergeant, Morgan and Knight slipped under the cordon to join him.

"Have you seen Lewis?" asked the Guards officer.

Morgan nodded. "We have. She's badly beaten, but alive."

"Thank God," De Villiers sighed. As head of royal security, Lewis fell under his command, and there was no doubt in the Private agents' minds that De Villiers truly cared for Lewis's well-being.

"And Cook?" the man asked hopefully.

Morgan said nothing. Knight shook his head.

"Morgan, I'm so sorry."

Morgan's mind was miles from sympathies. A million miles from them. It was only concerned with retribution.

Perhaps De Villiers saw as much.

"Get into the car, Morgan," he ordered as if to a soldier. "Not you," he said to Knight as he tried to follow. "I need to speak with Morgan alone."

Chapter 62

AS THE RANGE Rover's door closed behind them, Morgan was about to ask De Villiers what he wanted to speak about. Instead, he watched with surprise as the Colonel slammed his fist into the headrest of the empty passenger seat.

"Bastards!" he snarled. "Spineless, gutless bastards!" He punched again, breathing heavily. "They'll pay for this— Lewis is one of mine." The head of royal security inhaled deeply. "An attack on her is…It's an attack on the *Crown*, Morgan." De Villiers shook his head. "And Cook? She was awarded an OBE for what she did in Afghanistan. She's done as much for her country as any other person."

"Why are you telling me this?" Morgan asked, his manners blunted by emotion.

"Why?" De Villiers choked, as if it were obvious. "Because I want to help you."

"You can't help in this. Our work for the Princess is over. We found Sophie. We found her killer."

"It's over, is it?" De Villiers shook his head. "Not when

Lewis is in the hospital it isn't. Not when…" He left Jane Cook's name and fate unspoken. "Look, Morgan, you may not have the highest opinion of me, that's clear enough, but I am a soldier—a British soldier—and we believe in honor and justice. Someone out there has murdered a former army officer, and badly beaten one of my police officers. I want whoever did it *found*."

"Then look for them."

"I don't need to, because you already know who it is, don't you? You're like a bulldog straining at the leash, Morgan. You're not sniffing for clues—you're ready to tear out a throat."

"I don't know who it was," Morgan lied.

"Bullshit! Total bullshit!"

"And what if it is bullshit? Do you think I'd tell you, so that you can get in my way?"

De Villiers laughed. "Get in your *way*?" He shook his head. "Morgan, Lewis is *family* to me. I want to help you. I want you to find these people before anyone else does. Do I have to spell out why?"

Morgan looked into the officer's eyes, and believed him—De Villiers wanted justice. The kind that couldn't be delivered in a British courtroom.

"No," Morgan answered.

"Good." De Villiers nodded with finality. "Now. I expect you've been wondering where to find a gun?"

Chapter 63

PETER KNIGHT WATCHED as Morgan emerged from the back seat of the Range Rover. No sooner had the door closed than the vehicle pulled away quickly up the street.

"Our own car's here." Knight gestured to a black Audi dispatched from Private London. "Where to?"

"Headquarters." Knight recognized from his boss's tone that it was not a good idea to dig for further information right now.

As they crossed to the waiting car, Morgan threw one more forlorn look toward the building that housed Jane Cook's body. It would be some time before the pathologists and crime scene investigators were ready to take her away, and it pained Morgan to know that Cook was alone and cold on a kitchen floor. He knew from experience that there was no dignity in death, but Cook's fate seemed exceedingly cruel. The fact that his own life was in danger did not even enter into his mind. Instead, Jack Morgan's emotions swung from crushing sadness to red-hot rage.

"I'm going to rip his throat out," he promised as they climbed into the car, repeating the image that De Villiers had put in front of him.

"We'll get him," Knight promised.

"We'll *finish* him," Morgan corrected. "This doesn't end in an arrest, Peter. I understand if you don't want in on that, but those are the rules."

"I'm with you," Knight said, meeting the hard stare of his friend and leader. "I'm with you, Jack," he vowed again, his mind then catching on the crux of what Morgan was saying—this was not an ordinary case. The rules had changed. *No,* Knight caught himself thinking, *not just the rules. The entire game.*

"We have to think like Flex," said Knight. "The man's clearly got no limits. No boundaries. What else is he capable of?"

"Anything. He's sick. You should get hold of your family, Peter. Have them brought into Private HQ."

"My God, you're right." The icy fingers of fear reached up from Knight's stomach and into his throat. It was with a near shaking hand that he made the call to his children's sitter, and asked for them to be brought to his place of work. "We should bring in all of our staff," Knight then urged. "No guessing who else he could target."

"Do it. He targeted Jane because of what she and I did to him in the gym, but I don't put anything past him."

Knight made the call, ordering Private London's watch manager to bring in all members of staff, emphasizing the need for vigilance.

"What now, Jack?" he asked, his phone calls made.

But there was no reply from the American. None in words, at least, but Morgan's eyes told Knight all he needed to know.

Now would be payback.

Chapter 64

MORGAN WATCHED ALMOST in a daze as their car slid through the rain-slicked streets of London. Traffic became a blur. Faces were meaningless. It was a procession of life—hundreds, maybe thousands of people—but all Morgan could think about was death.

Jane.

Gone.

He blinked hard to try to clear the image from his eyes. It was the picture of Jane, her face pleading and terrified as Flex held the gun to her head. Then Morgan had seen that most beautiful face turn to ruin as Flex had pulled the trigger.

"Pull over," he instructed the driver. "Pull over!"

The man did so, drivers honking angrily as Morgan pushed opened the door and threw up onto the curb.

"Are you all right?" Knight asked as Morgan stepped back inside the car.

Morgan ignored him. Instead he closed the door and waved for the driver to go on.

"Jack, are you all right?" Knight insisted.

Of course he wasn't all right. He had fallen for Cook, hard, and then he had watched helplessly as her brains were blown out onto the floor. Who could be all right after that? But he was Jack Morgan, after all. He almost laughed to himself, thinking of how Private's agents saw him as both the unstoppable force and the immovable object.

Hadn't he seen enough death? He could still remember the helicopter crash in the Afghan mountains. He could still remember the screams and the smell of burning flesh. He could still remember the nightmares and bed sheets soaked in sweat. He could still feel the guilt that hung from his shoulders like the heaviest rucksack he had ever carried as a Marine. And now this? Now Jane's death, too?

"Why are we doing this?" Morgan asked himself, but the words came out loud enough for Knight to hear. The Englishman frowned in confusion, as if the answer were so simple.

"For justice."

"For justice." Morgan smiled. What justice could there be for Jane Cook? Her life was worth a million Flex Gibbons. How could her soul and presence ever be replaced? How could there be real justice when the world was an emptier place without her?

"I miss her already," he confessed to Knight. "And it hasn't even hit me yet. Not really."

"We're here for you, Jack," Knight promised. "All of Private London. We're here for each other, as a family."

Private London. So caught up was he in his own loss that Morgan had yet to consider the wider ripples of Jane's tragedy. Cook was beloved of every member of the London office, he knew. She had family there, and family in the wider world. What of her comrades from the army? People who had fought and lived beside her in the hardest of circumstances. Flex's actions would cause distress and grief to hundreds of people. His attack had been not just on Cook and Lewis, but on hundreds, maybe thousands of people. He was a monster, and he had to be stopped.

No matter the consequences.

"Peter, are you ready to step up? If the time comes, are you ready to step up, for Private?"

It took Knight a moment to grasp the implications of what Morgan was saying. "I am, Jack," he promised. "But I won't need to."

We'll see, Morgan thought.

Because he knew this was only going to end one of two ways—with the death of Michael "Flex" Gibbon, or with the death of Jack Morgan.

Chapter 65

MORGAN FELT THE shrouded looks and pity-filled smiles as he walked into Private London's HQ alongside Peter Knight.

"My children are upstairs," Knight sighed, shoulders slumping in relief.

"You should stay with them," said Morgan. "I can handle this alone."

Knight didn't reply, but there was no chance he would leave this for Morgan to handle alone. "How are we doing on the headcount?" he asked his watch manager.

"Almost everyone is accounted for," she advised Knight. "We've got them either coming into here or safe houses if they're in other parts of the UK."

"How is it affecting ongoing ops?" he asked.

"Minimally. Sir Tony and Sophie Edwards were our main investigations. We have a fraud case in Scotland, and a widow in Sheffield has asked that we look over her husband's death, but other than that, the decks are clear."

"Those cases can wait," Morgan said evenly. "Right now, Private only has one case."

The watch manager nodded. No one needed telling what that case was. "There is just one person we haven't yet been able to contact," she said.

"Who is it?" Knight asked, instantly fearful.

"Jeremy Crawford," she replied. "Hooligan."

Chapter 66

MORGAN AND KNIGHT sprinted for the Audi. Knight relieved the driver and jumped in behind the wheel. Within a moment they were tearing out into traffic.

It had been less than ninety seconds since the watch manager had informed them that Hooligan was the only Private employee who hadn't been contacted. She put this down to his being at the West Ham game, where phone coverage was always pitiful due to the number of users in one place, but Knight and Morgan had darker thoughts.

"Flex won't have had time to get him before the game started," Morgan worked out. "But he could be waiting for him. Hooligan was one of the team that worked on the case to rescue Abbie Winchester, so if that's his list, we have to find him before Flex does."

"How much do we know about the man Hooligan's with?" Morgan asked.

"Perkins? He was sent from De Villiers to coordinate with

them on the tech side of things. No one's been able to get hold of him either. You think he could be working with Flex?"

"He's not one of ours, so I'm ruling nothing out."

I'm not losing anybody else, Morgan promised himself as he picked up his phone, the call going straight to Hooligan's voicemail for the tenth time. "Come on, dammit! Connect!" He hit his fist against the car's dashboard.

Chapter 67

JEREMY "HOOLIGAN" CRAWFORD streamed out of London Stadium with thousands of other downcast West Ham fans, having been drubbed 2–0 by the visitors in a pre-season friendly.

"I can't believe you pay for a season ticket to watch that dross," said Perkins, the Millwall fan.

"Been paying for the past seventeen years." Hooligan shook his head. "I must be a sucker for punishment."

"If you're into paying to be miserable, there's ladies that will do that for you in Soho."

"Black leather doesn't suit my complexion," Hooligan laughed. "And I've got too much important stuff to say to have a ball-gag in my mouth."

For a moment, Hooligan thought that the grimace on his new friend's face was an indication that he had taken the joke too far, but he quickly realized something was seriously wrong as Perkins crashed to the ground. "Crap! Perkins! Help!" he shouted to the crowd around him.

He felt a rush of relief as he saw a police officer only steps away.

"Help! Officer! Help!" Hooligan gestured frantically. "My mate's collapsed!"

Only then did he see the taser in the officer's hand.

Chapter 68

HOOLIGAN'S EYES WENT wide in horror as he saw the mouth of the taser flicker to life. Crouched to help Perkins, he knew there was no way he could spring clear before the man disguised as a police officer struck. The crowd had allowed the "policeman" to close on them unseen, and now it hemmed Hooligan in like a trapped fish.

Killed by my fellow fans, he thought as the taser jabbed toward his throat and he closed his eyes.

But the expected pain of the electric shock did not come. Hooligan realized he was somehow untouched and opened his eyes. In front of him he saw a beautiful sight.

A ruptured pie slipped lazily from the side of the man's head, gravy spilling down his neck as all about him laughed and cheered.

"On your head, pig!" a voice in the crowd shouted.

The hard-core football fans had no love for the police, and seeing a fan tasered, they had lashed out. The thrown food and shoves into the man's back had bought Hooligan seconds, and now he used them, scrambling to his feet and pushing his way through the scrum of bodies. A flash of guilt struck him for abandoning Perkins, but a quick look behind was enough to tell him what his gut already knew—that the "officer" was there for Hooligan. Sure enough, the big man was now pushing his way through the crowd like a barracuda through a shoal of fish.

Hooligan knew damn well that the man was no police officer. It wasn't so much that he had attacked without reason, but because Hooligan had seen into his eyes—that was not the face you sent to reassure a grieving family, or to talk to local shopkeepers after a theft. It was the face of a killer, plain and simple.

Hooligan ran and shoved as if his life depended on it, because he knew that it probably did.

Chapter 69

NATHAN RIDER WAS not a happy man. In fact, he was furious. When the pie had hit his head, his first instinct had been to find the man who threw it and to shove his thumbs into that man's eyes. It was with some internal struggle that he had fought off the urge, and in those few seconds the ginger bastard had escaped.

Not escaped, Rider corrected himself, but made life difficult. The ginger was pushing through the crowd, but Rider could see how the man was already breathing like a beached whale. He was unfit, and he was panicked—his lack of fitness would drop him into Rider's hands as easily as the taser would have done, and then it was simply a case of dragging him away into the "police car." From there it would be a short drive to a garage full of power tools, and the beginning of the ginger's real nightmare. Flex planned a show—"something that would make even the Mexican cartels look like pussies," he had said—and Rider was the kind of man who enjoyed such work.

Rider was not what anybody could consider a nice person.

Those who had known him in his childhood would politely describe him as "difficult," while those who knew him as an adult would describe him as a "total bastard." Those who *truly* knew him would use the words "dangerous" and "killer."

He had been twenty years old when he left Britain to join the French Foreign Legion. For a man with Rider's violent disposition, fighting had always seemed like a good way to earn a living, and so, when the British Army couldn't take him due to his long criminal record, he had set sail across the English Channel. To him, one army was as good as the next.

Tough men join the French Foreign Legion, and the Legion makes them tougher still. By the time Rider had completed twenty years' service, he was fluent not only in several languages but in killing. He left the service with a reputation, and was headhunted by Flex Gibbon, who had once worked with Rider on a shady operation in West Africa. Flex knew from those bloody days that Rider was a man who would carry out a mission first and ask questions later, so he had been the perfect candidate to run Flex's operations in Africa. Over the past ten years the two men had built a firm friendship, and so when Flex told Rider that he had a score to settle, Rider had not needed reasons—only instructions. That was how he had come to be hunting down the Private tech guru.

He knew now there was nothing that would come between him and the ginger. He simply walked on, confident that his size and face would clear a path for him like the parting of the Red Sea. For those too slow to move, there was always a shunt in the back, or a shove to the shoulder.

Rider was blocked by one of those oblivious idiots now. "Out of my way, you cock," he growled, taking hold of the West Ham supporter's shirt and shoving him aside. He hadn't spent weeks tracking Hooligan's habits to lose him now.

Chapter 70

HOOLIGAN COULD HEAR shouting behind him and turned to see the "policeman" only meters away, the huge man violently shoving a West Ham supporter out of the way. Then he saw a knife pulled free of its hiding place. He saw it drive forward and plunge into flesh.

His pursuer's flesh.

"Arghhh!" the man screamed as the blade pierced his stomach. "You bastard!" he growled at the football fan who had stabbed him.

No—Private's tech guru corrected himself. Not a football fan. A football *hooligan*. A real one. And here came his friends, scarves pulled up over their faces as they hurried to form a barrier between him and who they assumed was an officer of the law.

"Run, you wanker!" they shouted at their friend and Hooligan's unwitting savior, who took off quickly. "Run!" they urged.

Hooligan also decided to take their advice, as the stabbed

man was getting to his feet. Hooligan cursed that he appeared mostly undamaged—his stab vest had taken most of the blow, and only a small amount of blood was leaking into his hand.

"Out of my way!" the man raged. "Out of my way or I'll arrest you all!"

And as Hooligan pressed through the crowd, he saw the football fans slowly obey. In the near distance there was now the sound of shouts and whistles: above the heads of the West Ham supporters, Hooligan could see two mounted officers entering the horde on horseback. A quick calculation told him they would never get to him before the fake officer. Hooligan's only chance was to keep running and to find his own safety. So he shoved, swore and sprinted his way between his fellow fans, ignoring the constant insults and occasional fists that came his way.

"I'm sorry!" he pleaded as he staggered on. The crowd began to thin as Hooligan reached the head of the exodus from London Stadium.

"Watch where you're going, you knob!" a fan spat, instinctively kicking Hooligan's legs from beneath him as he barged by him and the woman with him. Hooligan hit the ground hard, the tarmac peeling back the skin on his hands and bringing with it a sensation Hooligan hadn't felt since his childhood—scraped knees and gravel burn as he dreamed of one day taking the field for West Ham.

No, he thought to himself. *It can't end here. I'm not ready.*

But no amount of adrenaline or dogged determination could rouse his spent muscles and heaving lungs. Hooligan had run to the limit of his endurance—he had nothing left to give.

And then his phone began to ring.

Chapter 71

"IT'S GOING THROUGH!" Peter Knight shouted excitedly, as the sound of ringing came over the Audi's speakers. "Come on, Jez, pick up! Pick up!"

Beside Knight, in the passenger seat, Jack Morgan sat tight-faced and impassive, his emotions shoved deep inside his chest as he tried to think only of the safety of his people that still breathed, and not the ones who were beyond help.

It was an impossible task. And as the phone continued to ring, Morgan could not help but think of Hooligan as Cook had been—forced onto his knees, with a pistol to his head.

"Goddammit, Hooligan, pick up!" shouted Morgan, the veneer of his outward calm breaking.

Through the windows, both men saw the beginnings of the football crowd seeping through the streets and away from the stadium that loomed in the middle distance. Around them, traffic began to calcify as car parks emptied.

"Pick up!" Morgan roared again, knowing they would soon be deadlocked.

The call connected.

"Help me!" The East Ender breathed heavily through the car's speakers. "Please!"

"Where are you?" Morgan asked, holding up his hand to cut off the same question coming from Knight. "What do you see around you?"

"The White Swan pub." The tremor of terror was clear in Hooligan's voice. "Please! I've lost sight of him!"

"Get to the pub!" Morgan ordered. "Stay in a busy place!"

"It won't stop him!"

"Just do it, Hooligan!" Morgan shouted. Knight was already turning the car in traffic to head back in the opposite direction.

"I saw that place on the way in," he explained. "It's only a few hundred meters back."

But it may as well have been a few hundred miles back. The road heading away from the stadium was a parking lot, West Ham supporters weaving their way through the cars and making it impossible for them to drive at faster than walking pace.

"I'm going for him," Morgan declared, opening the door.

"Jack, wait! It could be a trap! They're using him to draw you in!"

Morgan heard the truth in Knight's words, but he couldn't care less—he would not sit idle as one of his own was in peril.

Instead he ran toward that danger.

Chapter 72

HOOLIGAN SHUFFLED AS quickly as he could to the packed White Swan pub. He was so busy throwing terrified looks over his shoulders that he never saw the bouncer in front of him, and recoiled as his head bumped off the big man's chest.

"Watch where you're going," the bouncer warned.

"Can I come in?" Hooligan asked. "I've got friends inside."

The bouncer shook his head at the disheveled man. "Not a chance, mate. You're shit-faced."

"I'm not!" Hooligan pleaded. "I swear on me mum! I'm not drunk!"

"Well, you've been scrapping then. Either way, you're not coming in."

"Can I stand next to you?" Hooligan asked, swallowing. "Someone's trying to get me."

"Get out of here, you smackhead," the man growled, "before I stick my fist down your throat."

The red-hot anger in the man's eyes told Hooligan that he would back up his threat. Caught between a rock and a hard place, Hooligan scuttled along the pub's wall, trying to have at least one side of himself covered from the approach of his stabbed assailant.

Hooligan scanned the crowd and saw no sign of his attacker. The closest uniforms were a hundred yards away—two mounted police who were craning their necks at something as they patrolled along the roadside, where vehicles sat bunched and lazy, awaiting their turn to slip away from the stadium's neighborhood.

"Where are you?" Hooligan asked hurriedly into his phone. "They won't let me in the pub!"

"Stay next to it," Knight replied. "Jack is coming for you. Jez, listen. Who is following you?"

Hooligan opened his mouth to reply, but the words died in his throat.

The "officer" was on the opposite side of the crowded street. A gray hoody was now pulled up over his head, but there was no forgetting the man's grim, ominous face.

"He's here," whispered Hooligan as the man spotted him and began to cross the pedestrian traffic, a sick smile creeping across his ugly face. "I need to run!" Hooligan hissed into the phone.

"Stay where you are," Knight insisted.

"But he's coming!"

"Hooligan, if you run, we may not be able to find you again."

"Peter! He's getting close! Where's Jack?"

"Stay where you are!"

"Peter! Peter!"

His pursuer was now halfway through the crowd. Halfway, and gesturing toward Hooligan's position—the assailant was not alone.

"Help!" shouted Hooligan to everyone and no one. But the revelers ignored him, seeing either a smackhead or a drunk. "Help me!" Hooligan begged, but they did not. They shook their heads or smiled as they walked by.

It was only when another man began to shout in the crowd that the smiles began to slip, and were replaced with panic, and something more powerful than fear.

Terror.

Chapter 73

"BOMB!" JACK MORGAN shouted as he sprinted toward the White Swan pub. "Bomb!" he roared, hoping to sow confusion and chaos.

He got it. London was a city where terror attacks were a question of when, not if, and now dozens of panicked fans began to run, some screaming, others echoing Morgan's frantic calls.

"Bomb!" they yelled, scrambling to get clear.

The stampede began moments later.

It took only seconds for word to pass from one mouth to another, twenty meters at a time. In under thirty seconds, it had reached the tail end of the crowd, who now surged forward, sideways and backward. What had been a steady flow of fans became a torrent, and no amount of cajoling by police or stewards could stop the flood.

"Out of my way!" a man screamed at Morgan, shoving him aside.

Others battered their way past him, many carrying

children. The White Swan was only a dozen meters from Morgan, but the wave of fleeing spectators turned his approach into that of crossing a raging Rocky Mountain river.

"Hooligan!" he shouted. "Jeremy!"

Between the flashes of hustling claret-and-sky-blue shirts, Morgan caught sight of Hooligan sheltering by the pub's wall as if from a storm, but it was a tidal wave of people that rushed by him.

"Over here!" Morgan shouted. "Over here!" His words were getting lost in the din of the crowd, but he kept calling. "Look! Jeremy! Here!"

And finally Hooligan did look, his eyes caught by Morgan's motion, which was counter to the direction all others were moving. "Jack!" he called, his voice cracking. "Jack!"

Morgan saw Hooligan waving and pushed forward with more force, his sole focus on reaching Hooligan's side. When he burst from the crowd, it was almost as a newborn, tossed from the frantic motion of fleeing fans into a tranquil haven.

"Where is he?" asked Morgan.

"I haven't seen him since the stampede started." Hooligan hugged Morgan as if he were a long-lost father. "That was you who started the bomb scare?"

Hooligan was not the only one to have figured that out, and now the alert mounted police, who'd been drawn to Morgan by his rushing through the crowd, pointed fingers in his direction and turned their horses into the press. The steady flow of fleeing fans broke around the beasts like river rapids.

"They're coming for us, Jack! Thank God!"

Morgan felt no such elation. Flex was owed retribution, and Morgan could not deliver that from a Metropolitan Police cell. The mess could be cleared up, but it would take time.

Time where Flex could be hunting more of Morgan's people, or disappearing.

"Up and over the fence," Morgan ordered, his eyes on the wooden fencing that stood between them and the back of the pub. "Go! Put your boot in my hand, and I'll push you up!"

Hooligan knew better than to argue with Jack Morgan. In seconds he was over the fence. Morgan chanced one look over his shoulder before he followed.

The horse troopers were surging forward, eyes narrowed in pursuit as they talked into their radios.

Morgan was a wanted man.

Chapter 74

MORGAN DROPPED DOWN into the backyard of the pub.

"Gate over there!" He pointed the direction to Hooligan, and the two men began to twist and turn their way between empty beer kegs that gleamed silver in the evening's sunlight.

"What's happening, Jack? Who's that bloke chasing me?" Hooligan asked over his shoulder.

"Just run! I'll explain later," Morgan told him. "Run, and don't stop!"

But Hooligan did stop—the gate was locked. Morgan was about to boost the tech up and over when both men's phones rang simultaneously. The anomaly was enough to stop Morgan, and have him answer. "Peter," he said into the phone.

"Don't worry about the police," Knight's voice bounced back. "Get out of the front of the pub, Jack. I'm waiting here."

"We can't," Morgan protested. "The police saw me start the stampede. We can't—"

"Don't worry about the police!" Knight urged. "Just get out front. Hurry!"

Morgan felt Hooligan's eyes on him, expecting orders from his leader. Every instinct told him that they should run, but...

"Inside," the American told Hooligan, putting his faith in Knight and leading his tech man toward the back door.

As they stepped inside they saw the pub had pretty much cleared out except for a few stubborn patrons.

"You've gotta love the British." Hooligan couldn't help but smile with pride as he caught sight of one pensioner who was still sipping bitter at the bar, damned if he would move from his usual spot for a bomb threat.

Morgan's eyes were on the doorways and windows. Through the glass he caught sight of Knight behind the Audi's wheel, and pushed Hooligan through the nearest exit toward it.

Emptying out onto the street, Morgan half expected to be instantly assailed by police. Instead, he saw the two mounted officers moving away at speed in the opposite direction.

"Get in!" he yelled at Hooligan, opening the rear door and bundling him inside. He was about to follow when a roaring voice stopped him like a sledgehammer to the chest.

"Jack!" the voice bellowed. "Jack!" The sound of the familiar voice he so hated ignited every inch of his body in furious fire as he turned to face the owner.

Flex.

The muscle-bound man stood in the street as the final panicked remnants of the stampede hurried by him. By his side was a tall brute in a gray hoody.

Morgan wanted to kill them both.

Flex knew it, and smiled.

Then he simply walked away.

"Flex!" Morgan roared at the man's back, his mind too full

of anger to formulate threat or insult. "Flex!" he shouted, his call cutting away as he realized he was immobile, something holding him back from charging at the man who had killed Jane Cook.

"Help me hold him!" Knight shouted at Hooligan, who stretched from the back seat to reach out the door, taking hold of Morgan's belt. "Hold him!" Knight demanded, struggling with his own grip as he twisted from the driver's seat.

"Get off of me!" Morgan ordered.

"It's a trap!" Knight shouted back.

"I don't care!" the American argued.

Knight lifted his foot from the brake and hit the accelerator. He let the car leap forward a few feet before he stopped it. It was enough of a distance to yank Morgan off balance and give Knight and Hooligan a chance to pull him backward. Morgan's head hit hard against the door frame as he was bundled awkwardly into the passenger seat, side on.

"What the hell are you doing?" he roared.

But Knight was not about to answer. With his friend and leader safely in the car, he drove up onto the pavement and hit the accelerator.

They were clear.

Chapter 75

JACK MORGAN WAS still furious as Knight eased off the gas and drove them back onto the roads.

"Have you gone crazy?" the American shouted. "Flex was there, Peter! I had him!"

"He had *you*." Knight spoke calmly. "He was pulling you into a trap, Jack. They could have had Hooligan if they wanted to. Think about it. This was a trap for *you*."

"It felt like they wanted me," Hooligan protested as adrenaline and shock shook his body. "Who the hell are they?"

Morgan was in a silent rage. Nostrils flaring, he turned his head to look out the window but all he could see was the image of Flex as he taunted him, within reach. Deep inside, Morgan knew that Knight was right—it had been a trap, with Hooligan the bait—but that didn't make it any easier to swallow the fact that Flex still drew breath.

"Flex Gibbon's behind it," Knight answered Hooligan from behind the wheel, with a concerned look toward Morgan.

"Flex Gibbon?" Hooligan asked, fishing in his memory for

the name. "He was the SAS guy that Jack and Jane beat up to find Abbie Winchester?"

"He was."

"Where is Jane?" Hooligan then asked, cautiously, his intellect connecting the dots between Morgan's behavior and Cook's absence. "Guys? Where's Jane?"

The silence told Hooligan all he needed to know.

"Oh God. Oh God, no," he uttered, slipping down his seat. "Not Jane." He trembled, his lip shaking violently.

"Flex killed her," Morgan pushed out through clenched teeth, his eyes like lasers as he stared out the window. "And he's still out there."

"You'd be dead if you'd have followed Flex," Knight ventured, as neutrally as possible. "What use is that to her, Jack? That's not what she'd want. Think about it like this: when Flex goes down, do you want hundreds of witnesses?"

"No," Morgan replied. No witnesses. Not unless he wanted to spend a lifetime in a British prison.

"Flex will get what's coming to him," Knight promised. "But when *we* decide. Not him."

For a while the car was silent. In the back seat, Hooligan held his head between shaking hands.

"You're a good man, Peter," Morgan finally said. "You too, Hooligan."

"I ran," Hooligan stammered. "I left Perkins out there."

"Perkins will be OK. The police will have got him to a hospital," Knight reassured him. "They didn't want Perkins, they wanted you. You did what you had to do."

"You lived," added Morgan. "And now you can help us finish this."

Chapter 76

THE AUDI PULLED to a stop in Private London's secured parking, and all men exited simultaneously.

"I've gotta go to the loo," Hooligan told the others, and scuttled off.

Knight looked at Morgan over the top of the car.

"I'm sorry I went against your orders," Knight offered. "I know you're the boss, but I couldn't let you go after him. It would have been suicide."

"You're my friend, Peter. And you probably saved my life." Knight managed a weak smile.

"I'm going to contact the Met," he told his leader, having been debriefed by Hooligan on the journey. "Let them know that there's someone masquerading in convincing police uniform."

"Hooligan said he had all the gear," Morgan agreed. "Hooligan couldn't tell them apart. You think Flex has links in the police? Could he have called off the mounted officers to draw me in?"

Knight shook his head. "That was Denise. She was following it all on their system. She hacked in and gave orders for all officers to make their way to a bogus mass casualty event."

"Good work. Better make sure she covers her tracks."

As Knight stepped away from the car, his investigator's instinct read Morgan's body language. "You're not coming inside, are you?"

Morgan shook his head. "I'm not. Keys, please."

Knight tossed them over. "Will you tell me where you're going?"

"I won't." Morgan walked around to the driver's door and offered Knight his hand.

The Englishman shook it. "Be careful, Jack. I told you I'm ready to step up, but I don't want to have to."

Morgan patted his friend on the shoulder. Then, without a word, he climbed into the car. The sleek black machine glided from the garage and into the London night.

Where Jack Morgan would hunt.

Chapter 77

PETER KNIGHT SLOTTED his ID card into the garage's door, and followed it with the biometric data of his thumb print and retinal scan. Only on the authentication of all three did the heavy deadbolts click open, Knight raising his hand to the cameras that monitored his every move. The security of his headquarters was more than a match for any building in the UK.

It was with a clouded mind and heavy feet that he walked Private's hallways. He had known Jack Morgan for years, and he had never seen the American act this way. Morgan had always been a focused, driven individual, headstrong, even—how else could he have built the world's biggest private investigation firm?—but his single-minded desire for revenge was worrying Knight. Knight knew that he and Hooligan had saved Morgan's life by pulling him back into the car and keeping him from rushing after Flex and into an inevitable trap. Now Morgan was out again, who knew where, and without anyone to stop him from making any rash moves. Flex was ex-SAS and highly trained in tactical warfare. In order to beat him and achieve the justice Morgan so desperately wanted, they needed to be as cold and calculated as he was.

Justice, he thought. What did that mean to him? Peter Knight had worked for a long time as part of the British criminal justice system. He had seen innocent people go to prison, and evil ones go free. The system was flawed, he knew, but overall he believed in it. What kind of society would it be where people felt the need, and the right, to dispense their own justice? Knight had studied cases from Indonesia to Venezuela. He knew what happened when law broke down and vigilantism took over. Inevitably, those vigilante groups descended into becoming gangs and cartels and murderous groups just like the ones they had at first stood up to, and Knight had no wish to see that on London's streets.

And yet.

And yet, he had done nothing to stop Jack Morgan taking the car and leaving on what could only be the pursuit of Flex Gibbon. A pursuit that, deep down, Knight knew would not end with Flex being handcuffed and put into the back of a police car. It would end with a casket, and spadefuls of dirt.

Knight strode toward the tech lab. "We need to track, Jack," he told Hooligan.

"Already on it," Hooligan replied intently.

"He didn't disable the tracker?" Knight asked, frowning. As head of Private, Morgan was aware of all standard operating procedures. One of the most basic of which was to tag and track all of the Private fleet.

Hooligan shook his head. "He didn't, surprisingly."

Knight was confused—why would Morgan go it alone,

unwilling to disclose his intent, but leave the electronic signature of his whereabouts?

"Where is he now?"

"Well, that's odd." Hooligan frowned, looking again at his screen, and then to Knight. "He's at Horse Guards."

Chapter 78

JACK MORGAN PULLED his car off Whitehall and into Great Scotland Yard, where he spied a parking space beside the Clarence pub. It was a private spot, but Morgan took care of that by giving the pub's bouncer a handshake loaded with a couple of fifty-pound notes. Then, with the lightest of rains falling on his skin, he walked back onto Whitehall, and in the direction of Horse Guards Parade.

The majesty of London had always impressed Morgan, and its effect was even more striking at night. The buildings that lined Whitehall had been part of the seat from which the British Empire had been ruled. It was now home to the Ministry of Defence, the road itself watched over by statues of men who had led British armies to great victories overseas. Morgan's eyes glanced over the brass plaques as he walked, recognizing the names from lessons he had been taught as a young Marine Corps officer: Earl Haig, who had presided over the slaughter in the trenches; Viscount Montgomery, who had turned back Rommel's Africa Korps, before serving beneath Eisenhower in Europe; the Viscount Slim, who had routed the Japanese in Asia. All leaders who had been blessed with remarkable men and women to serve under them, just as Morgan had. Looking at their faces, Morgan wondered if they suffered as he did when any one of the people under their command were hurt, or died in the line of duty.

Morgan looked away from the statues, his eyes drawn to a brilliantly lit up structure in the road's center. It was the Cenotaph, Morgan remembered—the central point of remembrance for all British and Commonwealth fallen soldiers. Jane had told him that when they had walked these streets together, looking for vulnerabilities in security ahead of the Trooping the Color parade, where kidnappers had threatened to execute Abbie Winchester should a ransom for her release not be paid. It was during those hours alone with her that Morgan had begun to develop an attraction for Jane Cook that was more than physical, and her memory had drawn him here. Their time together had been as short as it had been electric, and Morgan wanted to feel her presence as he sought out the road ahead. He wanted to recall memories of her that were exciting and promising, rather than the grotesque images of her death.

His feet crunching on the stone of Horse Guards Parade, Morgan closed his eyes and tried to imagine her own set of footsteps beside his. Then in the center of the square he halted and raised his face to the sky.

"I'm sorry, Jane," he whispered to the night. "I'm so sorry."

He breathed deeply, holding back tears behind closed eyelids. He knew he had become a runaway train, and that he had to hold back his emotions—or at least channel them—if he was to bring justice to Jane's killers. *Killers*, because now he knew the face of Flex's accomplice.

Morgan breathed out and opened his eyes. The square about him was deserted, the magnificent buildings surrounding him standing as proud as Guardsmen in their lit-up glory. Such a sense of history and scale helped to focus Morgan's mind. How many men who had stood on this square had gone on to war, never to come back? They had taken on danger and death because they had believed in a cause—a mission. Morgan's mission was one he believed in with every fiber of his being: to avenge Jane. A strange sense of calm settled upon him as he realized, without the slightest trace of doubt, that he would die to avenge her.

"There's no other way," he said out loud.

And so, resolved to his mission, Morgan's boots crunched the gravel as he strode toward the arched gate of the parade ground, and out into his war. If he was going to win it, though, he'd need firepower.

He pulled out his phone and called an unlikely ally.

Chapter 79

THE SUMMER RAIN had stopped by the time Morgan had walked to the Thames Embankment, the few puddles left in its wake shimmering beneath the street lights, as the breeze coming off the wide river plucked at their surface.

He was guided to his destination by the stone structure that stood sentinel over the river. At the monument's head was a gilded bronze eagle. It was the Royal Air Force's memorial, and Morgan had met a man here before, two summers ago.

That same man was here again to greet him now. "Good evening, Morgan," he said.

"Good evening, Colonel," he replied to De Villiers. "How's Lewis?"

"She's demanding we let her out of the hospital so that she can go after them. She's a bloody trooper."

"And Perkins?"

"He'll live. He's damn lucky not to have been trampled to death in that stampede."

"That's good to hear," said Morgan. "I don't think the Princess is in danger, but you should probably hold back on public appearances until this is over."

"Of course," De Villiers agreed. "She's already been moved to a safe place."

"Where?"

De Villiers ignored the question.

Morgan turned to face the Thames. On the opposite bank stood the huge wheel of the London Eye—how many happy couples on there? Morgan wondered. How many couples for whom death would be something to be confronted in their eighties, and at a bedside?

"Have you brought me what I wanted?" he asked.

"I haven't," the Colonel replied.

Morgan turned his head sharply toward the other man. "Then why are you here? I don't have time to waste."

"And it won't be wasted," the Colonel promised. "But this isn't Texas, Morgan. One doesn't simply walk into Walmart and leave with a trolley full of guns."

"You wouldn't need to go to Walmart, Colonel. You're the head of royal security, and a solider. You have access to armories."

"Well-secured and -monitored armories," De Villiers added.

Morgan's burning glare prompted the Colonel to explain himself, and in a hurry. "Do you want the police and the army's special branch breathing down our necks from the moment I walk out of the armory? You'll get your weapon, but you'll do things my way."

De Villiers pushed a folded piece of paper into Morgan's pocket.

"What's this?"

"The address of a place where you can find what you want." Morgan raised an eyebrow in question.

"It's an illegal-club-slash-drug-den," the Colonel explained. "High end. I've had to pull a few of our wards out of there over the years."

"How do you know I'll find weapons?"

"Because I've had the bloody things pointed in my face when I came in the back door unannounced. Believe me, Morgan, you'll find what you need there. Their security will be holding them."

Morgan considered it for a moment. "What about police?" he asked.

"I told you, it's high end. The people there are people that matter. The police give it a wide berth."

"You're sure?"

"I once saw the retired head of Scotland Yard in there, Morgan. I'm sure."

Morgan shook his head and snorted. The hypocrisy of the world and the establishment never ceased to amaze him. And yet, he had to remind himself, there were many good men and women in such archaic institutions, doing good work in a corrupt system. Despite first appearances, Marcus De Villiers was showing himself to be one of them.

"Thank you for doing this for me," Morgan told the man.

"No offence, Morgan, but this isn't for you. This is for Lewis and Perkins, and for Cook."

Morgan felt as though the Colonel was holding something back. "Go ahead," he pressed.

"Lewis told me what happened," De Villiers admitted. "She remembered names, Morgan. She told me about Flex."

"You know him," Morgan muttered.

"Of course I know him. He's from the regiment, and he

runs one of the biggest private security firms in London. At least, he did."

Morgan looked at the man, and let his eyes ask the question.

"His business has taken a dive over the past couple of years. Word got out that he was beaten down and had his knee blown out by a couple of civilians, one of them a woman, the other an American."

Morgan said nothing.

"He's had the first part of his revenge, Morgan, but he won't be satisfied until you're dead."

"The feeling is mutual."

"Good. Flex is not only a murderer, but by virtue of who he was, he is a national disgrace. Better he be dealt with quietly, rather than dragged through the courts."

"You're helping me because you want this kept quiet?"

"I'm helping you because it's the right thing to do. There are two pieces of paper in your pocket, Morgan. One is the address, and the other is a copy of my letter of resignation. Lewis and Perkins were hurt under my command. As I can't take their place in the hospital—which I wish I could—I can only give up my command. I'm staying in my post only to be useful until this bastard is dealt with, Morgan. Then I will resign my commission."

"We have to deal with Flex first," Morgan replied.

"We do," De Villiers agreed. "So you'd better go get your gun."

Chapter 80

COLONEL DE VILLIERS walked eastward along the Thames' northern bank, his eyes on the pavement as the wind began to whip off the water, finding every opening in his clothing.

"It's supposed to be bloody summer," the man grumbled to himself as he reached inside his Barbour jacket for his phone.

"Yes?" the voice asked as De Villiers' call connected.

"I met with Morgan," the Colonel replied after a look over both shoulders. "I gave him the address."

"Will he go?" the voice asked.

"He will. He's on a rampage. You could see it in his eyes."

For a moment there was silence, all quiet in De Villiers' ears except the slap of his brogues against the Embankment's damp paving stones.

"Did he buy your resignation?" the voice finally asked.

"He did," De Villiers replied.

"Good. It's important he trusts you."

"I don't know if he trusts me, but he believes me. With the state of mind he's in, I think that will be enough."

"Very good, Colonel. You'll see this through for me, won't you?"

"Anything for you, Your Highness."

Chapter 81

JACK MORGAN STARED intently through the Audi's windshield, his fingers tight on the wheel. The car's navigation system told him that he was one minute away from the destination given to him by De Villiers, and Morgan intended to make his first reconnaissance in the car.

The venue's location was in Knightsbridge, which struck Morgan as no surprise. Given that the streets were dotted with Ferraris and Maseratis, where better to hold a private party for London's mega-rich and ultra-connected?

It was the appearance of a tall woman that first gave away the location. She was every inch the Russian millionaire's wife, with blonde hair piled on top of her head, and fur over her shoulders. Knightsbridge was home to rich clichés, and Morgan watched as she was followed out of the golden Lamborghini by a bearded man whose clothes were twenty years too young for him, and two chest sizes too small. Morgan slowed and watched the couple as they climbed the steps to a black door. The bearded man gave his woman a helpful grab on the ass as she slipped slightly in her heels, then knocked on the door. The couple waited patiently to be admitted. As there was no one else outside the building, one thing was clear to Morgan—the security, and the weapons he wanted, were behind that black door.

"Dammit," Morgan swore softly, pulling his car into a side street a block away so that he was clear to think—how the hell could he get inside there without starting World War Three?

And then he had it.

"Hello," Morgan said into his phone when it was finally answered. "I know, it's been a long time," he went on politely. "Listen, I'm calling because I need a favor."

Chapter 82

AFTER MORGAN HUNG up the phone, he drove to the nearest twenty-four-hour superstore to collect what he would need to turn that favor into weapons. By the time he had arrived back at the Knightsbridge location, the American had received a text that told him he was "all good." Armed with that piece of information, he began the short walk to the party. With each step he prayed that the rain would hold off and he could ascend the steps dry, his freshly purchased clothes spotless. Despite knowing what was soon to come, Morgan fought back his adrenaline and took the steps slowly, trying hard to appear as cool and calm as possible. He needed to look as though he belonged at that party.

He knocked and counted to ten.

Nothing.

He knocked again.

Eight . . . nine . . . ten . . .

"Yes?" a female voice buzzed from the intercom beside the door.

"I'm here to see Albert," Morgan announced, using the phrase he had been given in his phone call.

"There's no Albert here," the voice answered through the intercom.

"Yes there is," Morgan insisted. "Abbie Winchester told me to come and say hello to him."

The intercom went silent. Morgan pictured how the woman within would be looking on her phone for confirmation that the well-known socialite Abbie Winchester had indeed invited a guest.

"She's not here," the voice came back, and Morgan wondered what his chances were of knocking down the thick door—zero, he reckoned.

"I'm visiting from out of town," he explained, smiling, certain that he was on camera. "Abbie recommended this place. I don't really know London." He shrugged, with another disarming smirk.

A second later the electronic bolts of the door clicked open, and Morgan found himself looking into an empty hallway, the dull thud of bass drifting down from above.

He stepped inside, and sense told him to wait. Moments later he was met from an adjoining room by the owner of the intercom's voice, a petite young woman with tattoos teasing up her neck.

"You're too clean-cut to be a friend of Abbie's, mate," she assessed, looking Morgan over.

"I'm American." He smiled helplessly. "We're not known for our fashion."

"True." The girl smiled. "You got a phone?"

Morgan shook his head. "Abbie told me to leave it in the car."

"Good. No photos allowed here. Lifetime ban if you do."

"Any other rules?" Morgan asked.

"Just don't be a dickhead." She shrugged. "Three hundred quid, please." The girl put out her hand.

Morgan reached for his wallet and pulled out the notes.

"Next time bring a girl and you'll get in easier. Or don't." She shrugged with a smile, playing the game.

"Here's another two hundred for your trouble," he told her, playing it himself.

The girl held his look before finally nodding her head. "Upstairs. You can't miss it. Just follow the music."

"I'll see you later," Morgan promised, and walked toward the staircase. As he moved, he looked through the open door that the girl had walked out of. He saw two muscular men on a sofa, their eyes on a bank of CCTV screens that showed what must be the party upstairs, and the building's exterior. They were big men, Morgan thought to himself, dismissing the idea of rushing them immediately. Better to bide his time, he decided, and to think of a plan.

Knowing that there was only one place in the building to do that without attracting attention, he followed the thump of bass and walked up the stairs.

Chapter 83

AS YOUNG MARINES, Jack Morgan and his comrades had enjoyed letting their hair down, short as it was. As head of Private, a multimillion-dollar business, Morgan had been invited to plenty of parties.

He wasn't sure if any of those experiences had prepared him for the sight that greeted him at the top of the staircase.

It was not one of Caligula's orgies, by any means. It was more just the sight in front of him was...*bizarre*, like a wild, wacky dream.

To begin with, the building itself was a marvel. What appeared on the outside as a Knightsbridge home was actually a party space as well appointed as any London club. There were lasers, flashing lights and smoke machines. There was a DJ, a packed dance floor and a bar running across the back wall. Morgan realized that the building didn't end there, and a quick look into the other corridors showed him a maze of rooms filled with bean bags, smoke and beautiful people.

Having got his bearings, he turned back to the main

room, first scanning the crowd for anyone known to him—in his position, it was always a possibility that he could run into a former client at a high-end establishment like this. Morgan saw none of them, but he did recognize an international football star sweating and grinding his jaw as he raged on the dance floor. In the room's back corner, a toppled TV presenter was doing bumps of cocaine from the fingernails of a Page Three model. Little wonder they wouldn't allow phones and cameras inside, thought Morgan. And little help these people would be to him in his attempt to liberate the guards of their weapons.

Or maybe not, he thought, remembering a British show-biz scandal that had made the American news.

Morgan stopped at the bar and ordered a virgin daiquiri. "Dress it up," he asked the bartender. "I like flowers in there." He slipped the man a note as tip once the glass was brimming with decoration.

Then, having watched the TV presenter take another snort from his companion's nail, he made his way over.

"Hi." Morgan smiled at the pair, directing his biggest grin at the presenter. "I'm Jack."

"I'm Natalie," said the model.

The presenter simply greeted Morgan with a nod, arrogant enough to believe that everyone knew his name.

"You're Matthew Alexander, right?" Morgan offered his hand as he named one of the man's biggest rivals.

"Matt Lloyd," the presenter corrected, unable to take his scowling eyes from Morgan's flowery drink. "What the fuck is that?"

"It's a daiquiri." Morgan smiled. "Would you like some?"

"Looks like something from the Chelsea Flower Show."

Morgan allowed his smile to drop and his shoulders to slump slightly. Natalie noticed.

"Aw, don't be a dick, Matt. You've hurt his feelings." She stepped over to Morgan and put a protective hand onto his shoulder. Matt Lloyd saw the picture in front of him, and realized that the attractive woman's attention had now switched to the American.

"Are you gay?" he sneered.

Morgan looked taken aback. "And what if I am?"

"Yeah, Matt. It's not a big deal," Natalie opined.

But it was a big deal for Matt Lloyd, Morgan knew. In fact, it had been a big part of the reason that Lloyd had lost his seven-figure contract with the BBC—a homophobic tirade that had been captured on smartphone and leaked to the media. The LGBT community had been outraged, and demanded Lloyd's head. They'd got it, and Morgan was certain that Lloyd would have spent tens of thousands on PR gurus and therapists to clean up his image, and his act. There would be no more public slip-ups from Matt Lloyd; no more loose tongues.

Of course, cocaine had a way of changing all of that.

"It's a big deal to me," Lloyd rumbled, the drug divesting him of any tact or inhibition. "Your rainbow-loving freak mates cost me my job."

"I'm sorry?" Morgan asked, feigning ignorance.

"You and the rest of the queers. You pushed me out of my job."

"He said some things about gays," Natalie confessed. "They weren't very nice."

"True though," the bigot smirked. "So why don't you take your flowers and piss off."

"Wow. I'm sorry I upset you. Really I am. I'll go now."

Lloyd was halfway back into his chair when Morgan delivered his mental right hook: "Natalie, would you like to dance?"

Lloyd was jumping to his feet in an instant. "You don't ask my girl to dance!" he shouted, pulling Morgan back by the shoulder. Deliberately, Morgan dropped his glass, and heads turned to look at the commotion.

"What are you doing?" Morgan shouted, feigning helplessness.

"You do not dance with my girl!"

"*Your* girl?" Natalie shouted. "I'm no one's girl."

"Oh, really? Who bought you those clothes? You think you're special? You're no use except for getting your tits out. Those pics will be fish and chips wrapping by next week, and you'll be forgotten!"

By now a small crowd was gathering as people recognized the turbulence in their midst.

"Don't talk to her like that," Morgan demanded.

"Or what, *faggot*?" Lloyd spat, using the most offensive American term he could think of.

Morgan said nothing publicly. Instead, he leaned close to Lloyd and spoke words into his ear that only they could hear.

It was the final straw for the bigot—he threw a punch.

It was an angry punch, sloppy, mistimed and misdirected. Morgan ducked it without even thinking, his own hands never leaving his sides. Lloyd swung a second haymaker. Morgan easily stepped out of its way.

The disgraced man never had a chance to throw a third. The two security men that Morgan had seen downstairs had been patiently watching the situation develop, hoping that it would fizzle out. Flare-ups between the stellar-sized egos at

the establishment were not uncommon, and would be toler-
ated so long as they kept to chest-beating and insults. Once a
punch was thrown, however, the security contingent would
sweep in on the perpetrator within moments. During their
phone call, Abbie Winchester had told Morgan as much.
Now he watched as the two men expertly restrained Lloyd,
one on each side of him, exerting enough pressure to hold
him in place, but not to cause damage.

"I'll have your face cut off!" Lloyd raged at Morgan as he
thrashed to break free, his rage escalating higher as Natalie
threw a drink in his face and the watching room cheered.

"I'm really sorry, sir," one muscular security man apologized to Morgan as he and his partner turned Lloyd to the
stairs and prepared to march him out.

"I'm sorry, too," said Morgan, the security man's face
dropping as Morgan's hand shot up under his jacket. Morgan
stepped back and clear before the bouncer had a chance to
decide if he should defend against the American or keep hold
of the thrashing Lloyd.

Now it seemed the answer was clear: there was only one
true threat in the room, and that was Jack Morgan.

Who had a gun in his hand.

Chapter 84

WITH THE SECURITY guy's back turned to him, Morgan had liberated the pistol from his hidden shoulder holster with ease. In one smooth motion he had pulled the weapon clear with his right hand, using his left to cock back the pistol's top slide, chambering a round. Within two seconds of Morgan beginning his theft, the pistol was ready for use and aimed.

"Don't kill him!" the robbed security man begged, bravely trying to put himself between Morgan and Lloyd, who was now weak-kneed with terror. "It's not worth it!" he urged.

"Your weapon on the floor," Morgan told the man's partner. "Do it!" he shouted, seeing in his peripheral vision a steady flow of revelers abandoning the scene, rushing with hushed panic for the exit. "Finger and thumb on the grip," he ordered.

Slowly, very slowly, the second bouncer reached inside his jacket. With his finger and thumb gripping the handle, he pulled out a six-shooter revolver and placed it on the floor. Behind him, the room had all but emptied. Morgan flicked his eyes quickly to assess who remained, seeing Natalie shaking uncontrollably close by his side.

"Pick it up like he did," Morgan instructed her. "Now!"

Natalie scuttled forward and picked up the gun.

"Put it in my jacket pocket," he instructed. "Keep holding it exactly as you are, or I'll blow his head apart."

"Oh God," the woman sobbed, black mascara running down her cheeks like a polluted river.

Morgan backed away as he felt the reassuring weight of the second pistol entering his pocket. "All of you on the floor. Facedown. Do it!"

They complied. Lloyd was the slowest to do so, almost paralyzed with terror. "I'm sorry," he begged. "Please don't kill me."

"On your face!"

"I have a daughter!"

"On your face!"

Dribbling with dread, Lloyd joined the others on a floor awash with panic-spilled drinks.

"Interlock your fingers behind your heads," Morgan ordered the four remaining people in the club, his voice suddenly seeming so loud, and bouncing around the room—the music had stopped, he realized. The last song put on by the DJ had played out, and now the lights and lasers flashed eerily in the silence.

"Your security tapes. Where are they? Tell me exactly where!"

But there was no reply, because the bouncers had heard the same thing that Morgan now did—footsteps on the staircase.

Before Morgan could move, gunshots filled the air.

He threw himself into a shoulder roll and scrambled for

the bar as bullets chewed the furniture and decor in the room. He heard someone scream in pain as the shots flew wild, none coming within a foot of his refuge.

"Stop shooting!" Morgan shouted, his gut telling him who the firer would be.

Two more rounds smashed into the wall above him. Morgan scuttled behind the bar and peered around its far side— as he expected, the tattooed girl from downstairs stood at the head of the staircase, a semi-automatic pistol held in her hand. Of the security guards, Natalie and Lloyd there was no sign, only the flapping door of an open fire exit, and a trail of blood made dark beneath the disco lights.

Morgan drew his pistol up to aim. The girl's shots had been wild, showing her lack of experience at firing a weapon, and he was exposing no more than his head and the top of his shoulders. At twenty yards, the chances of her hitting him were almost non-existent, while his own accuracy was a dead cert.

But Morgan couldn't kill her.

"Drop it, goddammit!" he shouted.

The girl fired instead. Across the bar, ten feet away, a bottle of Gran Patrón tequila paid the price.

"I don't want to shoot you!" Morgan shouted as the liquid and glass bounced around him. "But I will, if I have to!"

"You fucked up our club!" she screamed back. "The police will be on their way!"

Morgan ducked back into cover, expecting the shot that puckered the bar's wood. The police were a far bigger threat in his mind than the girl's marksmanship. The exodus from the front door would have been enough to alert a nosy neighbor or an alert bobby. If by some miracle that had gone unnoticed, then the gunshots would do the rest—the club room had been soundproofed for house music, but the open fire escape had seen to that precaution against sound complaints.

That fire escape was now Morgan's only chance, he knew. He couldn't kill an innocent person, and contrary to the belief of politicians and activists, there was no such thing as not shooting to kill. Sure, Morgan could aim for the girl's shoulder, but when that bullet entered the body it would hit bone. It could send slivers of bone and steel anywhere, including into the girl's heart. A shot to the arm? She could bleed out from her brachial artery. Then there was the chance of her moving as Morgan fired. The only non-lethal shot was the one you didn't fire, so that was the option Morgan took.

But how the hell would he make it to the fire escape?

It was half the distance between him and the girl, on the right-hand wall. He would be ten yards from her, and his full height, not head and shoulders behind cover. Seeing him coming, the girl was bound to let rip with everything she had left, and only one of those bullets would need to find him to put him down, and from there into handcuffs, or a coffin.

It couldn't end here, Morgan swore to himself. His promise of retribution could not die in an illegal club, surrounded by broken bottles of liquor, and washed over by lasers.

Lasers.

"Will you let me surrender?" Morgan tried.

"Piss off, you wanker! You think I'm stupid? You're staying there until the cops get here!"

Morgan had assumed as much, but he had used the girl's tirade to maneuver himself to the other end of the bar, hoping to emerge where she would not expect him.

Her words done, the room was silent. Silent enough for Morgan to hear shouts in the street and sirens in the distance.

It was now or never.

He stepped from cover, and took aim.

Morgan fired four times, the pistol rounds sparking as they hit the metal chain and fixture that held the light mounting in the room's corner. The structure toppled downward and in front of the staircase, its thick cord catching it at chest height before it could crash into the ground. Now with an obstacle between him and the girl, Morgan was already running.

She fired—shots snapped from beneath the obstruction—but her view had been robbed from her. Within seconds of opening fire, his shoulder was hitting the partially opened door, and he was on the staircase.

He took a moment to collect himself at the top, not wanting to plunge from one trap into another. With no obvious ambushes ahead of him, Morgan left the first metal platform, traversing the fire escape like a parkour runner, clearing a flight at a time. The shock of the impacts shot through his ankles and up into his body, his face grimacing with each descent.

But the pain saved his life. No sooner was he on the second platform than the girl appeared on the platform above. Morgan gritted his teeth, expecting the impact of bullets to smash into his exposed back. Instead he heard two clangs, like a hammer hitting metal, two bullets puncturing the sheet metal of the staircase beside him. Then there was only the sound of swearing as the girl realized that her ammunition was spent.

"Wanker!" she shouted, hurling the pistol at Morgan in frustration. Her throwing aim was better than her shooting, and the pistol narrowly missed his head. He moved. He ran as fast as he could through the darkness, dogs barking and security lights snapping on as he fled, and the sound of sirens growing ever closer and more imminent.

Morgan felt at the reassuring lumps of metal in his pockets. He had done what he needed to do, and he was not sorry that he had terrified others to obtain the weapons.

But someone else would be.

Chapter 85

PETER KNIGHT LOOKED at the papers in his hand. It was a printout of the premier security companies in the country. These were not businesses that advertised in the local job center, but who recruited directly from the Special Forces and army. Minimum entry requirements were tours of duty, combat experience and solid references from former commanders. They were the kind of people who had worked with Flex both in and out of uniform, and now, Knight hoped they'd be the ones to lead him to the murderer.

He was wrong.

"Come on, Ryan," Knight beseeched the man at the other end of the line. "We've used your company for years. Where's the loyalty?"

"Well, that's exactly it, Peter. Even if I knew where Flex was, I couldn't tell you. Me and him were in the regiment together. Maybe if you told me what this was about."

"I can't," Knight said, closing his eyes in frustration. "Just trust me, Ryan, this is not a guy you want to be associated with."

"I do trust you. But Flex has built up a lot of trust with me too. We were in the sandpit together, so you understand why I can't rat him out, even if I did know."

Knight rubbed at his face. The blind loyalty of the soldiers running these companies was a brick wall that a civilian could not penetrate.

"What if I told you he hurt another soldier?" Knight tried, tiptoeing around the subject. "A decorated one."

"Then get them to call me. If we have a few friends in common, and they vouch for them, then we'll see."

Knight swore under his breath.

"Something big is about to happen," Knight told the man, sensing failure. "And you're about to fall on the wrong side of it."

"Nah, mate. I'm standing back from it, well out of the way."

"Goodbye, Ryan," Knight said, hanging up the call. "Bollocks!" he shouted out, crossing off the last name on his list. Not one of the companies' leaders would speak about Flex.

Frustrated, Knight screwed up the paper and threw it at the wastepaper basket. It missed. Swearing, he crossed to pick it up, but as he did so a red mist of anger descended before his eyes, and instead of picking up the paper, he kicked the basket as hard as he could and let loose a howl of rage. A rage that had built inside him since Jane Cook had been killed in cold blood. *His* agent. *His* friend. Killed in cold blood.

"Bastard!" Knight roared, wanting nothing more in that moment than to rip Flex's heart out with his own hands. "Bastard!"

Eliza Lightwood had done a good job of destroying Knight's office. Now the angered man did the rest. He threw books, kicked cabinets and punched the walls. He grabbed at his face, pulled at his hair and cried down his cheeks.

He remembered Jane.

"No!" he shouted at everything and nothing. "No! No! No!"

The grief and rage that he'd bottled up hit him like an avalanche. He had been so caught up—so busy protecting Morgan and worrying about him—that he'd ignored his own emotions. Now, faced with the dead end from the security companies, he could no longer hold back the irrepressible savagery of his heartache. As his chest heaved and swelled like an angry ocean, Peter Knight sank to his knees and wept.

Chapter 86

AS WAS HIS plan, Jack Morgan abandoned the Audi parked on the Knightsbridge street, instead leaving the area by foot and collecting a bag of clothing bought at the twenty-four-hour supermarket that he'd secreted in a dark alleyway that led to a park. There, he quickly changed jacket and trainers, and pulled tracksuit bottoms over his trousers. A peaked cap was the final item to complete the outfit change, and with the pistols in his pockets, Morgan struck out of the park.

He pulled a phone from his new jacket—a black windbreaker. The phone was a cheap model bought at the store, and kept with the change of clothes—the one that it had replaced now resided in a drain. Morgan knew that the Audi would eventually draw suspicion. Even if he dispatched someone from Private to collect it, the vehicle would show up on the CCTV footage that officers would scour as they investigated the shooting. Of course, by the time they did, Morgan believed he would have carried out his mission, or died trying. To that end, he dialed a number from memory.

"I need to meet you, and off the streets."

Morgan then listened as he was given an address.

It wasn't a hard one to remember, and he flagged down the first black cab that he saw.

"Where to, mate?" the cabbie asked.

"I'll give you directions."

Chapter 87

COMPARED TO THE modern behemoths that arched toward the sky, the Tower of London seemed hardly fitting of its name. More a collection of buildings, walls and ramparts than a singular tower, its tallest point stood at twenty-seven meters. By contrast, the Shard, on the opposite bank of the river, climbed to three hundred and ten. Even the neighboring apartments dwarfed the building in height, but scale was only half the story, and what the Tower lacked in vertical bombast, it more than made up for in history and sheer regal majesty. Heavy black gates sat daunting in the stone walls. Flags flew proudly above the lit-up towers and ramparts, snapping in the wind as if to attention.

Morgan stepped out of the cab—the third he had taken, anxious to avoid being followed—and took in the building that sat with gravitas alongside the Thames, the river itself spanned by the grand vision of Tower Bridge, lit-up cables hanging between its iconic twin towers. Jack Morgan had visited the place before as a tourist, and such history reminded him of how small was his own place in the world, and the events of man. The oldest parts of the building were almost a thousand years old, and within the walls, enemies of the state had awaited judgment and been delivered to death. Beneath the beauty was a nation's past soaked in treason, blood and violence. Morgan could not help but wonder if De Villiers had asked to meet him here for just that reason.

The chance to ask him arrived as the Colonel removed himself from the shadows.

"Why here?" Morgan asked.

"It's secure," De Villiers replied. "Police. Soldiers. These walls? You won't find a safer place in London. You found what you were looking for?"

Morgan evaded a direct answer. "I don't have anything on me," he told the man, having hidden the weapons between cabs.

"Good." De Villiers turned and led Morgan toward a door that was set in the stone beside one of the imposing gates and flanked by armed guards, who stood to attention at the approach of the Colonel, clad in civilian attire though he was.

The cold stone tunnel was ten feet deep, and as Morgan emerged at De Villiers' back, he saw that much of the interior was cast into darkness.

But there were voices in the night.

"Stop for a moment," said the Colonel, his voice calm.

"What is it?" Morgan asked quietly.

"Just be quiet."

Then, clear as day, Morgan heard a young voice cry out into the night. It was a confident voice. The voice of a soldier.

"Halt!" he demanded. "Who comes there?"

A second voice answered, rich with years. Following the sound, Morgan saw the uniform of a Yeoman Warder—a Beefeater. "The keys!" he replied.

"Whose keys?" the young sentry questioned.

"Queen Elizabeth's keys!"

"Pass then!" the soldier allowed. "All's well!"

And Morgan watched silently as the Yeoman, under escort of bayonet-toting soldiers, their silhouettes made long by tall bearskin hats, marched by the young sentry and out of sight.

At that moment, Morgan realized he'd been holding his breath, and let it go silently. He could not explain why he had done so. Only that he knew he was watching something ancient, archaic and special. A moment that was timeless. A throwback to past days.

"What was that?" he asked De Villiers, as the tramp of the men's boots faded into the darkness.

"The Ceremony of the Keys," the man explained. "They're locking up the Tower."

"They do this every night?"

"For centuries," De Villiers confirmed. "The only thing that changes is the monarch's name. You're very lucky to have seen it. Very few do."

The majesty of the moment had not been lost on Morgan, and he nodded, but the movement was cursory. A punctuation at the end of one conversation, and the beginning of the next. He had come to the Tower for a reason that was not one of ceremony.

"Something's been troubling me," Morgan admitted to the Colonel. He didn't need to say that it was something other than the death of Jane, which burned through his soul with more torturous intent than any of the contraptions that had been used to bring misery to the Tower's former occupants, and traitors.

"What is it?" De Villiers asked.

"The shooters knew my hotel in Brecon. They knew where

to find us at the waterfall. It's fair to say by now that those gunmen were Flex and an associate. Maybe more than one."

"Are you saying you think Flex had inside help?"

"I know he did."

"And do you know from whom?"

"At first I thought it was Lewis, but I know now that's not possible."

"Then who?"

"The Princess told me you have SAS troopers on the security detail?"

De Villiers nodded. "Of course. They're the best of the best."

"They're also people who are loyal to Flex, he being one of their own."

"I don't like where you're going with this, Morgan."

"But hear me out anyway. I'd like you to look into the service records of the SAS men on the Princess's detail, to see if any served alongside Flex."

"They're all younger men on this detail, much younger than Flex. He has been out of the regiment for a while now. I doubt it's possible."

"But we need to consider it."

His business at an end, Morgan gave De Villiers the number that he could now be reached on.

"But we're not done yet," the Colonel said suddenly, surprising him.

"We're not?"

"No, Morgan. There's a reason I wanted you to come to the Tower, and I'm afraid you can't leave without knowing it. Follow me."

Morgan allowed himself to be led by De Villiers into the heart of the Tower, emerging in a courtyard that was lined with small terraced houses older than the American's home nation.

"Who lives here?" Morgan asked.

"The Beefeaters," the Colonel answered.

"They're trusted to live inside the Tower?"

"More than trusted. They're the soul of the place, every one of them a former warrant officer with twenty-two years' service or more. They come from the army, air force and navy, each of them as dedicated and patriotic a person as you'll find."

Morgan listened, interested to find out where De Villiers' speech was heading.

"Many of them joined the military at sixteen," De Villiers added. "And they'll serve until they retire. Duty to their country is all, to them."

"And duty to the Crown?"

"You'll not find a Beefeater who doesn't see them as one and the same. After you, Morgan." The Colonel unlocked a door and stepped aside so that the American could walk in first.

He did, and came face to face with a man holding a gun.

Chapter 88

THE ARMED MAN made no move as Morgan entered, a Heckler & Koch MP5 machine gun held downward across his chest. After a moment, Morgan recognized him as one of the men who had talked to Lewis at the gate of the royal residence in Wales, what felt like a lifetime ago. The man acknowledged Morgan with a jut of his chin.

"Up here." De Villiers pointed over Morgan's shoulder. Morgan brushed by the armed man as he made his way through the cramped corridor and up the narrow staircase. Behind him, De Villiers stooped so that his head avoided the ceiling.

When Morgan reached the top of the short flight he turned and found himself in what amounted to a studio apartment, the walls thick with books, the antique wooden desk piled high with papers.

There was a woman sitting at it.

"Your Highness," Morgan greeted Princess Caroline, his outward appearance giving away nothing of his surprise. He had expected De Villiers to be taking him to some intelligence briefing—or to detain him, had he developed cold feet. Instead, Morgan now found himself in the top-secret hiding place of Princess Caroline. Hearing footsteps behind him as De Villiers walked back down the steps, it became apparent that this reception was to be for Jack Morgan alone.

Princess Caroline turned to face the American at the top of her tiny staircase. Her initial expression was one of grief, mourning the loss of her beloved Sophie, but then he saw something else in her face, too—shock. Perhaps fear.

"Jack." She rose to her feet and removed her reading glasses. "Jack, you look like a different man."

Morgan said nothing and stood as still as the Tower's bayonet-carrying soldiers while Princess Caroline crossed the small room. She stopped in front of him and embraced him. It was the embrace of someone who had experienced the deepest pain of loss, and who could see that same emptiness of grief in him.

"I'm so sorry," the royal told him, her words muffled by Morgan's windbreaker. "I'm so very sorry." In her words, he could feel the Princess expressing her sadness and regret for her own loss as much as his. They had both had the woman they loved taken from them. Perhaps, that night, there were no two souls more alike than the British royal and the American investigator.

Morgan hugged her back.

There was no awkwardness in the moment. They were two people. Two people trapped in grief. Consumed by it. United by it.

"I'm reviewing grant applications," Caroline said suddenly, breaking the embrace and moving back to her desk. "I need some good to come from today, Jack. When I close my eyes tonight, I want to know there's good in the world, and not just evil.

"Here." She picked up a sheaf of papers. "This one's for a well in Africa." She picked up a second proposal. "This one for a girls' school in Pakistan. Do you think it will make a difference? I hope so. The thought of improving the lives of children struggling in such impoverished conditions is the only thing that could possibly help me sleep tonight."

Morgan said nothing. They both knew that a good night's sleep was impossible for either one of them.

"I didn't even know about him," said Princess Caroline, taking a seat on the room's small bed and gesturing that Morgan sit beside her. "*Mayoor Patel.* I'd never even heard that name before, and now it will be with me forever. What does he look like?"

Morgan told her.

"I picture this ogre in my head," she said. "Is he the monster I picture him to be?"

Morgan shook his head. "I don't know," he answered honestly. "But I don't think he ever intended to kill Sophie. It was a crime of passion, a situation he lost control of. It wasn't planned or calculated. Some people kill when they don't mean to. Others do it because they're sick."

"You've met a lot of people like that," Caroline guessed.

"Too many."

"I suppose Sophie kept secrets from everyone. Even from me. I think she knew that, had I known she had a love for someone else, it would have broken my heart. I'm telling myself that she kept her relationship with him a secret so that I didn't get hurt."

"She loved you," Morgan assured her, his eyes telling her that it was the truth. "Patel told me as much. He tried to make her blackmail you, but she wouldn't do it. That's when he realized it was love."

"And that's when he killed her."

There was nothing Morgan could say to that.

"People will say that we were lucky to have loved, even if for a short time," she tried, desperate to be stoic.

Morgan didn't answer in words, but he couldn't hide the answer on his face.

"Fucking bullshit, isn't it?" Caroline uttered with a sad laugh. "Absolute bullshit. I would die on the spot to bring Sophie back."

"But it wouldn't," Morgan replied.

"No. It wouldn't."

"I should go. It was good to see you, Your Highness."

"Whatever help I can give. Whatever help my people can give. It's yours, Jack."

As Morgan reached the bottom of the narrow staircase, he found the proof of that vow: De Villiers was waiting for him.

"I found something," said the Colonel.

Chapter 89

MORGAN FOLLOWED DE Villiers down a stone staircase and into a cellar. The air was cold and dank, and Morgan sniffed at the smell of mothballs. The cellar was now a store-room for tables and chairs draped in dust sheets, and a home for spiders, their cobwebs littering the space, clinging to the ceiling's wooden beams like the torn sails of some battered warship. De Villiers frowned at the unkempt space, then turned his attention to the American.

"I cross-referenced Flex's record with the SAS men on the Princess's security detail," the Colonel explained. "I started with the oldest first, as they were most likely to cross paths."

"And you found one?" Morgan asked.

"Second name I tried. I've got my most trusted people checking the others, but until then, I told Corporal Joyce to meet us down here, so that we can have a chat."

Corporal Joyce, of the Special Air Service Regiment, arrived in the cellar a few minutes later. Having been called from rest, he was unarmed, wearing only a tracksuit and a frown.

"Colonel De Villiers down here?" he asked the room's sole occupant, Jack Morgan.

"He's not," Morgan said simply.

"Oh. All right. Wrong bloody room." The man was about to turn away when Morgan's words stopped him.

"You know who I am, don't you?" he asked. "I saw it in your face. You know who I am, and now you're about to run upstairs, to tell your boy Flex."

Joyce tried to snort at such a ridiculous notion, but his shifting feet and awkward posture paid testament to his guilt. "I don't know who you are, mate. And I don't care." He turned, coming face to face with Colonel De Villiers.

Who held a dusty chair by its legs.

"Bastard!" the Colonel roared, swinging the piece of furniture down on the treacherous man. Joyce raised his arms to protect himself, but the Colonel was tall, and his swing fierce. The blow smashed against Joyce's arm with the sound of cracking bone.

"Jesus!" the man gasped, dropping to one knee.

"Colonel!" Morgan shouted, shocked at the attack. "Colonel! Stop!"

But De Villiers would not stop. He brought the chair down on the man again, this time over Joyce's back. He was about to swing the remnants of the now-broken chair a third time, but Morgan wrestled it from his grasp. Denied, De Villiers settled for delivering a kick into Joyce's stomach.

"He did it! It was all over his face, Morgan! You piece of shit, Joyce! I'll beat you to death for this!"

Morgan held the Colonel back, and spoke evenly into his ear. "Colonel. We need him to talk. We need him in one piece, so he can talk. That's how we find Flex. That's how we get justice for Lewis, Perkins and Cook."

"You'll talk," the Colonel growled at the man on the floor.

Morgan, knowing the SAS's training to withstand interrogation, did not expect the man to give it up easily.

He was wrong.

"I didn't know he was gonna do what he did!" the soldier spat between gritted teeth. "I didn't know, sir!"

"What did you do?" De Villiers hissed. "Why were you helping him?"

"He said this one had tried to kill him over money," Joyce replied, pointing a hand at Morgan. "He came into Flex's gym and attacked him, but Flex beat him off. I was helping him get even."

"'Get even'?" De Villiers roared. "A former army officer is dead! Lewis—your teammate!—is in hospital, beaten to within an inch of her life!"

"Flex said that *he* did it," Joyce said meekly, looking at Morgan. "He said it was a set-up."

De Villiers was unable to stop himself, and slapped the soldier hard around the head. "Have you got shit where your brains should be, Joyce? This is all Flex's doing! He used you, you idiot! He used you to kill one of us, and to put two others in hospital!"

"Oh God…" Joyce swallowed, as the horrible truth crashed down on him. "Sir, I'm so sorry. I'm so sorry." He looked to Morgan.

Morgan made no reply.

It was De Villiers who spoke for them. "You have blood on your hands, Joyce."

The man made no move to deny it, simply nodding with stunned guilt. "Just tell me what to do to make it right," he begged them. "I'll do anything, sir. Please. Let me help you catch Flex."

Chapter 90

MORGAN WALKED OUT of the building and into the cool summer air. Blood pulsed in his temples. It wasn't from the admission of the soldier that he had planned to help Flex do harm to Morgan—in his line of work, he was used to that enough not to take it personally. The quickening of his heartbeat came at the thought of being one step—a big step—closer to Flex.

Morgan pulled out his phone. A few seconds later, he called Peter Knight's personal number.

"Jack, are you OK?" Knight asked, hopeful.

"Yeah. How are things going back there?" Morgan replied.

"Everyone's safe, but we're banging our heads against a brick wall trying to find leads."

Morgan could hear something in his friend's voice. Something that hadn't been there when they had parted company. Was it suppressed anger? Grief?

"How are you holding up?" he asked.

"I'm OK," Knight replied. Morgan was sure then that he was lying. "But we need a lead. Anything to get this moving."

"I'm taking care of it," Morgan told him, then regretted his choice of words. "We're going to take care of this," he assured his friend. "I've found out who was leaking information to Flex. Maybe he can lead us to him."

"I'll come with you." Morgan could swear he heard the sound of car keys being grabbed.

"No. I need you to organize eyes onto Flex's London offices. There's always a chance he's hiding in plain sight."

"The hell with organizing, Jack. We have staff who can do that for us," Knight protested firmly. "I'm not sitting here whilst you're on the street doing God knows what. I sent an agent out to check on the car's location, expecting to find you dead behind the wheel, and they come back telling me that two streets over was cordoned off by police because of a shooting. I suppose that's totally unrelated though, isn't it?"

"I need you calm, Peter."

"And I need you alive, Jack. *Private* needs you alive. Hundreds of people, all counting on you. You can't do this alone."

Morgan knew that was the truth, but he pushed it from his mind. One person who had counted on him was dead.

"Watch Flex's office, Peter. And track this phone if you need to, but don't interfere," he ordered as he heard footsteps coming toward him.

"Hooligan's already tried, but the system must be throwing false echoes. It says that you're in the Tower of London."

Morgan almost smiled. "Then the system is working perfectly. Goodbye, Peter. I'll contact you soon." He ended the call and turned to face the source of the footsteps.

"Your Highness," he greeted Princess Caroline, surprised to see her alone.

"Don't worry about me," she told him, sensing his unease.

"This is the safest place on earth for me. The Beefeaters are as loyal as anyone can be."

"So Colonel De Villiers told me. What can I help you with, Your Highness?"

"Just take a short walk with me. I've run out of grants to sign, and I think some air would do me good."

Morgan looked toward the door of the building that housed the cellar. There was no sign of De Villiers and the answers he would bring, so Morgan agreed, falling into step alongside Princess Caroline as she paced the courtyard between the Beefeaters' tightly packed homes.

"There are thirty-five families here," she told the American beside her. "Some have children, and they live in the bigger houses. Then there are the smaller apartments, for the single ones. There's more and more of them, I'm afraid to say. Service in the military seems to take a terrible toll on families."

"It does," Morgan agreed, his eye following a large black raven that hopped across the open courtyard, pecking between paving stones.

"Legend says that if the ravens leave the Tower, then the kingdom will fall."

Morgan sensed that the royal was making small talk to delay divulging what was really on her mind. "You can say what you need to say. It's just us here, Your Highness."

"OK then, Jack. I've lost someone whom I loved. Thanks to you, the person responsible for taking her from me is now in custody. He will receive justice, and he will do so through the British legal system."

The implication of the words was clear for Morgan, and he held the woman's gaze. "Of course."

"Do you know who brought law and order to this country, Jack? It was the monarchy. It was the Crown. Sophie? Jane?

This all started with me, Jack, and I want to end it before violence is brought to our streets. I am hurting, Jack—*you* know how much I am hurting—and the only thing that can hurt me more is to see more blood spilled."

Morgan took a deep breath. He respected Caroline, and his words came out evenly and under control. "I will not stop looking for Flex."

"I'm not asking you to stop looking. It's what you plan to do when you find him that's scaring me. Please, promise me that when you do find him, you'll let the police take it from there. Promise me that you'll let the British legal system do its job."

Morgan could see genuine concern in the woman's earnest eyes. Concern for his own safety, but also for a greater cause—that of law and order in the country she was sworn to serve.

"Does your country have the death penalty?" Morgan asked.

"It doesn't."

"Then I won't make a promise I can't keep. I want justice, and that isn't it."

"Then we may find ourselves at odds, Jack."

"Maybe we will. And I'm sorry if we do."

"So am I." She smiled sadly. "Good night, Jack. Whatever happens, thank you for finding Sophie."

Morgan tried to smile in return. Then Princess Caroline turned and walked away.

Chapter 91

MORGAN STOOD ALONE in the center of the courtyard for some time after his conversation with the Princess. Except for the occasional tramp of a sentry's feet, or the caw of a raven, the place was quiet. The Tower's walls muted London's traffic, giving it the serene sense of being a place of calm amidst the city's storm. Of course, for Morgan, that was exactly what it was. Soon it would be time to go out into that storm.

De Villiers' tall frame appeared in the doorway of one of the buildings.

"You could have waited inside," the Colonel told him.

"I wanted to think," Morgan replied.

And think he had done. Of Jane Cook. Of Sharon Lewis. Of Jeremy "Hooligan" Crawford. Of Peter Knight. All wards in his care. All people that, on some level, he had failed. In Cook's case, Morgan's actions and lack of foresight had led to her death.

"Whatever you're thinking, it's not good for you." De Villiers frowned, reading Morgan's features like a map. "You need your head on straight, Morgan. Come on, man, this isn't what I expected from you. Look at how you handled the people who took Abbie Winchester."

"I've lost one of my agents, Colonel." He didn't need to tell De Villiers that he had lost much more than that.

"I know you have, Morgan. And now you have this." He passed Morgan a sheet of paper.

"What are these?"

"Joyce has had no luck in contacting Flex directly, and he's heard nothing from him since Jane . . . He's heard nothing from him since then.

"What you have here," he continued, "is a list of addresses that Flex has been known to frequent. And these," he pointed, "are the details of Flex's expected accomplice, Nathan Rider. Joyce heard that Rider had been brought over from Africa by Flex. Apparently Rider isn't the kind of man who cares to be in a country where there is a higher kind of law than who has the biggest guns, and so the pieces fit that he's here for one reason."

"To kill me."

"To *try*. I'll walk you to the gate. I expect you'll want to make use of the night."

They walked in silence. Morgan left the way he had come in: through the small door set into the wall. As he emerged he found himself facing lengthways along the Thames, London's skyline brilliant in the darkness.

"You have everything you need?" De Villiers asked, emerging beside him.

"I do," Morgan replied, his eyes on the towers that were lit up toward the clouded heavens.

"Then I'll leave you with one last thought. I'm giving you

as much rope as I can, Morgan, you understand? Precise and deliberate retribution I will allow you, but . . ."

"I get it."

"Good. Just remember that this is London, not Afghanistan. If you bring war onto our streets, you'll be in our sights as much as he is. This city's suffered a lot these past few years. Our security forces are on a hair trigger."

Morgan nodded.

"Thank you for your help, Colonel." He put out his hand and De Villiers took it in a firm grip.

"Get the bastard, Morgan. Get him, and put him down."

Chapter 92

JACK MORGAN WALKED a mile from the Tower using back streets, main roads and alleyways. Happy that he was clear of tails, he'd put a call in to Hooligan, passing him the few addresses given up by Corporal Joyce. "Get CCTV in those areas if you can," Morgan had instructed. "Have surveillance teams stood by, but no one is to leave Private HQ unless I order it."

Then he had given his London team a second set of instructions. Thirty minutes later an old Ford Focus pulled up at exactly the spot Morgan had requested, the driver getting out and walking away without a backward glance. Taking a few seconds to check his surroundings one more time, Morgan pulled a carrier bag from where he had shoved it into a hedge, felt the weight of the pistols inside, and walked to the car. He entered the driver's side, found the key in the ignition and started it up.

A few seconds later he was on his way to the first of Flex's addresses.

Chapter 93

TWO YEARS AGO, Michael "Flex" Gibbon had run his security enterprise from atop a beautiful glass building that sat alongside the Thames. So great were the views, and so heavy his workload, that he had lived in the same building.

A lot had changed since Jack Morgan had beaten the SAS soldier down, blowing out the man's knee and sending the rumor mill wild. *Flex was a soft-arse. Flex couldn't cut it anymore. Why were the heads of two security firms fighting in the first place? I'll take my business elsewhere.* Now Flex's operation was run out of a town-center office in Tottenham, sandwiched between a chartered accountants and a failed business whose windows were covered with wood panels and graffiti. It was a big fall for a big ego.

Peter Knight sat lonely in his car, looking at the bricks-and-mortar reasoning that had driven Flex to seek out Morgan and cause him pain.

"All because of his bloody pride," Knight said sadly, shaking his head.

He was in a small car park a hundred yards from the buildings that showed no signs of life. Even if Flex still ran operations around the globe, Knight guessed that the smaller-scale business would now employ a duty manager that worked from home, or wherever his laptop and phone happened to be. It was that way for many of the smaller security companies, of which Flex's business had undoubtedly become one.

Knight looked down to his lap, where he held a dossier on Flex Gibbon. It was possible to read it by the street lights, and he thumbed through its pages, marveling at how a solid SAS trooper could go from national hero to murdering monster.

It was ego, Knight decided. All ego.

That and pride had pushed Flex to join the army as a young man, after being beaten his whole childhood by his father. Ego had pushed him further, to volunteer for selection for the SAS. Ego had kept him going over the arduous hills phase of training in the Brecon Beacons. Ego had kept him going in the jungle. Ego had kept him going during escape and evasion, where he had been beaten and waterboarded. Ego had allowed Flex to endure so much. It had allowed him to build a thriving business. But then, when that ego had been damaged, it had exploded.

Knight turned the next page.

It was a picture of Flex's children, now young adults, one studying at Liverpool University and the other in Manchester. The kids looked bright and athletic. A note in the dossier said that custody of the children had gone to their mother. The grounds of divorce had been that Flex was forever away on service for his country, and that when he'd returned he'd be angry and violent. On one occasion he had locked his wife in the bathroom for a day to "teach her some respect"—the police in Herefordshire had dropped the case in deference to Flex's meritorious service. In what then looked like a trade with his wife, Flex had not fought the divorce.

Knight looked again at the picture of the man's children. What effect had their father's choice of career had on their lives? Were they able to live like their other classmates at university? Were they able to settle disputes with calm words, or did they fly to anger and violence? Did they feel abandoned, or resentful? Were they ambivalent toward their father, or did they hate him? Was he a part of their lives, or was he forever estranged? Forgotten.

Knight rubbed at his eyes as he realized he was asking these questions as much about himself as about Flex. Though Peter Knight could say honestly that he had never intentionally caused his children any harm, they had been harmed because of him. The death of their mother had been traumatic enough, but Knight's role as head of Private London brought with it a constant threat of danger. He thought of how he'd almost lost them six years ago when they were kidnapped as part of Cronus's vicious attack on the London Olympic Games. How could Knight live with himself if his children were brought into this? He couldn't, he knew.

And the children were growing older. They were understanding more and more each day. They were reading moods, and reacting to them. Danger aside, Knight's workload at Private was enormous. He could not have it any other way, as he was responsible for the lives of other people, but did he want to be just another absent father who put his business life before his children? With his beloved wife gone, did Knight really want to continue risking his own life, and potentially orphan Luke and Isabel?

He didn't know the answer.

But one thing was clear: once this mission was done, Knight would have to seriously evaluate his life. He would have to choose between being the father he wanted to be, or Private.

Chapter 94

JACK MORGAN DROVE slowly into the suburban estate in the borough of Wandsworth, south of the Thames. Unlike parts of central London, the homes here were detached, sat back behind manicured lawns, and nestled amongst trees that were heavy and lush with summer rain. Morgan smiled as he saw the surroundings, but not out of any sense of romance—it would make his job of getting close to the buildings easier. He would need to move quickly, as there were three addresses listed to Flex on the paper. Morgan had chosen the closest to the Tower to begin his search, but he was aware that the cover of night was in short supply in summer. Estimating time to travel between each, he had less than an hour for each location.

He was a hundred yards away from his target now, so he pulled his car to the curbside and got out next to a narrow alley that led between two patches of greenery. Checking Google Earth, Morgan saw that the alley led to a pathway that ran behind the houses, before emerging onto a park and sports field. He turned the bright screen of the phone off, put it into his pocket and followed the path used by dog walkers and football-mad children during the day. Tonight, it would serve a darker purpose, and Morgan took the semi-automatic pistol in his right hand before pushing it into his jacket pocket. If need be, he could fire through the material and off the hip.

Counting off his paces, as taught to him in Marine training, Morgan measured the distance, the practice accurate enough for him to know that he had come to a stop behind the correct building, a two-story brick home that showed no light and emitted no sound. The house was separated from the footpath by a thin fence and a few trees, and it was no effort for Morgan to raise himself over the fence and drop quietly into the back garden. There he waited. There was nothing. Deep in suburbia as it was, Morgan did not expect Flex to have the garden defended as if it were Fort Knox—nothing drew suspicion like a big musclehead with sirens in his garden—but even so, he inched slowly across the open space to the back wall, his hand twisting the pistol's grip so that the barrel was aimed through the material at the back door.

Morgan was halfway across the small garden when the sensor light flicked to life. He had expected it, and now covered the remaining distance in a split second, pressing himself against the back wall. He was cloaked from view from the windows, but he would be looming proudly on any CCTV screens that were inside the building—Morgan was willing to take a chance on that, having seen no flicker of lights inside to indicate that anyone was awake. He could only hope that the house wasn't empty.

It wasn't. Morgan saw him as he peered through the

corner of the window, nothing but a pair of feet raised up at the end of a sofa. Confident that the man was sleeping and not watching TV, Morgan moved to the door and considered the lock—it was garden variety, the same as almost any suburban home. He reached into his left pocket and pulled out one of the items he had instructed to be placed in the old Ford's glove box—it was a lock-picking kit, and Morgan made short work of the old Chubb. Then, pressing delicately, he depressed the handle and pushed open the door.

The house alarm sounded shrill and violent in the calm night. Morgan had been prepared for it, and as the first note pierced his eardrums he ditched his plan A of quiet calm and resorted to plan B, keeping in mind the three principles of close-quarter battle.

Surprise: Morgan had taken the sleeping man unaware, and he had a few seconds to act before the man regained full function of mind and body.

Speed: Morgan raced across the threshold and into the living room like a charging bull, pulling the pistol free of his jacket.

Violence of action: before the man could even raise himself off the sofa, Morgan had gripped him by the throat and pressed the cold steel of the pistol's muzzle into the man's ear.

"Alarm," Morgan hissed. "Turn it off. Now."

Gripping the man by his trachea, he lifted him to his feet. The man saw that his situation was hopeless, and he used his wide white eyes to guide Morgan to the alarm box, jabbing his finger awkwardly at the digits. Within ten seconds of the door opening, all had returned to silence but for the man's gasped breaths. Morgan shoved him to the floor and trained the pistol onto the back of his head. Only then did he notice the man's left arm and shoulder were bandaged.

"You got shot in the forest," he guessed.

The man said nothing, but when Morgan delivered a blow onto the recent gunshot wound, he groaned like an animal.

"I'll open up another one in the back of your head if you don't start talking," Morgan promised. "You know who I am, and you know I'm working outside the law, so talk. Are you Rider?"

"I'm not," the man spat through clenched teeth.

"Then who the hell are you?" Morgan demanded, pressing the gun into the back of the man's skull.

"Herbert. Chris Herbert."

"You work for Flex?"

"I work for myself."

A finger into the recently sutured gunshot wound convinced the man to change his answer. "Yes! Flex! Yes!"

"You're a mercenary? Well, I have a proposition for you. You help me get Flex, and I pay you back by not blowing your brains out over the carpet."

"Ram it, you Yank tart."

Morgan pressed his thumb into torn flesh and broken bone. Then he let Herbert tell him everything.

Chapter 95

THE THOUGHT OF his children, and the implications of a life without them, weighed heavily on Peter Knight as he watched the row of offices in Tottenham. He rubbed at his eyes, certain that the long hours and excitement had got to him, but he was not wrong in what he was seeing.

Flex.

There was no mistaking the size and shape of the muscle-bound man as he slinked quickly inside of his building. Fingers almost fumbling, Knight tried Morgan's phone. It went straight to voicemail.

"Dammit, Jack," he cursed. He then tried Hooligan's number, and it connected. "Jez? Flex has shown up at his office. Keep trying Jack from your end. I'm going to call Elaine and see if she can move some units closer, without us having to spill all the beans on why."

"All right. But stay safe. Don't do anything stupid, Peter."

"I'll watch from the car," Knight promised, hanging up. A moment after he did so, he heard a metallic object tapping on the glass of his driver's window.

In that split second Peter Knight knew the game was over. And he was the loser.

Chapter 96

HERBERT HAD SPILLED some good information as to who Flex was working with. There was always the chance he was lying, but Herbert swore blind that the former Foreign Legion man Nathan Rider was the only other man Flex trusted to stand by him during outright murder. Rider had been waiting in London during the shootings in Wales, should opportunity arise there. Once Herbert had gone down to Lewis's gunshots—treated by Flex, a deft medic from long experience—Rider and Flex had ridden together, and Herbert's part in the actions had been reduced to watching the news channels, and reporting to Flex anything of interest.

"He thinks it was you that caused the Knightsbridge shooting," Herbert told him. "Thinks you went in there looking to get yourself a piece."

"And what do you think?" Morgan asked, pressing the steel of the stolen pistol against the man's head.

"You know you shot someone? You're in as much shit as me."

The only shots Morgan had fired were to take down the lighting fixtures. It must have been the girl's wild shots that had found flesh, and left the dark blood trail on the dance floor.

"Who was it?"

"Some bellend TV presenter. It clipped off a few fingers, apparently."

Morgan didn't feel too bad about that. He was relieved that it wasn't Natalie or the security men who'd been hit.

"Look, mate," Herbert tried, "I've been in enough bad situations to recognize a *really* bad one, and the only way I see of getting out of this is by working with you."

No honor amongst thieves, Morgan thought to himself. *Same goes for scumbags.*

"Talk."

"I'll testify. I'll tell them everything they need to know about Flex. I just need looking after, because he'll kill me if we end up in the same prison."

But Morgan shook his head. "I don't need testimony. I need him brought out in the open. I need him in front of me, so I can deal with him myself."

"But—"

"Look, you've seen this guy's capacity for revenge. You think being in a different prison is what's gonna save you from him? No. If you're going to live past tonight, you need to help me. And if you're going to live after that, then you need Flex in the dirt."

"Shit," Herbert hissed, knowing that it was the truth. "Shit. What is it you need me to do?"

Morgan bundled Herbert into the back of the Focus. Already wounded, and with his wrists bound in tape, there was little

Herbert could do to escape. A final piece of tape across his mouth had been enough to stifle the groans of pain—Morgan had not been gentle on the man.

The American scowled as he looked at the captive on the back seat behind him. In truth, he still had no concrete plan of how he would use Herbert to get to Flex.

Though it pained him to do so, Morgan knew he must take his foot off the gas, and allow thought to take over from action. He realized that the best place for him to do that would be in Private London's headquarters, where he could draw on the minds of his agents.

As if his thoughts were being read, he saw a familiar name flash up on his phone's caller ID. He took it on the second ring, his eyes in the car's mirrors as he pulled out of the Wandsworth estate and headed toward London's city center.

"Peter. I'm coming back to HQ. I'll meet you there in ten."

"No," Flex's voice answered him. "You won't."

Chapter 97

"DON'T DO IT," a strange voice had said from outside of Peter Knight's car, seeing his finger moving to redial. "I'll put one in your head before your call goes through."

Slowly, Knight had turned his head. He had not been surprised by what he'd seen, and had found himself looking into the barrel of a pistol. It was held by an ugly man in a dark hoody.

"You fuckin' amateur," the man had sneered. "Maybe you want to turn down the brightness of your phone next time you call in a sighting. Get out the car."

Knight had obliged, furious with himself. The man was right—Knight had acted like an amateur. Thoughts of his children had clouded his mind, and on seeing Flex he had acted quickly, without thinking. Now that impulse would probably mean he would never see Luke or Isabel again.

"Flex is the only one who's killed someone. You can get out of this if you turn him in."

The ugly man had half smiled, as if he'd felt sorry for the

Private agent in front of him. "You really should have stayed in the amateur leagues."

Knight had heard a sound behind him. Then had come darkness.

He regained consciousness in the back of a van. His head covered, he had no concept of where he was or for how long he'd been unconscious. All he knew for certain was that he'd been abducted, and that he was in serious trouble.

The van stopped, and he felt the suspension move as a significant weight departed, opened the door and climbed into the rear. A second later, what must have been a meaty hand swiped Knight's hooded head, sending it bouncing off the wooden floorboard.

"Are you awake?" Flex asked.

Knight said nothing. Flex hit him again. Already bruised from the hit he had taken in Mayoor Patel's home, Knight gritted his teeth against the pain.

"I said, are you awake?"

"I'm awake," Knight replied, tasting blood on his teeth. The hessian sacking of his hood smelled rank and musty as it pressed against his face.

"Morgan's on the phone," Flex told him. "Say hello."

"Morgan?" Knight asked, raising his voice so that it would carry, "I—"

Flex finished the conversation for him, savagely punching Knight so that the man's groans carried all the message needed. Then Flex stepped from the van's rear doors and shut Knight alone in the confines of his misery.

Chapter 98

"STILL THERE, JACK?" Flex said, climbing back into the passenger seat and motioning for Rider to drive.

"I'm here," Morgan growled down the phone. "Now what is it you want, Flex? You haven't killed him. There must be a reason. How much do you want?"

"This isn't about money, Jack. You should know that by now."

"I'll give you twenty million dollars."

Flex laughed, but beside him Rider frowned, tuning into the conversation. Flex tried to silence the man's piqued interest with a hard look, but it didn't work.

"This isn't about money," Flex said again, as much for Rider's benefit as for Morgan's. "The reason he's still alive is that I want to kill him slowly. And I want you to know all about it, Jack. I want you to see it. I want you to hear it. I want you to feel it. I don't like my chances of getting you alive, but he's close enough for what I've got planned. You I can deal with later."

"Why wait?" Morgan asked. "Deliver Knight unhurt, and you can have me. You can have your fun with me."

"I wasn't born yesterday, you dickhead."

There was a moment of silence on the line. Flex felt Rider's scowl—the man clearly unhappy that £20 million had been so quickly dismissed.

"Talk to him about the money," the ugly man urged, only shutting up when Flex strained against his seat belt like an angry pit bull.

"Well, if we've got nothing more to talk about, Jack—"

"How do you like loose ends, Flex? Because I've got one of yours in the car with me, and he's about to get dropped at Private HQ."

"Bollocks," Flex snorted.

"His name's Chris Herbert," Morgan announced, giving away the details of how, and where, he had taken the man. Flex's face grew more angry with each piece of information. "He's ready to roll on you. You may kill Knight, you may kill me, but this is solid evidence against you, Flex. You'll be on the run for the rest of your life."

It took every measure of Flex's self-control not to dash the phone to pieces. He had never expected to stay in the UK after enacting his revenge, but there was a big difference between being a suspect who quietly slipped off the radar leaving only theories and no evidence, and one of the culprits testifying to his guilt.

"Fuck!" he finally shouted, losing the battle with his rage and the synthetic testosterone that coursed through his body. "I'll give you your man back once you put a bullet in that useless bastard's brain!"

"Do your own dirty work," Morgan replied, the sounds

of a panic-stricken Herbert coming from behind him as he strained against the tape on his mouth. "Herbert for Knight."

"Done," Flex spat. "Be in central London. The meet will be at zero five thirty."

He didn't need to tell Morgan that he'd hold back the location of that meeting place until the last minute.

"Make it public," Morgan told him. "I'll be waiting."

Chapter 99

JACK MORGAN SPENT the wait in an industrial area of Battersea, placing him close to central London's many bridges, the Ford Focus pulled to the curb alongside steel fencing and litter.

"Flex wants me to put a bullet in your head and dump you." Morgan eyed the trash on the roadside.

Herbert tried to speak through the tape. His eyes had calmed, and they pleaded with Morgan to let him talk.

"Don't speak," Morgan told him. "Just listen."

The man ceased his movement and stifled words.

"You realize there's a chance Flex just puts a bullet in us both the moment we arrive?"

Herbert nodded.

"I have an idea, but you have to play your part."

The man raised his eyebrows.

"You'll find out when we get there. Just do as I say. Flex is who I want, understand?"

The man nodded. He understood. Just as Morgan had felt no great personal animosity toward Joyce for helping to conspire to kill him, neither did he feel it toward Herbert. Jack Morgan lived in a world where people tried to kill him on a regular basis—it was an occupational hazard. It was when they involved the people he cared about that he began to see things personally. Herbert had not been there when Flex had pulled the trigger and killed Jane Cook. If he had, he'd be dead already. The man couldn't know it, but being shot by Lewis had likely saved his life.

Morgan sighed, and looked along the empty street that was bathed beneath orange street lights. He thought about Peter Knight. How his friend was a captive of a man who had shown himself to be a murderer. How the father might soon make orphans of his children. How a professional investigative agent had allowed himself to be caught so easily by the people he was there to track.

With guilt, Morgan realized that he was *angry* with Knight. He tried to push the feeling away, but the sense that Knight had come between Morgan and justice for Cook would not shift. Hadn't Morgan told him to send other agents to watch Flex's office? Hadn't he trained Knight, taught him, and trusted him? Now, when he needed him most, and when he was finally getting ahead through the capture of Herbert, Knight had flipped the field back in Flex's favor. He was putting them all in Flex's hands, and giving the man a chance to play his endgame. Morgan had only a wild card left to play, and if that failed, he was at best back to the beginning in his search for Flex. At worst, he was on his back with a bullet in his head.

The next hour passed in waves for Morgan. One minute there was anger at Knight, the next guilt that he could ever think that way. Then came sadness, then came grief, then came rage that Flex was at large. That rage led to the obstacle that now stood in the way of justice—Knight—and so began the cycle once more.

To break it, Morgan attempted to distract himself through meticulous checking of his two pistols. He broke them down one at a time—one always with a bullet in the chamber, and close at hand, should he need to use it—and inspected and cleaned every part of them to ensure there would be no malfunction when he needed them most. Morgan's ammunition count stood at eight 9mm rounds for the semi-automatic pistol, and six .357 rounds for the revolver. Not enough for a protracted gunfight, but maybe enough to put Flex and Rider down if he drew first.

And was he willing to do that?

Rubbing the heel of his hand into tired, blood-red eyes, Morgan could not be sure. He hated Flex, and wanted the man removed from society, and the world, but Jack Morgan had always pictured himself as a defender—a man who took life in order to save others. Could he really draw his pistol first, and shoot Flex and Rider down in cold blood? For the sake of justice for Jane, he wanted that answer to be yes.

But deep down, beneath the anger and the pain, he admitted to himself that he just did not know.

Morgan finished assembling and reloading the pistol in his hands, cocked back the hammer, and pointed it at Herbert's startled face.

Pull the trigger, he told himself. *Pull the trigger. Find another way to get Flex. Find another way to rescue Knight. Knight put himself in this position. Why should Jane's killers go unpunished, for his mistake? Pull the trigger!* Morgan's anger screamed at him. *Pull the trigger, kill this son of a bitch, and then kill the others. Do it! Kill him! Now!*

Morgan lowered the pistol, and turned to the front.

278 • James Patterson

Behind him, having seen the murderous intent in the American's eyes, and believing his life to have run its course, Herbert began to whimper.

Before Morgan could tell him to shut up, his phone vibrated.

Chapter 100

THE FIRST LOCATION sent to Morgan was a waypoint. Morgan expected that Flex would hold the final destination until the last moment, but the muscle-bound murderer needn't have worried—Morgan had no intention of alerting anyone who could stand between himself and Flex. His mind was as set as a Marine charging an enemy machine-gun nest, focused on nothing but the result of his actions—his own safety an afterthought unworthy of consideration.

Flex's first direction sent Morgan to Brixton. The second, to Waterloo. Morgan was then instructed to proceed to Lewisham, until Flex called back with the location of the true meeting place: London Bridge.

At first the site of the meeting point surprised Morgan. It was public. It had limited access. Perhaps Flex really did intend to honor the swap? Or perhaps, like Morgan, he was ready to die to get what he wanted, and the bridge was the best bottleneck to make sure that happened.

"We're going to go in on foot," Morgan told Herbert,

remembering the barriers that had been put in place to stop terrorists from driving vehicles into pedestrians, and knowing that any stopped car on the structure would draw instant scrutiny from the security services.

"You realize your best chance to live is by doing what I say?" he asked the man again.

Herbert nodded, and Morgan ripped away the tape that had covered the man's lips. Herbert grimaced as pieces of skin tore away with it. The tape on the man's hands would stay, covered by a coat, the hood pulled up over the man's head and zipped in place to act as an impromptu straightjacket.

"I've counted my rounds. You mess this up, I'm holding one back for you."

"I won't," Herbert promised. "All that crap that mental bastard told me about unit loyalty and honor, and then he goes and tells you to stick a bullet in me? Give me a gun and I'll shoot him myself."

Morgan smiled at the idea. "Out the car."

They left the Focus in a disabled parking bay next to London Bridge station. Morgan had no intention of coming back to it, and had pushed the revolver into the front of his trousers, the semi-auto in the back. Herbert had said that Flex expected Morgan was behind the Knightsbridge shooting, and so it was safe to assume he knew Morgan would be packing heat as a result. What Morgan couldn't guess was whether or not Flex would ask him to expose those firearms on the bridge, and to draw the inevitable attention that would bring.

"He won't give you your mate." Herbert shook his head. "He's a nutter, and all he's talked about for months is killing you."

Morgan ignored him, instead taking in his environment.

The area was quiet, but slowly breathing its way to life—early birds in suits made their way toward the station. A street sweeper cleared plastic glasses and cigarette ends from outside a pub. Looming above all this was a thousand-foot-high sentinel, the Shard, looking like it had been plucked straight from one of Tolkien's fantasy worlds then clad in glass.

Morgan looked at his watch—5:28. They would hit the bridge's center at exactly the time of Flex's request. The bridge itself was a flat expanse, the pedestrian pavement on each side as wide as its two traffic lanes. Across it came a dribble of cars and lonely pedestrians, people ensconced in their own worlds, with no idea that life and death was about to pass them by within meters.

"Keep on my left side," Morgan told Herbert, wanting to keep the firing line of his right hand free. "You see any of Flex's people?"

"It will only be Rider with him. It was only me and him that Flex brought in."

Morgan kept looking over the people ahead of him nonetheless. He wasn't about to make assumptions based on the word of a man who had tried to kill him.

"Where the hell is he?" Morgan growled as they reached the center of the bridge's long span.

There were no stopped vehicles. No sign of Flex's bulky form, or Rider's rangy figure.

"Where the hell are they?"

"Traffic?" Herbert suggested.

Morgan shook his head. At this time of the day the roads were almost bare.

Too late, he saw the trap that had been set.

"Shit!" hissed Herbert as he saw the same. "We've got to run!"

But Morgan did nothing.

He simply watched as the police car came slowly across the bridge, and indicated that it was about to pull up alongside them.

Morgan had been set up.

Chapter 101

"WE NEED TO leg it, now," Herbert urged. "If they catch you with those guns you're done!"

Morgan knew it, and yet he remained where he was, his eyes tracking the police car that was gliding along the curb-side, now only ten meters away.

"Move and I'll kill you," he told the man beside him.

"What are you going to do? Kill me, then the coppers?"

Could he? Morgan asked himself. Could he shoot police officers acting in the line of duty, so that he could bring his own brand of justice to Flex? Could he bring that same heart-break that he now felt to the families and loved ones of these officers?

No, Morgan knew. Not a chance in hell.

And so his options were to run, or stand—he chose to stand, and Herbert hissed that he was an idiot.

Morgan said nothing. Maybe he'd be proved wrong, but he was listening to his gut, and his instinct told him that Flex would not be happy with Morgan simply being arrested and imprisoned. Flex wanted Morgan's blood as badly as Morgan wanted his.

No, Morgan told himself, growing more certain. Flex wouldn't send the police, and though Morgan believed in coincidence, he did not believe that a squad car would happen to pull up on him the moment he walked onto London Bridge, and single him out, when dozens of other pedestrians were walking across the length of the bridge.

There was something more going on here, and as the car drew close enough for the early morning light to illuminate the occupants, Morgan saw that his gut had been right.

Flex.

There was no mistaking the bulk that sat in the car's passenger side, and who now emerged onto the roadside, clad head to foot in police gear, his equipment accurate down to the shoelaces. Behind him the rear door opened, and Rider stepped forth, equally tailored. So dressed, neither the men nor their car would draw unwanted attention—security was a part of London life, and nowhere more so than at its iconic locations.

Flex had taken the precaution of turning off the car's interior lights so that they did not come on with the open doors, and Morgan could only just make out the shape of the figure in the car's recesses. Behind the wheel sat the face of another "police officer," and Morgan chanced a glance to Herbert, who gave a quick shake of his head—he didn't know him.

"You keep your mouth shut, you fucking rat," Flex snarled at Herbert. "Did the regiment teach you nothing?"

"Taught me that you'll blow the bridge to save yourself," Herbert replied.

"Shut up," Morgan told him, as calmly as he could in the

presence of Jane's killer. Then to Flex, "Take Knight out of the car, and Herbert's yours."

"Change of plan on that one." Flex shrugged his massive shoulders. "Knight can go, but you're coming with me."

Morgan held his tongue. He'd expected the gambit, and now ignored it, instead taking in his options, and his chances. Flex and Rider were both armed, pistols holstered on their hips. As seasoned pros, neither man was impinging on what would be the other's aim—Rider stood aside and staggered from Flex. Morgan was a quick draw, but he couldn't expect to take down both men before he was hit himself. Was he willing to die to kill Flex? Was he willing to give Knight's life, too?

"Let's talk money," Morgan said. "You said no to twenty million. Let's make it thirty."

"Thirty million to walk away?" Flex sneered.

"To walk away from this bridge," Morgan corrected him. "We both know that this doesn't end until one of us is dead, Flex. I'll give you thirty million to give me Knight, and leave this bridge."

Flex scoffed, and Morgan looked to Rider. "You may not want the money, but maybe your men do."

"They want what I want," Flex growled, taking a pace forward. "Honor. Respect."

But the look on Rider's face told Morgan different. "Thirty-five million."

"Let him speak, Flex," Rider said from behind his boss. "That's a lot of money."

"He's trying to confuse you, you soft bastard," Flex snarled, turning back to Rider.

"I'm trying to save my friend's life, and to get us off this bridge." Morgan now spoke to Rider directly. "Thirty-five million, or a lifetime as a wanted murderer. Your choice."

The look on the former Foreign Legion man's face said it was a simple one. "Let's get back in the car, Flex. Let's get out of here, and at least talk about this."

"We're not going anywhere."

"It's a lot of money."

As the two men scowled at one another, Morgan chanced to look at the police car's driver—the man was pale with nerves, his hands gripping the wheel hard.

"You can't stay on this bridge forever," Morgan said to Flex and Rider. "The real police are going to smell something, and when they get here, there's no getting off this bridge."

"The real police?" Flex snorted. "How often do you want to underestimate me, Jack? *Insult* me? Why dress up as coppers when I can just buy dirty ones? This is a Met Police car, and it works this beat. If I say we have all day, we have all day. All. Fucking. Day."

Morgan shook his head, and flicked his eyes to the east—the sun was rising higher in the sky, and with it would come more pedestrians. More scrutiny. They could not stay on this bridge all day.

"Into the car!" Flex ordered Morgan and Herbert.

"Thirty-five million," Morgan replied.

"Get in!"

"Flex, think about the money!" Rider pressed from behind him.

But Flex would not. He could only think about reputation, and how Morgan had stolen his. And so he reached into the car's back seat and pulled Peter Knight out by his hair. Morgan watched tense as his battered friend was shoved toward the side of the bridge.

"I'm sick of your shit," Flex spat at Morgan, confirming the American's fears. "Either you get in the car, or he goes in the river."

Morgan could see the handcuffs on Knight's wrists, and knew that a fall from this height into the water with hands bound was a death sentence.

"If he dies," he said evenly, "there will be no money, Flex. Only death."

"Get. In. The. Car."

For a moment all was silent. Then Morgan turned his hate-filled eyes from Flex's face to Knight's, the man he had been so angry with for putting them in this position, and for coming between Flex and Morgan's justice. But the true spirit of Morgan's soul broke through, and he knew that, no matter what, he could never put his own desires before the safety of his agents, and friends.

"I'll get in the car," he told Flex, stepping forward. "But Knight goes free."

Flex smiled, moments from victory.

"Don't!" Rider called out as Morgan stepped forward. "Stay there. Flex, we're taking the money!"

"Enough!" Flex snarled.

Everything happened instantly, at once, and at speed.

Morgan watched on horrified as Flex used his massive arms to bundle the handcuffed Knight up and over the bridge's side. In the same motion, Flex was already dropping to one knee and pulling his pistol.

But Rider had been faster—*No honor amongst thieves, scumbags or killers*—and his first 9mm round chipped stone from just above Flex's head, the second striking Flex in his armored chest plate.

Rider didn't get the chance to fire another. His eye was

drawn to the figure of Morgan, who was pulling his own pistol free, and that split second of indecision cost Rider his life. Flex fired a double tap from his kneeling position, one round hitting the man in the neck, and the second clipping the side of his head. Rider went down, but his finger remained depressed on the semi-automatic trigger, 9mm rounds blasting and smashing into the police car's windows and metalwork. Morgan saw in his peripheral vision a spray of blood on the windshield as the driver took one in the back of his head.

Two deaths had occurred before the large splash below announced that Knight had hit the chopping river, where now, handcuffed, he would have only moments to live.

And it looked as though Morgan *had* those moments— Flex was still twisted away from him, facing Rider, and now Morgan had a half second to sight in on the man and fire.

It was all he'd need. He would have justice and revenge.

His finger touched the trigger.

Chapter 102

AS MORGAN TOOK aim at Flex, Herbert launched himself into Morgan's back and landed on top of him. The pistol fired but the shot was spoiled, the bullet smashing into one of the ammunition pouches on Flex's hip.

"Run, Flex!" Herbert shouted at his leader. The man then bit down onto Morgan's neck like a feral dog.

Herbert felt Morgan writhe in agony beneath him, and he used his legs as he had been taught in jiu-jitsu classes, hooking them over and under Morgan's. With his hands still tied behind him, and his arm wounded, Herbert wormed and snapped like a lamprey, blood running into his mouth as he sought to save Flex, who he knew would never truly abandon him. They had been through too much together. They were mates. They were comrades, with an unspoken bond. Herbert had known Flex's words about killing him for what they were—a ruse to get Herbert back by his side, no man left behind.

Herbert had never liked Rider. He had never understood

why Flex employed him in the first place—so he hadn't been surprised to see the man put money before honor and draw on Flex. Now, like a dog trained for blood sport, Herbert was eager to serve his master. His friend. He was eager to serve the man who had told him that he would never abandon him, and that he would be there for him always.

Chapter 103

TIME, LOCATION AND reality had melted for Flex. He was oblivious to the fact that he was in the center of a gunfight on London Bridge, pedestrians running screaming and cars crashing into one another as they sought to escape the carnage. Flex had been overtaken by the red mist, his anger and rage all-consuming. His endgame was a distant memory now. All he wanted to do was kill. Kill. Kill.

Throwing Knight over the bridge had been a good start. He hoped that the weasel suffered a long death. It was a shame he couldn't have given the same end to Rider, that greedy shitheaded bastard, but blowing out his throat would have to be enough. Turning through his arc to draw aim against Morgan, Flex briefly noticed the slumped body of his dirty cop behind the steering wheel, what little there had been inside the man's head now gray jelly against the windshield.

Completing his arc, Flex was surprised to see that Morgan was not up and standing in the aim position, ready to pull his own trigger, but struggling on the ground, with someone biting and writhing on top of him as the American howled in agony.

Herbert, Flex realized. *You were actually loyal to the end.*

Flex pulled the trigger.

Chapter 104

JACK MORGAN FELT the thud of rounds chew into the body on top of him. He heard the screams of pedestrians as they ran, joined by the drivers of vehicles desperate to flee the death on the bridge.

Morgan fought his urge to black out from the pain. He had never known anything like it. He had suffered several unpleasant injuries, but never before had a man tried to bite into his arteries like a zombie.

The pressure of the bite gave up suddenly as the bullets began to hit like sledgehammer strikes against flesh. Morgan guessed that the man who had assailed him, and who now acted as his unwitting human shield, was Herbert, the idiot loyal to the end and believing Flex cared about anyone but himself.

There was little need to guess the identity of the shooter, and Morgan braced himself for the round that would find its way through Herbert's flesh, missing bones, and instead coming straight and true to lodge in his own body.

It didn't come.

The firing stopped.

Chapter 105

FLEX LOOKED AT the pistol in his hand. The top-slide was held halfway back by an ejected round that had failed to properly clear the weapon, the empty bullet case now stopping the slide from coming forward to chamber the next round. To clear it would take the experienced Flex only two seconds, but as the wails of sirens and cries of "armed police" sounded behind him, the man realized that it was two seconds he didn't have. Flex's mission had been to kill Jack Morgan and those close to him—not to die himself. Looking at the leaking tandem of bodies on the pavement, Morgan silent and unmoving, Flex was content that the first part was done.

Now he had to escape.

Chapter 106

THE TIME FOR playing dead was over.

Morgan pressed himself up and rolled Herbert's limp body off him. As he looked at the body he saw that Herbert had been killed by a round in the skull. The bullets that had ploughed into his torso had been stopped by the bulletproof vest Morgan had pulled onto Herbert in Battersea. The man's assurances that he be protected against Flex had ended up saving Morgan's life instead. Without the barrier of Kevlar and flesh on top of him, Morgan would have been bleeding to death on London Bridge. For now he was alive, but time was running out for others.

Having lost his pistol in the struggle with Herbert, Morgan now stood empty-handed, his mind struggling to take in the chaos of the scene around him: Rider lay dead in a pool of his own blood. The dirty police officer was dead and slumped behind the car's wheel. Herbert was no more than a bag of chewed flesh and bone. Flex was gone.

And Knight...

Morgan ran to the bridge-side and peered down. There was no sign of his friend in the swirling gray-brown waters.

Morgan swore, then looked left and right along the bridge. He saw panic. The bridge itself was a rout of abandoned vehicles. The center of the span was empty of civilians, the press of their running bodies cleared to the bridge's ends. There sirens announced the arrival of the inevitable, London's security services rushing to the point of attack like blood clots to a freshly opened wound. Morgan saw a flash of movement between the cars and vans that stood abandoned on the bridge—he saw Flex, using cover from view and fire as he fled to the south bank.

As he fled from justice.

On instinct, Morgan turned to follow, but his friendship with Peter Knight stopped him as suddenly as if they'd been attached by a chain. He looked down at the wind-churned waters once more. There was no sign of Private London's leader. Morgan looked to his blood-smeared watch, and saw that the time was 5:33. Less than three minutes since Flex and his crew had arrived in the police car. In those short moments, at least three men had died. Morgan prayed that it was not four.

Knight could be alive, he knew. He could be alive, and if he was, there was no way Morgan could abandon him. Not when there was hope, no matter how slim.

Morgan took one last look at the fleeing shape of Flex. Knowing that his chance of bringing vengeance down on Jane Cook's killer may be lost forever, he turned back to the river, and prepared to jump.

Chapter 107

"STOP!" MORGAN HEARD coming from a car's loudspeaker as he climbed onto the stone. "Don't jump! Don't jump, Jack!"

It was hearing his name that stopped Morgan, his toes teasing the edge of the ledge as he turned in the direction of the police van that slewed to a halt beside the scene of carnage. Armed officers spilled from its back like pepper from a shaker, their weapons up, ready and searching for targets—Morgan could not be a more inviting one. He felt the press of the revolver in the small of his back, and wondered if it was visible.

"Don't move!" one of the masked officers shouted at him.

But Morgan did move. His eyes moved. They moved to the shape of an unmarked police car that skidded to a crunching halt between the officers and Morgan.

The doors flew open. The first man that Morgan recognized was the armed man who had stood guard for Princess Caroline inside the Tower. The second was Colonel De Villiers, clad head to foot in tactical gear, a pistol on his hip.

"Go!" he shouted at Morgan, waving in the direction of the south bank. "Get Flex!"

"Knight..." Morgan began, looking to the waters.

"I've got him!" De Villiers promised. "Go! Run! Get Flex!"

Morgan took one more look at the empty water beneath him, before turning his predatory eyes to the south.

Flex's figure was almost clear of the bridge. Once he hit the mass of streets, Morgan knew, the chances of finding him would be almost zero.

And so he ran.

Chapter 108

COLONEL DE VILLIERS watched as the bloodied apparition of Jack Morgan leaped down from the bridge-side and raced off toward the southern bank of the Thames.

"He's with me!" the Colonel shouted to a pair of officers who began to take off in pursuit. The men pulled up short with a look to each other, but knowing well enough that orders were orders.

De Villiers ran to the bridge's edge. He knew police boat units were already rushing to the scene, but Knight had been in the water for almost two minutes now—his time was running out, if it was not already up.

The Colonel had watched the man get hurled by Flex into the waters. He had seen Rider shot, and the struggle that followed. He had seen all this from a drone feed. Morgan had sent word at 5:28 of where the exchange would take place— Jack Morgan, still a Marine and servant to others, had put his own desire for vengeance after what was best for others. He had put his own head in a noose to draw Flex out so that the police could swoop in at the right moment and arrest Jane Cook's killer.

De Villiers should have known better than to put faith in a plan to survive contact with the enemy. They had made the difficult decision to stand back, and allowed traffic and pedestrians to continue on the bridge—to do anything else would have alerted Flex. What they had not counted on was Flex's temper causing him to throw Knight into the Thames, and to begin a shootout that had turned London Bridge into the Wild West.

With no other option, Colonel De Villiers shed his gear and jumped from the bridge.

Chapter 109

JACK MORGAN, DRENCHED in Herbert's blood, launched into his run like a sprinter at some ghastly Olympics. Unlike Flex, he made no effort to weave between the stalled traffic for cover, instead running along the bridge's pedestrianized side.

As he ran, he passed some of the city's early risers who had pressed themselves against the bridge's scant cover, paralyzed by fear, or too old to run. They looked at him with terror-filled stares, but his eyes were locked on a figure a hundred yards ahead, the bulk of Flex pushing conspicuous even from a distance.

Flex had a head start, but Morgan had seen Rider's bullet strike the man in his armored chest plate. Even the greatest athlete would be winded after such a hit, and Flex was made of sixty pounds more muscle than his heart and lungs had been built to carry—in effect, he was running with a ruck-sack. In his SAS days, that was exactly what Flex did as his bread and butter, but he was older now, and Morgan could bet that Flex's gym time was spent pumping up his muscles in the mirror, rather than on the cardio machines.

The result of all this was that Morgan was catching up.

The American was at the end of the wide bridge now, and saw Flex fleeing eastward with the tail end of the bridge's terrified fugitives.

"Out of my way!" Morgan heard the man bellow. "Police! Get out of my way!"

The wide-eyed pedestrians moved aside for the human bowling ball, who knocked to the ground any who were too slow to clear a path. As Flex reached a set of elevators that carried passengers down to the ground level of London Bridge station, a young woman was sent tumbling forward by the muscleman's barging shoulder. People screamed, and Morgan used those shouts as beacons whenever he lost sight of the man. The foot of the open bridge was now twisting into steps and staircases that entangled into the concrete jungle of buildings, roads and train track. Morgan had closed the distance, but as the urbanity built up ahead of him, he knew he could lose his quarry from as close as twenty yards away.

"Flex!" Morgan called, willing to set himself up as a target if that's what it took to halt his prey. "Flex!"

The second shout reached the man's ears. The fugitive turned, scowled, and snapped off a double tap from his pistol. The bullets zipped by Morgan's head as he continued to run forward in a crouch, ducking behind a low wall. The sound of panicked civilians was everywhere, but no more shots, and so Morgan risked a look around the end of the wall. There was no sign of Flex.

Morgan rushed onward, preparing for the final showdown. He reached behind his back and pulled free the revolver—he had six shots.

Six shots to kill, or be killed.

Chapter 110

FLEX USED A backhand to clear a fear-stricken young man from his way, the youth falling backward with a whimper as Flex barged through the narrow alleyway.

Bastard, he growled to himself. *Bastard*. He could not believe Morgan had survived the fusillade of bullets that he had pumped into Herbert's torso. Now the American was clinging to him like the parasite he was, the chances of Flex's escape diminishing with each yard of ground that the man gained.

The bastard was harder to kill than a cockroach, he railed. Flex needed him dead. He needed him dead more than he needed almost anything else in the world.

The only thing more important than Morgan's death was Flex's own survival. Caught up in moments of red mist and rage, he had lost sight of that. Rider's greedy treachery had pushed him to the edge and over it, but now Flex was calming, and becoming more calculating—escape and evade, he told himself. *Come on, you old bastard*, he goaded. *You were trained for this. Escape, evade, and then track the Yank down and cut his throat. It doesn't have to be today, it doesn't have to be tomorrow. Let him suffer a bit. Let him remember how you blew that bitch's brains out on screen. Let him remember how you chucked his mate into the Thames like he was an empty tracksuit. Let him suffer for a bit, and then kill him.*

Yes, Flex told himself. *That's what I'll do.*

But first he had to escape.

To that end, he took a wide berth around the train station, knowing there would be coppers there. Instead he circled it two streets over, running eastward, the roads all but empty of onlookers now. Those that Flex did pass stood still in wide-eyed bewilderment—they saw a running cop, they heard a siren, but they had no idea why. In the Big Smoke it could mean a house fire or a terrorist massacre.

"What's going on, officer?" an elderly man asked plaintively as Flex thundered past.

But Flex had no time to play cops, because he was looking at two real ones coming down the street toward him. They pulled their BMW motorbikes to a stop and dismounted.

Flex saw his opportunity.

"Thank God!" he shouted, cursing inwardly as he saw that the men were armed, and cautious. "I got attacked! He's armed and on a rampage, and he's right behind me, covered in blood!"

"Just stop there, mate!" one of the cops called, hand on his pistol. "What's your name and police number?"

Flex said nothing. Instead he cursed his own stupidity. He should never have used the police gambit again after their trap at the London Stadium. Word must have gone out to the police about imposters in uniform, and Flex was not the kind of person people forgot in a hurry—his huge bulk and disheveled appearance taking these police to the logical assumption that this man might not be what he seemed.

"Move your hand away from your weapon," the second cop told him, moving his own hand to his holster.

Flex didn't give him the chance, and drew. A double tap cracked the officer in the chest. Flex turned to draw down on his companion, but that officer had already dropped into cover, positioning his bike between himself and the shooter.

Flex snarled. He didn't have time for this. So he turned and ran. He ran for the only building he could see with an open entrance. He ran for a building he knew was a dead end, but would at least give him a place where he could take hostages, and negotiate, for with a professional's eye, he saw that its top reaches would be almost impossible for his former SAS comrades to assault.

And so Flex ran for the Shard.

Chapter 111

JACK MORGAN HEARD the gunshots but did not break stride. They were away to his right, echoing from the street where he had seen Flex disappear. He flinched at the thought of Flex taking more innocent life, and braced himself for what scene he would come across in his pursuit. Morgan prepared for a decision he might have to make between saving that person's life, or catching the murdering monster.

But then he heard a second set of gunshots crash through the streets, closely overlapped by others, and that overlap could mean only one thing: Flex was in a gunfight.

Morgan waited then—a patient hunter behind the low wall of a staircase, steadying himself, and waiting for his shot.

It came seconds later. Flex barreled out of the street with a quick look over his shoulder, closely followed by a gunshot. Any people in the locale who were not already running and screaming took off like a burst of frightened partridges, obscuring Morgan's view as he brought up his pistol and tracked Flex's progress—he was coming closer, running at an oblique angle to the American, who remained undetected, ready and waiting.

Morgan pulled the trigger.

The first round went wide, impossible to tell how far, but the sound was enough to draw Flex's attention. The fugitive fired back a trio of shots without breaking stride. One of the bullets struck close, sending chips of brick into Morgan's face and eyes, scratching him and forcing him down into cover. He cursed and wiped his eyes with his fingers to clear his vision.

When he looked again Flex was out of pistol range, charging like a bull ahead in the direction Morgan knew there would be no escape from—the Shard. With a flash of realization, Morgan understood Flex's intention: he would take captives in one of the country's most difficult buildings in which to effect a hostage rescue, beginning a siege that would end only in the death of innocents, or in the government-sanctioned escape of Flex.

Morgan could not allow either of those things to happen.

He ran onward.

Chapter 112

FLEX DIDN'T LIKE running with his back exposed, but with the armed copper in the street, the inevitable backup on its way, and Morgan taking his own shots, he had decided the best thing for him to do was to put his head down and just go.

Get to the Shard, he told himself. *Get in there, grab a hostage, take a breath, work this out.*

Despite the death and the carnage, Flex was confident he could escape the situation alive. He knew that the government line on not negotiating with terrorists was bollocks—he had seen it with his own eyes in countless failed states and backwaters around the globe—so he was sure they'd be willing to come to an agreement. After all, Flex had likely trained some of the men who would be orchestrating any planned rescue—he already knew their probable moves. There wasn't much Flex could do to prevent them gaining access to him eventually, but with a few hostages, he could make a convincing enough argument that there would only be bodies to greet the would-be heroes. With limited options, Flex charged toward the Shard and the endgame that had been forced upon him.

"You!" he shouted to the top-hatted doorman, who was cowering behind a flower pot. "Take me upstairs! Now!"

If the police uniform was not enough to convince the doorman to comply, the pointed pistol was. "OK!" he stuttered in accented English. "OK!"

Flex grabbed the man by the collar of his greatcoat and shoved him toward the golden glimmer of the elevators. "All the way up!" he ordered. He backed into the opening doors so that the doorman was between himself and the outside, Flex's gun over the man's shoulder with a clear aim. As the doors began to slide closed, he saw a shape bounding from cover to cover outside. The figure moved too quickly for Flex to be certain it was Jack Morgan, but he fired a double tap anyway. Glass from the building's front cracked and sent frosted spider's webs outward.

A split second later, the elevator's doors closed.

Chapter 113

MORGAN PICKED HIMSELF up off his stomach and looked at the cracked glass that had saved his life—the shatterproof windows of the Shard's lower floor had absorbed the impact of Flex's shots.

"Stop!" Morgan heard as he broke back into a run. "Get down! Armed police!"

Morgan turned to look over his shoulder and saw a running officer eighty yards away. The revolver was clearly visible in Morgan's hands, and one look at the officer's face told the American that he was serious, and trying to close the distance before he fired.

"Armed police!" he shouted again.

Morgan ran. He could not let him close that gap.

The Shard lobby was empty as he squeezed between the slowly opening automatic doors, not stopping until he hit the elevator call button. When it didn't open at once, Morgan hit the deck on instinct. He was right to.

Two bullets cracked through the building's open doors,

which were now closing once more. The officer rose from the firing position on his knee, and began to bound forward. Morgan knew he could never bring himself to shoot the man, but the officer didn't know that.

He raised his pistol and fired.

The first bullet went a foot wide of his target. The second hit dead center, and the police officer dropped to the ground.

Then crawled to cover.

Morgan had shot out the power box above the glass sliding doors, and now they were immobile, a six-inch gap between them. It would be enough to buy Morgan moments for his pursuit, before the police response teams could access the building's industrial entrances. It would buy him moments to stop Flex from beginning what could turn out to be one of the country's most bloody hostage situations. It would buy Morgan the time to offer Flex the one thing that could halt his course of action.

Morgan's own life.

Chapter 114

THE DOORMAN WHIMPERED as the elevator shot upward. The muzzle of Flex's pistol was pressed into his cheek so hard that he could feel it against his teeth.

"Please," the man begged, his accent Eastern European, "I have a family."

Flex said nothing. His eyes were on the numbers on the elevator's controls. "How many floors in this building?" he demanded.

"Seventy-two."

"Then why does this lift only go up to thirty-four?"

"It goes to the hotel," the terrified man explained. "Then there is another set of lifts."

Flex swore. His plan had been to ride the elevator to its highest level, grab a few more hostages, and then to ensconce himself somewhere that had a good view of the entrances, but was clear of windows that would allow him to be taken out by a helicopter-borne sniper. He also didn't put it past the regiment to land on the top of the narrow building before abseiling down and smashing their way through the glass. In fact, they'd probably love that, Flex thought to himself, a sense of pride in his past life reaching up momentarily through his anger and hate.

He had been a part of something once, Flex knew. He had been a part of something greater than himself, and not as a cog in a machine, but as a brother amongst pilgrims. Eventually, when push came to shove, he had chosen that band of men over his own wife. She hadn't been able to understand what it was he did, and why he was the way he was. After losing friends in Desert Storm, the last thing Flex needed to hear was her moaning about him having a couple of beers with his mates instead of driving her to Tesco. As much as it had hurt when she'd taken the kids, Flex had seen it as just one more sacrifice to be made in the service of his beloved regiment, and his country.

And what had happened then? He'd served his years, and though he'd felt fit and able, and had had no wish to leave, the army had had other ideas. Thanks for your work. Sorry about your dead mates. Here's a shit pension, now piss off, will you, and drink yourself to death somewhere nice and quiet. There's a good man.

Not Flex. He had joined the most elite unit in the world to prove a point—that he mattered. That he was good enough. The chip on his shoulder was still there when he left the service, only it had been joined by the vicious things he had done—and enjoyed doing—in the name of Queen and country. Flex had found he was bloody good at killing people, and as the West had capitalized on the spoils of war, Flex had thought it only right he take his own share.

And so he had started P-C-Gen Security, using his network of Special Forces contacts across the world to bid for the lucrative contracts spawned by the wars on terror and drugs. As he'd snapped them up like a greedy dog, Flex had reached out to men he'd worked with in the world's most dangerous corners. As the money had rolled in, Flex had moved into offices on the Thames—literally—and though he was not in the regiment any longer, he'd had what he wanted—pride. Respect. A career that kept him in the center of the world's web of violence, and the men who administered it.

Jack Morgan had ruined all of that. The beating in the gym had been embarrassing enough—and had left Flex with a ruined knee that had required long and arduous reconstruction—but what had followed from Private was worse than any smackdown.

It was the whispers. *Flex is a pussy. Flex got his arse beat. Flex is crooked. Flex can't be trusted.* Flex *knew* that Morgan had started those rumors, and soon P-C-Gen was losing contracts hand over fist. Reputation was everything in this game, and Flex had lost his. What made it most unbearable to such a proud man was that no one had even been hostile about it. They'd simply stopped calling. And like guilty lovers, they'd stopped answering his calls.

And there was Morgan, the charismatic American twat who had whispered in the ears of CEOs, politicians and agents. Morgan was no soldier, Flex fumed to himself. He was a pilot who'd stuck his chopper into the ground, and hadn't had the common courtesy to die with it, despite toasting his comrades. He was a schmoozing bastard, not a warrior, and Flex fumed at the thought of the prick's smug face as he had stood over him in the gym and demanded—*demanded*—answers.

"Please don't hurt me," the doorman in Flex's grip begged, sensing the rising swell of anger.

Flex obliged by smashing the man's head into the

elevator's polished mirror. The man slumped to the floor, a smear of blood left behind by his ruined skull.

Flex looked dispassionately at the body. Another life taken because of Morgan. *He* was the instigator in all this. *He* was the one who didn't have the decency to stand, fight and die.

"Bastard!" Flex roared in the confines of the elevator. "Bastard!" he fumed again, as the doors pinged open.

Chapter 115

EARLY MORNING WAS a quiet time in the Shangri-La, customers of the five-star hotel asleep in their comfortable beds, or admiring panoramic views from their rooms over coffee. There were only a small number of people in the hotel's reception, an international collection of the establishment's workers, and all were pressed up against the glass of the floor-to-ceiling windows, their fearful eyes zoned in to the pandemonium on London Bridge below, where sirens wailed and lights flashed, dozens of police officers swarming about the bridge like ants on a log.

"I can see bodies," a sharp-eyed receptionist gulped.

"Is it a terrorist attack?" one of the breakfast chefs asked, logging into Twitter.

"I hope not," the duty manager prayed. The sound of the elevator doors pinging open behind them caused the group to turn. They stood frozen as they saw an armed police officer emerging, the body of the hotel's doorman crumpled at his feet.

Chapter 116

AS FLEX EMERGED from the elevator, he saw the fear on the faces of the people stood huddled in front of him. *No,* he corrected himself—not people. *Sheep,* just waiting for one of their flock to make the first move before the others followed. Flex could see their tiny minds trying to work out what was going on—a man lying slumped dead on the elevator's floor, and a police officer—a symbol that they had been told all of their lives was a force for *good*—standing over him.

Flex decided he would help the sheep make up their minds, and shot the duty manager in the face.

Chapter 117

JACK MORGAN PRESSED himself as tightly as he could into the elevator's front left corner. As soon as the doors opened, he expected incoming fire from Flex. Morgan would have a couple of seconds at most before the door was fully open, and he had less than half a foot of cover to hide behind. If Flex was waiting in ambush, Morgan would have a split second to decide if he would gut it out against all odds, or if he would hit the button to close the door and return him to ground level. Deep down, Morgan knew the decision had already been made.

For the memory of Jane Cook, there would be no retreat.

He watched as the elevator's numbers crept upward, hitting thirty-four in a smooth stop. He pulled the pistol up to his shoulder, ready to punch out and aim immediately as the doors opened.

They did so with a pleasant ping, and Morgan prepared himself for a fusillade of gunshots.

None came. All was quiet but for the sobs of a chambermaid

who leaned back against a high glass window. She was cradling someone in her arms. Morgan only needed one look at the limp body to see that the person was dead.

"Is he in here?" Morgan shouted, maintaining his position. "Is he in here?"

The woman shook her head and sobbed. Morgan stepped out, his eyes drawn to the body of a suited man who lay dead on the floor. Suddenly, Morgan's ear was drawn to the sounds of relaxing, melodic music that continued to play in the reception area, despite the carnage that was playing out beneath the hidden speakers.

He swept his pistol left and right, but all was clear.

"Where is he? Where did he go?"

The chambermaid was incapable of speech, but she pointed in the direction of a second set of elevators.

"Does he have hostages?" Morgan asked, reaching into the woman's pockets and coming up with her access card.

She nodded, sending tears dropping down onto the face of the young man in her arms. Morgan had no time to comfort her. He left, and ran in the direction of the elevators.

"Please don't hurt me!" a man shouted. Morgan turned to see a businessman huddled shaking beneath a table. "Please!"

"Did you see who went in here?" Morgan asked sternly.

The man nodded.

"How many people with him?"

"Three, I think. Maybe four. Please don't hurt me."

"I'm not going to hurt you. There's a woman over there." Morgan pointed back toward the sobbing chambermaid at the window. "Grab her, and get downstairs. Go!"

After swallowing the lump of fear in his throat, the man scuttled away, and Morgan turned his attention to the elevator. It had only one destination: the highest floor.

He looked once more at the fleeing man, who had stopped at the sobbing woman, and was now moving her toward the elevator that would take them down to safety.

Morgan sucked in a deep breath to calm the nerves and adrenaline that pumped through his system. Then he cast a cool glance out at the magnificent vista of London.

Morgan had seen worse places to die. With that thought in his mind, he stepped into the elevator that would deliver him either to revenge or to his death.

Chapter 118

"GET OVER THERE!" Flex ordered his six captives, brandishing his pistol. Four of them he had herded like the sheep they were from the thirty-fourth floor. Another two, both cleaners, had been acquired as they'd arrived in the building's viewing rooms, and the highest reaches of the Shard. The viewing rooms were confined, Flex realized, and unsuited to his purposes—he couldn't keep point of aim over all entry points, and he certainly couldn't cover all angles in the room by himself, the layout stretching around the elevator at its center.

He realized there was only one true option for him. He dragged a hostage by the hair, moving the short distance to the window so that he could see the towers and buildings below, some reaching as high as the Shard's waist.

"Look at the flags!" Flex told the younger woman. "What are they doing?"

"The flags?" she mumbled, confused.

Flex slapped her hard to sharpen her senses.

"I'll look for you!" a young man offered bravely.

Flex didn't need people deciding they were heroes. That could be trouble down the line, and so the young man's offer earned him a bullet in the chest.

"What are the flags doing?" he demanded again, against the screams.

"Blowing! They're blowing!" the woman bawled.

That was what Flex had seen, but his eyesight wasn't what it had been, and he didn't want to wager his life without a second opinion. Knowing that the winds were high, he made a calculated gamble. Chances of the commanders signing off on their snipers taking a shot in high wind speed, with hostages? Low. Chances of them storming the floor from a direction that Flex wasn't facing, and killing him before he could react? High.

"We're going up on the roof," Flex ordered.

He was just about to give a second command when the single elevator pinged, and its doors began to open. On instinct, Flex raised his pistol and fired.

Chapter 119

JACK MORGAN DIDN'T see Flex open fire, but he heard him well enough, the pistol's reports crashing around the small space of the elevator as the bullets went zipping toward Morgan.

Who survived every shot.

Knowing that Flex would likely cut him down as soon as the doors opened, Morgan had stacked the elevator with tables behind which he could take cover. The five-star hotel had bought the best timber, and now Flex's 9mm bullets flattened and died against it, protecting Morgan from the storm of steel that Flex unleashed his way. When he heard the click of an empty magazine, Morgan sprang up and punched out the revolver, ready to fire.

He saw Flex, red-faced and angry, the man he longed to kill, but he saw too the young woman that Flex's left hand had gripped by the hair, pulling her close to him and using her as a shield.

Eyes went wide. Both men knew that, without using both hands, Flex would not be able to execute a quick enough reload to kill Morgan before Morgan killed him. Both men also knew that until Flex let go of the girl, Morgan would not fire.

It was a stand-off.

Flex began to back away. Morgan tracked him with the pistol, but he knew he could not fire and risk hitting the weeping girl. The revolver's short barrel was not made for accuracy, and so Morgan would have to kill Flex up close.

"He's out of ammo," Morgan told the girl. "Be calm."

"Don't try and run," Flex whispered venomously into her ear. "I can drop this pistol and draw my knife long before you get free. I'll cut your throat like it was butter."

"Why don't you use that knife on me instead of a defenseless woman?" Morgan tried, as Flex stepped back toward the maintenance doorway that would lead them to the final flight of stairs, and the building's thousand-foot peak.

"You know what I regret? That I didn't rape that bitch of yours. That I didn't smash her before blowing her brains out."

Morgan needed every piece of his concentration to force down the black rage that built inside of his chest and threatened to consume him.

"I should have let the other lads have turns too," Flex goaded, backing through the doorway. "Don't follow me."

"Fuck you, Flex. I'm the one with the loaded gun here."

"What was your favorite part of her?" Flex asked, as Morgan followed him into the bare utility of the maintenance stairwell. "The tits? Her face? I didn't see much of them, but I did see her brains, Jack. There was a lot of them. Made a hell of a mess on the floor, they did."

Morgan willed his mind to shut out the words, but the cloud of rage was rising, trying to push him into recklessness.

"Your hands are shaking," Flex laughed, seeing the

slightest of trembles in Morgan's aim. "You should be thanking me. You'd have got tired of her and chinned her off soon enough anyway. At least this way no one else gets inside her. Well, unless the guys at the morgue are a little—"

"You shut your goddamn mouth," Morgan hissed, the veneer of his cool cracking, and revealing lava beneath.

"Or what, Jack? You goin' to get this girl killed too, just like you did Jane?"

Flex was at the top of the staircase.

"Open the door," he told the girl, who squirmed awkwardly to obey. Flex kept her body between himself and Morgan. The girl's own frame wasn't enough to cover the entirety of his muscular bulk, but it was enough for Morgan.

"Let's just do this, you and me," Morgan tried again.

Flex spat at him instead.

Then he backed out onto the top of Britain's tallest building.

Chapter 120

ONE THOUSAND FEET above the country's sprawling capital, the wind slapped Morgan hard in the face as he followed Flex onto the highest level of the Shard, nothing between them and the elements but guard rails. Morgan kept the revolver trained at Flex's head, but he knew there was no way he could pull the trigger. The shot had been a difficult one before—now, with the wind, it was a near certainty the girl would die first.

"Let her go and I'll put my gun down," Morgan said, his voice raised against the wind.

Flex backed himself into an area of the roof where the glass panels that gave the building its name would cover his back from heli-borne snipers.

"You're out of options, Flex. London is covered in cameras. Your crimes are on tape. You can go to prison, or you can die."

Flex snorted, and Morgan knew he was holding out for a third option—to keep the girl as a hostage, and bargain his way out.

Morgan hadn't considered that there could be a fourth.

Suddenly, with no warning, Flex shoved the girl forward at Morgan, the massive muscles of his chest and arm propelling her like a rag doll. The girl's arms flailed and her hair was blown in the wind as she stumbled and tripped the few meters toward the American. Morgan knew instantly what Flex's ploy was: to buy himself two seconds to reload his empty pistol, and finish Morgan, so he made to sidestep and fire while Flex was reaching for his spare magazine. But the girl came at him like a lost child to her parents, her eyes wild with terror, unable to see that by grabbing at Morgan, she was sealing both of their fates.

"Off!" Morgan screamed at her, pushing the clutching girl away and expecting 9mm rounds to begin punching into the bodies of both of them. "Off!" he yelled again, grabbing a scruff of her jacket and sending her spinning toward the door. But her flailing arms knocked the pistol from his hand, and sent it skidding across the metal floor.

Now unarmed, he knew that he would die.

He looked to Flex. The murderer pushed the fresh magazine onto his pistol and was raising it up to face Morgan's body. As it came, the thumb of Flex's left hand moved to push down on the release catch, which would allow the top-slide to come crashing forward and chamber the round that would kill Jack Morgan.

Morgan knew there was no escape now, so he steeled himself to look Flex in the eye, desperate to avoid showing a single ounce of fear that the man could enjoy.

Flex's thumb hit the weapon's release catch.

Prepared for death, Morgan watched as the top-slide came forward.

And jammed halfway.

Chapter 121

FLEX LOOKED DOWN at the weapon in his hand, seeing the top-slide stuck halfway forward, the weapon rendered useless.

"No!" he shouted. The reason for the malfunction was instantly clear: Morgan's gunshot on the bridge. It had hit the ammunition pouch and caused enough of a bend in the magazine to pinch the top, which now stopped the spring from feeding up the bullet as the carrier came forward to collect and chamber the round. Even if he were to clear the obstruction, the same malfunction would occur over and over again. Without another magazine—which Flex did not have—the semi-automatic pistol was useless.

Looking across at the man he longed to kill, Flex realized that Jack Morgan had come to the same conclusion.

His eyes went to the floor, and Morgan's dropped revolver.

Chapter 122

JACK MORGAN HAD been ready to receive death. Now, seeing that Flex's weapon had been rendered useless, relief flooded into him like sunlight. Still, he knew his reprieve would be short unless he could put Flex down, so he lunged toward the revolver that the girl—now a memory rushing away into the stairwell—had knocked flying from his hands.

At least, that's what Morgan convinced Flex he was doing.

The big man took the bait, and went diving for the weapon like a linebacker onto a quarterback. Morgan had pulled himself up short and stayed on his feet, and now he delivered a crushing kick into the side of Flex's thick skull.

Flex roared in agony, but still he reached for the pistol. Morgan stamped quickly on his fingers, feeling something crack and give way. He was about to deliver another kick when Flex forgot about the pistol, and instead rolled toward Morgan's leg like a hungry gator, enough of his fingers unbroken to grab a boot in a vise-like grip, and his free hand moving to a knife on his belt.

Morgan threw himself forward. Flex lost his grip as Morgan bounced off his broad back, his hands going for the knife that was now free in Flex's left hand. Like a drunken rodeo rider, Morgan hooked his legs around Flex's own, attempting to keep the man's bucking body pressed down to the floor as he wrestled the blade from Flex's meaty hand.

"I'll kill you!" Flex screamed. "I'll kill you!"

Morgan had no doubt of it, so he resorted to the most basic of human instincts when life is in danger. A tactic taught to him by Flex's own comrade.

He bit, his teeth pressing down into the flesh of Flex's knife hand. The pinned man roared, and Morgan felt the knife twitch. A moment later, Morgan's vision began to blur from blood running into his eyes. Lots of blood.

He sank his teeth in deeper.

Flex howled and bucked, finally shaking Morgan loose. The American rolled clear with blood in his mouth and eyes.

And a knife in his hand.

Flex charged forward, taking Morgan in a bull-rush.

Morgan drove the knife forward at him, but the police stab vest absorbed the blow and the blade buckled from Morgan's hand. He was slammed backward by Flex's mad charge, and the lower guard rail hit across his kidneys, all air being driven from him.

Flex threw a headbutt into Morgan's face, opening a deep cut above his eye and adding to the blood already covering his face. Morgan tried to look at the man, but all he could see was a red haze through the blood in his eyes. As he saw the bulk of Flex's upper body pull back for another headbutt, Morgan realized this was the final chance for him to bring justice to Jane's killer.

As Flex made to drive his head into Morgan's face, Morgan gripped hold of his enemy, pushed up from his legs, and used the momentum of the muscleman's headbutt to bend himself backward over the guard rail, and to the thousand-foot drop below.

Chapter 123

AS JACK MORGAN'S body hit the narrow ledge ten feet below the Shard's upper deck, he was almost grateful that blood clouded his sight and saved him from seeing clearly the terrible truth that he was three hundred meters above London, with nothing between himself and the earth but the meter-wide shelf that he and Flex had crashed onto. Only a snagging of Flex's equipment belt had stopped them from bouncing from the ledge and into oblivion, and now Morgan was quickest to get to his feet as the big man sought to free himself of the entanglement.

Morgan scrambled free of Flex's hold, and now he used the bottom of his shirt to clear the blood from his eyes. As the red liquid was wiped away, Morgan's heart raced into his mouth—London was laid out below him like a three-dimensional Monopoly board. As a gust of wind shook the tower's top, Morgan wasn't sure if he'd ever been more scared in his life.

But he was alive.

He was alive and in the sky, and that was a place where Morgan knew comfort, as well as fear. The same could not be said of Flex, who now gripped for finger holds with terror in his eyes.

"Long way down," Morgan taunted, enjoying the man's panic.

"Help me up!" Flex begged, all grudges forgotten as he found himself inches from death.

Morgan smiled darkly, then jumped upward, his hands grabbing a hold of the metal fixtures that the tower's audacious work crew would use to clip in their belts as they descended to clean and maintain the glass leviathan. Morgan shut out any thought of the terrible possibility of what a mistimed jump or poor handgrip could mean. Instead, he focused all his strength and courage on leaping from hand-hold to handhold. Moving his feet closer to the tower's summit and safety in strides, Morgan pushed Flex from his mind, concentrating solely on his movement, trying to predict the wind, and to jump between its vicious gusts.

It was on his final leap—barely two feet from the top—that his luck ran out, and a savage thrust of air hit Morgan as he was free of his handholds. The gust blew him to his left, and his right hand snatched at the fixture that had been meant for his left. He caught it, but the movement spun his body, and he found himself facing outward, his back to the building, and nothing ahead of him but sky.

Below him, on the ledge, Flex saw his moment for victory and grabbed at Morgan's legs like a cat after a bird. Morgan was saved by Flex's inability to let go of his own handhold, and so only one hand reached up to grasp Morgan. He tucked his legs up to avoid Flex's grabs, but the movement left him even more vulnerable to the wind, his outstretched knees catching every gust. As Morgan moved his left hand to join his right and double his grip, he looked up and realized there was only one choice left to him—a movement that would either save his life, or take it. Without waiting a second more before the next gust could hit, he drew his knees up toward his chin and, like a gymnast, curled his body upward so that his feet went above his head, pushing through the movement until he felt his shins scrape against the metal of the floor above. Pushing with his hands, Morgan shoved his body up and back, and slid himself onto the upper deck. His chest heaving from exertion and the endorphins of near death, he looked down at Flex, helpless on the ledge below.

Then he turned his eyes to the revolver that lay beside him.

Chapter 124

MICHAEL "FLEX" GIBBON looked up at the revolver that was pointing down at his face.

"Put one in my head," he asked Morgan, knowing the game was over. "I don't want to fall, Jack! For God's sake, put one in my head!"

Morgan said nothing. He wasn't seeing Flex, and not because the blood was trickling into his eyes and blocking his vision—it was the picture of Jane Cook, seconds from death, that he could see in front of him. Then it was the image of her violent execution carried out by the man who now waited helpless below Morgan, begging for mercy.

"Put one in my head!" Flex pleaded.

Morgan did not. Instead, he used the pistol to trace out the other parts of Flex's body below him.

"No!" Flex begged, knowing that any wound that didn't kill him would certainly brush him from his narrow perch. "Please!"

Morgan's pistol hand shook with rage, adrenaline and

grief. It shook as another gust of wind hit the building's top. Flex dug his fingernails into the building's side as if he thought he could claw his way to safety.

"For God's sake, Jack!" he cried. "Shoot me before I get blown off here! Shoot me! Shoot me!"

Morgan felt the cold metal of the trigger beneath his finger. He had the bullets and he had the shot. Since Jane's murder, he had dreamed of this moment, the fate of the killer in his hands, his face filling the sights of Morgan's pistol.

Do it for Jane, Jack Morgan thought savagely to himself. *Do it for Sharon Lewis. Do it for Peter Knight. Do it for all those other people that Flex has left dead, ruined or scarred in his wake.*

Do it, Morgan told himself.

DO IT! his mind screamed.

And so he did.

Chapter 125

"CLIMB!" MORGAN ORDERED. "Now!"

"You won't kill me?" Flex asked in disbelief.

"I won't kill you," Morgan spat. "Now climb!" he shouted again, his pistol unwavering as the big man's shaking fingers searched for their first handholds.

Flex winced with pain as he put strain on the hand that Morgan had crunched beneath his boot. Grimacing, he began to haul himself upward. To stay on the shelf was to risk the wrath of the wind, but Flex was no more secure from it as he began his slow ascent, his big body buffeted by the gusts.

"Get me a rope or something!" he shouted up.

Morgan said nothing, and stared impassively.

Knowing that no help was coming, and seeing that he was alone in his efforts, Flex gritted his teeth and pushed higher. Morgan watched with grim satisfaction as he saw the pain that Flex's right hand was causing him.

"You're getting tired, Flex," Morgan taunted. "All that muscle, and one heart. Your blood's not getting around fast enough, Flex. Your muscles are filling with lactic acid, and soon you'll cramp. One big gust, Flex, and you're done."

"You said you wouldn't kill me!" Flex shouted up.

"And I won't," Morgan replied, his face devoid of emotion.

And that was the truth. Jack Morgan had decided to let Flex climb, and face justice. During the murderer's ascent the winds had calmed, and Morgan wondered if perhaps some force unknown to him wanted to see the man answer for his crimes in court.

He looked down at the struggling man below him. Flex's red face was a mere two feet from the ledge now. Close enough for Morgan to put a hole through his skull without thinking, but his finger remained away from the trigger because he knew without hesitation what Jane Cook and Peter Knight would tell him. They would want justice, but they would want it within the law of the country they loved so much.

"Help me, please," Flex pleaded, and one look told Morgan that the man's oversized muscles had run out of gas a mere foot from his refuge. "Come on, Jack, please! I can't keep holding on!"

Morgan looked into Flex's eyes and saw the big man's spirit wither as he realized that the American's mercy had extended to its furthest point.

"I don't want to die, Jack! Please, I have kids!"

"Peter Knight had kids," Morgan said evenly, taking a step backward to drive home Flex's predicament.

The former soldier grimaced and looked to his right hand. With two broken fingers, he could barely hold on. "I'll confess everything!" Flex shouted. "I'll confess! Just please don't let me die!"

"You'll confess?"

"Yes! Just get me up there!"

Morgan thought for a few seconds, during which Flex dug his fingernails into his hands as he sought to tighten his grip. Then Morgan pulled out his phone, and opened the camera.

"Confess," he ordered.

And Flex did. He told about how he had attacked Morgan and his team at the Brecon hotel, and in the forest. He told of how he had murdered Jane Cook, and beaten PC Sharon Lewis to within an inch of her life. He told of how he had feigned an attack on Hooligan to lure Morgan into a deadly trap. When that hadn't worked, he had kidnapped Peter Knight, and then thrown him into the Thames. From there, Flex told of how he had shot down innocent civilians in his bid to escape.

"How's your conscience?" Morgan asked the man.

"Just get me up!" Flex growled.

Morgan turned off the camera. Then he shook his head.

"We had a deal!" Flex begged.

Morgan braced himself as a gust of wind shook the buildings, and Flex's fingers began to slip.

"Don't do this, Jack! You can't let me die!"

Morgan knelt, and looked into Flex's dark soul.

"You're a good man, Jack," Flex pleaded.

"And she was a better woman."

Morgan held Flex's terrified stare until the next blast of wind rocked the tower top, and Flex's fingers slipped away.

Chapter 126

AS HE WATCHED Flex fall away into oblivion, the weight of Jack Morgan's grief came crashing down—her killer had received justice, but Jane Cook was still dead. Nothing would ever bring her back.

He sank to his knees, and closed his eyes.

That's how he was found by the armed men that burst onto the building's rooftop. Without an ounce of resistance, Morgan let himself be pushed face first into the cold metal flooring. He heard the men shouting, but he paid them no heed. Hands cuffed behind his back, Morgan was dragged to his feet roughly and a hood was pulled over his head.

Shoved and pulled by his captors, Morgan was taken from the roof and inside the building. There he was lifted and put onto a gurney, where he felt a second cuff attach to his right ankle. Morgan's world turned darker still as what felt like a blanket was laid over him.

Jack Morgan said nothing through all this. He felt the sensation of falling through air, and presumed it was the elevator.

He heard distant sounds of sobbing, sirens and shouts of command. He felt himself pushed and wheeled, the sudden bump of the gurney's legs tucking as he was slid into what he presumed was an ambulance. Seconds later, the siren blared and he felt the unmistakable movement of a vehicle travelling at speed.

He had no idea how long it was until the vehicle stopped, his gurney was unloaded, and Morgan was wheeled through quiet corridors. He had no idea how long it was until a man pulled away the blanket, and then the hood.

"Peter Knight?" Morgan asked, looking up at the man above him, desperate to know the fate of his friend. "Is he alive?"

"Knight is at Guy's Hospital," Colonel De Villiers told him, "but he's alive."

Morgan closed his eyes in relief. The Colonel pretended not to notice the tear that ran down Morgan's cheek. Instead he used a set of keys to take off the cuffs that bound Morgan to the gurney. The American pushed himself up, and took in his surroundings: he was in a bare corridor, the smell of bleach and disinfectant thick in his nostrils.

"I'm sorry you had to be brought in like this," De Villiers said as Morgan rubbed at his sore wrists. "Given the circumstances, we decided the best option was to convince MI5 to claim you as an operative. As far as everyone but the few operators from the rooftop knows, you were a British intelligence asset, who died heroically. Jack Morgan has been under my protection in the Tower this entire time."

"You said *we*?" Morgan asked.

"The Princess likes you," De Villiers replied, confirming Morgan's thoughts about who had been pulling the strings to keep him out of a British prison.

"Thank you, Colonel," Morgan said, putting out a hand.

"Marcus," the Guards officer insisted.

"You saved Peter's life?" Morgan asked as they shook.

De Villiers smiled. "He saved his own. I found him on one of the stone arches. He'd kicked his way there and was using his cuffed hands to grip a submerged mooring ring. His head was just above water."

"So you did save him." Morgan smiled.

"I helped him."

For keeping him from prison, Morgan had offered the Colonel a handshake. For saving Peter Knight's life, he put his arm around the taller man and embraced him.

"No need to make a scene, Morgan," De Villiers said, coloring a little.

"Jack," Morgan told him, standing back. "Thank you, Marcus."

De Villiers smiled and straightened his jacket.

"But now, if I'm not here to see Peter," Morgan asked, "then where am I?"

De Villiers cleared his throat, and told him.

Chapter 127

THE SMELL OF bleach and disinfectant hit Jack Morgan strongly as he pushed open a heavy door and entered the pathologist's lab, the room as still and lifeless as the woman that lay at its center.

Jane Cook.

He stopped as if shot when he saw the shape of the covered body on the metal table, the memory of his lover's contours etched into his mind so that even the silhouette of her was enough to trick him into believing it had all been a nightmare, and that Jane would now rise, smiling, and kiss him.

She never would, Morgan knew. Jane Cook would never breathe again. She would never laugh again. She would never crease the corner of her lip when she was deep in thought, a memory that now pushed a choked laugh of love from Morgan's dry throat.

He approached her.

De Villiers had warned Morgan not to pull the sheet away, and Morgan obeyed. He had seen her death. He knew what lay beneath the sheet, no matter how he wished he didn't. Instead, he reached under the material, and felt out Jane's hand. As he gripped her cold fingers, a quartet of tears trickled over the cuts and bruises of his cheeks.

"I'm sorry," he whispered. "I know that Flex's death can never bring you back, but you were a warrior. I wanted you to know that justice was done."

Morgan used his free hand to wipe at his red eyes. They were tired—so tired.

Behind him he heard the sound of the doors opening. "Give me five more minutes, Colonel."

"It's me, Jack," came the voice of Princess Caroline in response.

Morgan turned. The royal was dressed in dark jeans and a hoody, and held a baseball cap in her hands.

"I came to pay my respects. To her, and to you."

Morgan let go of Jane's cold hand, and delicately placed the sheet back over her still flesh.

"You got what you wanted, Jack."

Morgan shook his head. "I can never get back what I want."

The royal looked to the shrouded body.

"The city's going crazy," she told him after a moment. "Another lone-wolf attack. A troubled individual hitting out at a society they feel has failed them."

Morgan raised an eyebrow. "That's how you're writing this off?"

She nodded. "Flex is a dark stain on the British armed forces, and the country, and he's one that's best forgotten as quickly as possible. The story that we tell can make all the difference."

"And how will that happen?" Morgan asked skeptically,

thinking of the carnage left in Flex's wake—the lives taken, or blighted forever.

"People see what they want to see, and believe what they want to believe," Princess Caroline explained. "A tragedy, where a broken veteran went on a rampage before throwing himself to his death. The media will lap it up like milk."

"Why not the truth?"

Caroline shrugged. "Because there's nothing to gain from it. The SAS tarnished. The police tarnished."

"Yourself tarnished," Morgan added.

She met Morgan's eyes, and nodded. "You found Sophie's killer, Jack, and now you've avenged yourself on the man who killed the woman who was special to you. I think it would be best if you stayed away from the UK for a while. Flex may have more friends."

"They know where to find me," Morgan replied, causing Caroline to smile whimsically.

"How have you lived so long, Jack?"

Morgan smiled in return. "Thank you for coming to see me, Your Highness. I'll take your advice and change the scenery, but first, I have things to do."

"Colonel De Villiers will see you're taken care of," the Princess promised.

"Don't let him resign over this," Morgan told her.

Caroline gave an apologetic smile. "I'm afraid that was a lie, and my idea. We thought that you'd be more likely to believe his help was genuine if you saw him falling on his sword."

Morgan shrugged it off. Then he turned to take one last look at the woman who had taken his heart.

"I'll leave you to pay your respects to Jane," he said to the Princess. "She was a hell of a woman and a soldier."

"I know," Caroline confirmed. "I'll be sure that she's remembered as such. Goodbye, Jack."

"Goodbye, Caroline."

With those words, Morgan walked from the room, knowing that though the body of Jane Cook would be left behind him, her memory would be carried forever in his heart.

Epilogue

JACK MORGAN HAD been standing for a long time in the hospital's corridor. He had been driven there by Marcus De Villiers, the men saying their farewells with some sadness, a mutual respect and admiration having grown between them. During the drive across London, De Villiers had informed Morgan that the media was indeed lapping up the story circulated that Flex had been a troubled veteran who had gone on a rampage, before taking his own life.

"It's all very neat," Morgan had remarked.

"You don't leave much mess," De Villiers had replied.

Jack Morgan knew that wasn't true. Jane Cook was dead, as were a handful of innocent bystanders. So too were Flex and his crew. Morgan had not an ounce of pity for the dead killers, but even so, he wished he could have taken them down more cleanly, without so much blood being spilled.

He exhaled loudly.

And then there were Sharon Lewis and Peter Knight. They rested in the hospital toward the end of the corridor in which he was now standing, but Morgan could not bring himself to walk the short distance, and to face the two people who had almost died in a vendetta that had been targeted at Jack Morgan himself.

"You going to stand there all day?" Morgan heard from over his shoulder.

He turned quickly, and looked down. A man in a wheelchair had spoken the words, two young kids combining forces to push him.

"Luke. Isabel," Peter Knight said to his children. "Go and see Sharon."

"OK, Daddy!" They smiled, and raced each other to the end of the corridor.

"I thought you died," Morgan said as the children disappeared from sight.

"I didn't." Knight smiled.

He gestured, sensing Morgan's reluctance to talk in public.

"I thought you were gone, Peter," Morgan told his friend after pushing him to privacy. "Thank God."

"Thank my parents," Knight grinned. "Swimming lessons."

Morgan shook his head and looked at his hands. "I shouldn't have left you."

"De Villiers came in for me. That lanky bugger's a strong swimmer. He helped me into the police boat."

"Still…"

"You had to get Flex," Knight insisted. "You *had* to, Jack, for all of us. We *all* loved her. She was one of us."

"She was," Morgan acknowledged with love and pride.

"I know she meant more to you than maybe anyone, Jack, but she was a friend and a sister to everyone in Private London. I still can't believe it."

Morgan put a hand on his friend's shoulder. Knight

turned his head upward. The look that passed between the men was enough to say all that words could, and more. That they shared love and grief. Purpose and brotherhood.

Eventually Knight spoke. "I've got to leave Private, Jack. The kids. I can't…"

Morgan said nothing. He understood. A nod and a look told Knight as much.

"Let's go back to the room," Morgan suggested, forcing a smile. "I want to hang out with these kids that are stealing my best agent."

The sound of animated chatter grew louder as Morgan wheeled Knight along the corridor. "I'm OK to walk," Knight insisted.

"I'm sure you are, but there's a lot of pretty nurses here, Peter. Make the most of it while you can."

Knight snorted, and used his foot to push open the door.

The source of the raucous babble was revealed immediately: Hooligan, playing the fool for Knight's laughing children.

"All right, boss!" he grinned, spotting the American.

"Hooligan." Morgan smiled before turning his head to a bed in the room's corner. "Lewis."

"You got him, Jack." Her eyes sparkled with pride.

"I did."

The next few hours passed with laughter, some golden, some solemn. They made remembrance of their friend, and they looked to the future. Through it all, the grief of Jane Cook's departure banged on Morgan's soul like the battering ram of a besieging enemy, but he held the pain at bay with the love and company of his agents, with Lewis, and with the children of his friend.

It could never last forever, Morgan knew, and he was right: Hooligan's phone began to ring.

"It's for you, boss," he explained, passing it over.

"Jack Morgan."

Faces peered intently as Morgan received what could only be the briefing of a task newly dropped onto Private's desk. As the one-sided conversation drew on, Knight observed how Morgan's battered body began to fill with purpose. By the time he hung up the call, Morgan's back was straight, his eyes alive.

"I've got to go," he told the room.

"Is it a good one?" the newly retired Peter Knight asked.

"It is," Morgan told him, getting to his feet.

Knight looked from his playing children to the adults in the room. One group were his family, and the other group were his . . .

"Can I withdraw my—" Knight began.

Morgan cut him off with a smile. "You *are* Private London, Peter."

"*We* are," Knight insisted, taking in his friends. "*We* are."

They embraced. Then, with pride in his step and purpose in his soul, Jack Morgan walked from the room.

He was onto his next mission.

He was alive.

About the Authors

JAMES PATTERSON holds the Guinness World Record for the most #1 *New York Times* bestsellers, and his books have sold more than 355 million copies worldwide. He has donated more than one million books to students and soldiers and funds over four hundred Teacher Education Scholarships at twenty-four colleges and universities. He has also donated millions to independent bookstores and school libraries.

REES JONES is a former British Army soldier who deployed on three frontline tours of duty to Iraq and Afghanistan. Now a full-time writer, Rees also collaborated with James Patterson on the BookShot *Private: The Royals*. Rees is also an author of historical fiction and war memoir, under the name Geraint Jones. He can be found across social media at @grjbooks.

Acknowledgments

First thanks go to my incredible family—patient and supportive as ever. It goes without saying that the team at PRH were brilliant and insightful, and a pleasure to work with. Thanks to Gaz and Kat for allowing me to use their beautiful home when working on this book—truly inspirational. Love, as always, to the team at Furniss Lawton. And last, but most importantly, thank you James. It is a privilege to work alongside a master of the craft.

—Rees Jones

Books by James Patterson

FEATURING ALEX CROSS

The People vs. Alex Cross • *Cross the Line* • *Cross Justice* • *Hope to Die* • *Cross My Heart* • *Alex Cross, Run* • *Merry Christmas, Alex Cross* • *Kill Alex Cross* • *Cross Fire* • *I, Alex Cross* • *Alex Cross's Trial* (with Richard DiLallo) • *Cross Country* • *Double Cross* • *Cross* (also published as *Alex Cross*) • *Mary, Mary* • *London Bridges* • *The Big Bad Wolf* • *Four Blind Mice* • *Violets Are Blue* • *Roses Are Red* • *Pop Goes the Weasel* • *Cat & Mouse* • *Jack & Jill* • *Kiss the Girls* • *Along Came a Spider*

THE WOMEN'S MURDER CLUB

The 17th Suspect (with Maxine Paetro) • *16th Seduction* (with Maxine Paetro) • *15th Affair* (with Maxine Paetro) • *14th Deadly Sin* (with Maxine Paetro) • *Unlucky 13* (with Maxine Paetro) • *12th of Never* (with Maxine Paetro) • *11th Hour* (with Maxine Paetro) • *10th Anniversary* (with Maxine Paetro) • *The 9th Judgment* (with Maxine Paetro) • *The 8th Confession* (with Maxine Paetro) • *7th Heaven* (with Maxine Paetro) • *The 6th Target* (with Maxine Paetro) • *The 5th Horseman* (with Maxine Paetro) • *4th of July* (with Maxine Paetro) • *3rd Degree* (with Andrew Gross) • *2nd Chance* (with Andrew Gross) • *1st to Die*

FEATURING MICHAEL BENNETT

Haunted (with James O. Born) • *Bullseye* (with Michael Ledwidge) • *Alert* (with Michael Ledwidge) • *Burn* (with Michael Ledwidge) • *Gone* (with Michael Ledwidge) • *I, Michael Bennett* (with Michael Ledwidge) • *Tick Tock* (with Michael Ledwidge) • *Worst Case* (with Michael Ledwidge) • *Run for Your Life* (with Michael Ledwidge) • *Step on a Crack* (with Michael Ledwidge)

THE PRIVATE NOVELS

Princess (with Rees Jones) • *Count to Ten* (with Ashwin Sanghi) • *Missing* (with Kathryn Fox) • *The Games* (with Mark Sullivan) • *Private Paris* (with Mark Sullivan) • *Private Vegas* (with Maxine Paetro) • *Private India: City on Fire* (with Ashwin Sanghi) • *Private Down Under* (with Michael White) • *Private L.A.* (with Mark Sullivan) • *Private Berlin* (with Mark Sullivan) • *Private London* (with Mark Pearson) • *Private Games* (with Mark Sullivan) • *Private: #1 Suspect* (with Maxine Paetro) • *Private* (with Maxine Paetro)

NYPD RED NOVELS

Red Alert (with Marshall Karp) • *NYPD Red 4* (with Marshall Karp) • *NYPD Red 3* (with Marshall Karp) • *NYPD Red 2* (with Marshall Karp) • *NYPD Red* (with Marshall Karp)

SUMMER NOVELS

Second Honeymoon (with Howard Roughan) • *Now You See Her* (with Michael Ledwidge) • *Swimsuit* (with Maxine Paetro) • *Sail* (with Howard Roughan) • *Beach Road* (with Peter de Jonge) • *Lifeguard* (with Andrew Gross) • *Honeymoon* (with Howard Roughan) • *The Beach House* (with Peter de Jonge)

STAND-ALONE BOOKS

Murder in Paradise (with Doug Allyn, Connor Hyde, Duane Swierczynski) • *Fifty Fifty* (with Candice Fox) • *Murder Beyond the Grave* (with Andrew Bourelle and Christopher Charles) • *Home Sweet Murder* (with Andrew Bourelle and Scott Slaven) • *Murder, Interrupted* (with Alex Abramovich and Christopher Charles) • *All-American Murder* (with Alex Abramovich and Mike Harvkey) • *The Family Lawyer* (with Robert Rotstein, Christopher Charles, Rachel Howzell Hall) • *The Store* (with Richard DiLallo) • *The Moores Are Missing* (with Loren D. Estleman, Sam Hawken, Ed Chatterton) • *Triple Threat* (with Max DiLallo, Andrew Bourrelle) • *Instinct* (with Howard Roughan) • *Penguins of America* (with Jack Patterson with Florence Yue) • *Two from the Heart* (with Frank Constantini, Emily Raymond, Brian Sitts) • *The Black Book* (with David Ellis) • *Humans, Bow Down* (with Emily Raymond) • *Never Never* (with Candice Fox) • *Woman of God* (with Maxine Paetro) • *Filthy Rich* (with John Connolly and Timothy Malloy) • *The Murder House* (with David Ellis) • *Truth or Die* (with

Howard Roughan) • *Miracle at Augusta* (with Peter de
Jonge) • *Invisible* (with David Ellis) • *First Love* (with
Emily Raymond) • *Mistress* (with David Ellis) • *Zoo* (with
Michael Ledwidge) • *Guilty Wives* (with David Ellis) • *The
Christmas Wedding* (with Richard DiLallo) • *Kill Me
If You Can* (with Marshall Karp) • *Toys* (with Neil
McMahon) • *Don't Blink* (with Howard Roughan) • *The
Postcard Killers* (with Liza Marklund) • *The Murder
of King Tut* (with Martin Dugard) • *Against Medical
Advice* (with Hal Friedman) • *Sundays at Tiffany's*
(with Gabrielle Charbonnet) • *You've Been Warned*
(with Howard Roughan) • *The Quickie* (with Michael
Ledwidge) • *Judge & Jury* (with Andrew Gross) • *Sam's
Letters to Jennifer* • *The Lake House* • *The Jester* (with
Andrew Gross) • *Suzanne's Diary for Nicholas* • *Cradle
and All* • *When the Wind Blows* • *Miracle on the 17th
Green* (with Peter de Jonge) • *Hide & Seek* • *The
Midnight Club* • *Black Friday* (originally published
as *Black Market*) • *See How They Run* • *Season of the
Machete* • *The Thomas Berryman Number*

JAMES PATTERSON
BOOK**SHOTS**

The Exile (with Alison Joseph) • *The Medical Examiner*
(with Maxine Paetro) • *Black Dress Affair* (with Susan
DiLallo) • *The Killer's Wife* (with Max DiLallo) • *Scott
Free* (with Rob Hart) • *The Dolls* (with Kecia Bal) •
Detective Cross • *Nooners* (with Tim Arnold) • *Stealing*

Gulfstreams (with Max DiLallo) • *Diary of a Succubus* (with Derek Nikitas) • *Night Sniper* (with Christopher Charles) • *Juror #3* (with Nancy Allen) • *The Shut-In* (with Duane Swierczynski) • *French Twist* (with Richard DiLallo) • *Malicious* (with James O. Born) • *Hidden* (with James O. Born) • *The House Husband* (with Duane Swierczynski) • *The Christmas Mystery* (with Richard DiLallo) • *Black & Blue* (with Candice Fox) • *Come and Get Us* (with Shan Serafin) • *Private: The Royals* (with Rees Jones) • *Taking the Titanic* (with Scott Slaven) • *Killer Chef* (with Jeffrey J. Keyes) • *French Kiss* (with Richard DiLallo) • *$10,000,000 Marriage Proposal* (with Hilary Liftin) • *Hunted* (with Andrew Holmes) • *113 Minutes* (with Max DiLallo) • *Chase* (with Michael Ledwidge) • *Let's Play Make-Believe* (with James O. Born) • *The Trial* (with Maxine Paetro) • *Little Black Dress* (with Emily Raymond) • *Cross Kill* • *Zoo II* (with Max DiLallo)

Sabotage: An Under Covers Story by Jessica Linden • *Love Me Tender* by Laurie Horowitz • *Bedding the Highlander* by Sabrina York • *The Wedding Florist* by T. J. Kline • *A Wedding in Maine* by Jen McLaughlin • *Radiant* by Elizabeth Hayley • *Hot Winter Nights* by Codi Gray • *Bodyguard* by Jessica Linden • *Dazzling*

by Elizabeth Hayley • *The Mating Season* by Laurie
Horowitz • *Sacking the Quarterback* by Samantha
Towle • *Learning to Ride* by Erin Knightley •
The McCullagh Inn in Maine by Jen McLaughlin

FOR READERS OF ALL AGES

MAXIMUM RIDE

Maximum Ride Forever • *Nevermore: The Final
Maximum Ride Adventure* • *Angel: A Maximum Ride
Novel* • *Fang: A Maximum Ride Novel* • *Max: A Maximum
Ride Novel* • *The Final Warning: A Maximum Ride
Novel* • *Saving the World and Other Extreme Sports: A
Maximum Ride Novel* • *School's Out—Forever: A Maximum
Ride Novel* • *The Angel Experiment: A Maximum Ride Novel*

DANIEL X

Daniel X: Lights Out (with Chris Grabenstein) • *Daniel X:
Armageddon* (with Chris Grabenstein) • *Daniel X: Game
Over* (with Ned Rust) • *Daniel X: Demons and Druids*
(with Adam Sadler) • *Daniel X: Watch the Skies*
(with Ned Rust) • *The Dangerous Days of Daniel X*
(with Michael Ledwidge)

WITCH & WIZARD

Witch & Wizard: The Lost (with Emily Raymond) •
Witch & Wizard: The Kiss (with Jill Dembowski) • *Witch*

& *Wizard: The Fire* (with Jill Dembowski) • *Witch &*
Wizard: The Gift (with Ned Rust) • *Witch & Wizard*
(with Gabrielle Charbonnet)

CONFESSIONS

Confessions: The Murder of an Angel (with Maxine
Paetro) • *Confessions: The Paris Mysteries* (with Maxine
Paetro) • *Confessions: The Private School Murders*
(with Maxine Paetro) • *Confessions of a Murder Suspect*
(with Maxine Paetro)

MIDDLE SCHOOL

Middle School: Escape to Australia (with Martin Chatterton,
illustrated by Daniel Griffo) • *Middle School: Dog's Best*
Friend (with Chris Tebbetts, illustrated by Jomike
Tejido) • *Middle School: Just My Rotten Luck* (with
Chris Tebbetts, illustrated by Laura Park) • *Middle*
School: Save Rafe! (with Chris Tebbetts, illustrated by
Laura Park) • *Middle School: Ultimate Showdown*
(with Julia Bergen, illustrated by Alec Longstreth) •
Middle School: How I Survived Bullies, Broccoli, and Snake
Hill (with Chris Tebbetts, illustrated by Laura Park) •
Middle School: My Brother Is a Big, Fat Liar
(with Lisa Papademetriou, illustrated by Neil
Swaab) • *Middle School: Get Me Out of Here!*
(with Chris Tebbetts, illustrated by Laura Park) •
Middle School, The Worst Years of My Life (with Chris
Tebbetts, illustrated by Laura Park)

I FUNNY

I Funny: Around the World (with Chris Grabenstein) • *I Funny: School of Laughs* (with Chris Grabenstein, illustrated by Jomike Tejido • *I Funny TV* (with Chris Grabenstein, illustrated by Laura Park) • *I Totally Funniest: A Middle School Story* (with Chris Grabenstein, illustrated by Laura Park) • *I Even Funnier: A Middle School Story* (with Chris Grabenstein, illustrated by Laura Park) • *I Funny: A Middle School Story* (with Chris Grabenstein, illustrated by Laura Park)

TREASURE HUNTERS

Treasure Hunters: Quest for the City of Gold (with Chris Grabenstein, illustrated by Juliana Neufeld) • *Treasure Hunters: Peril at the Top of the World* (with Chris Grabenstein, illustrated by Juliana Neufeld) • *Treasure Hunters: Secret of the Forbidden City* (with Chris Grabenstein, illustrated by Juliana Neufeld) • *Treasure Hunters: Danger Down the Nile* (with Chris Grabenstein, illustrated by Juliana Neufeld) • *Treasure Hunters* (with Chris Grabenstein, illustrated by Juliana Neufeld)

OTHER BOOKS FOR READERS OF ALL AGES

The Candies' Easter Party (illustrated by Andy Elkerton) • *Jacky Ha-Ha: My Life is a Joke* (with Chris Grabenstein, illustrated by Kerascoët) • *Give Thank You a Try* • *Expelled* (with Emily Raymond) • *The Candies Save*

Christmas (illustrated by Andy Elkerton) •
Big Words for Little Geniuses (with Susan Patterson,
illustrated by Hsinping Pan) • *Laugh Out Loud* (with
Chris Grabenstein) • *Pottymouth and Stoopid* (with
Chris Grabenstein) • *Crazy House* (with Gabrielle
Charbonnet) • *House of Robots: Robot Revolution*
(with Chris Grabenstein, illustrated by Juliana
Neufeld) • *Word of Mouse* (with Chris Grabenstein,
illustrated by Joe Sutphin) • *Give Please a Chance* (with
Bill O'Reilly) • *Jacky Ha-Ha* (with Chris Grabenstein,
illustrated by Kerascoët) • *House of Robots: Robots
Go Wild!* (with Chris Grabenstein, illustrated by
Juliana Neufeld) • *Public School Superhero* (with Chris
Tebbetts, illustrated by Cory Thomas) • *House of
Robots* (with Chris Grabenstein, illustrated by Juliana
Neufeld) • *Homeroom Diaries* (with Lisa Papademetriou,
illustrated by Keino) • *Med Head* (with Hal
Friedman) • *santaKid* (illustrated by Michael Garland)

For previews and information about the author,
visit JamesPatterson.com or find him on Facebook or at
your app store.

JAMES
PATTERSON
RECOMMENDS

A PRIVATE NOVEL

JAMES PATTERSON

& ASHWIN SANGHI

COUNT TO TEN

COUNT TO TEN

I admit it: I put Private investigator Santosh Wagh through the wringer in his first outing. A combination of personal setbacks and a harrowing case almost did him in. Then I started wondering—is there something that can push him over the edge?

Santosh is ready to quit as the head of Private India. Except Jack Morgan, the global leader of Private, wants to open an office in Delhi, and Santosh is the only person he can trust. Still battling his demons, Santosh accepts and the agency takes on a case that threatens to destroy them. Plastic barrels containing dissolved human remains have been found in the basement of a house. But this isn't just any house. This property belongs to the state government. With the crime scene in lockdown and information suppressed by the authorities, delving too deep soon makes Santosh a target to be eliminated.

When the rich and famous
are in trouble, their first call isn't 911.

#1 *NEW YORK TIMES* BESTSELLER

JAMES PATTERSON

PRIVATE

NEW YORK · LOS ANGELES · LONDON · PARIS

& MAXINE PAETRO

PRIVATE

I've always been a curious person. It's one of the many reasons why I'm a writer. Something I always asked myself was: "What happens if a 'one percenter' gets into trouble?" The answer: Jack Morgan and Private. On Jack Morgan's agenda in his debut outing is investigating a multimillion dollar NFL gambling scandal and solving a series of schoolgirl slayings. Then, the unthinkable—his former lover turned best friend's wife is murdered. One thing you should know about Jack is that beneath his Lamborghini-driving, red-carpet-event-attending surface, he's a very smart guy. And he takes no prisoners. Just wait till you get to the end of PRIVATE. You'll see what I mean.

JACK MORGAN
IS WANTED
FOR MURDER

THE WORLD'S #1 BESTSELLING WRITER

JAMES PATTERSON

PRIVATE

#1 Suspect

& MAXINE PAETRO

PRIVATE: # 1 SUSPECT

Over the years, I've learned that reputation is everything when it comes to business. While Private's Jack Morgan has a reputation for being effective and discreet, he's also known for being quite the lady killer. But when an ex-lover shows up dead in his bed and all evidence points to him, Jack realizes someone wants to kill more than just his good name. To make things worse, another event threatens Private's stability, and Jack suddenly finds himself with his back against the wall. Characters will do the most shocking things when they have no other options, especially characters like Jack who are used to being in control. I won't tell you what happens, but I will say it'll blow your mind.

THE WORLD'S #1 BESTSELLING WRITER

JAMES PATTERSON

Was Hollywood's most
famous couple kidnapped?
Or murdered?

PRIVATE
L.A.

MARK SULLIVAN

PRIVATE L.A.

If you've ever wondered what celebrity power couples do behind closed doors, you can stop all of your conjecturing—they're all in PRIVATE L.A. America's most popular celebrity couple has made an exit...from their lives. No one knows where they went or why, and it's up to Jack and his Private team to breach the walls of security and hordes of paparazzi to find the power couple. But when has anything good ever come from a pile of secrets buried under miles of genius PR? Jack's about to find that out, up close and personal, and he's in for the shock of his life. Because in the city of big dreams, nothing is what it seems. Especially if I'm involved.

PRIVATE BERLIN

Every now and then, I find myself wanting a big change in scenery. Don't get me wrong. Jack Morgan and the Private team are great fun, but sometimes a little taste of the foreign makes life a bit more exciting. And by "exciting," I really mean dangerous. At Private's German headquarters, Chris Schneider—superstar agent—has gone rogue. He's the keeper of quite a few pieces of sensitive information, but one in particular could have earth-shattering consequences. Hang on tight and don't blink. This one is a rollercoaster of tension that'll leave you reeling.